"I admit, t
showing u

"You don't have to worry," Pierce said. "Because I'm confident he can't find me. I've done nothing that might enable him to locate me. I pay with cash, don't use credit cards or my debit card, and I don't post photos to social media."

The husky timbre to his voice made Cassie ache with longing. Clearly, he had no idea of his effect on her.

"I know. You're careful. I'd expect nothing less from a bestselling thriller author. I just want him caught."

"Me too." Again, that sexy flash of a smile. "I have to admit I'm also selfishly hoping when he is, he finally reveals which book and which antagonist he thinks is modeled after him." He shrugged. "Weird as it may be, I'd really like to know."

She smiled back. "I don't blame you. Hopefully, he will," she said, her smile fading. "The important thing is getting him locked up so he stops killing people."

"Agreed."

Dear Reader,

West Texas is a dry, dusty and windy place. The landscaping is flat, and the trees are often hunched into the unrelenting wind. Yet for whatever reason, I find the wide-open spaces and endless sky beautiful.

I've set numerous books in my fictional West Texas town of Getaway, where this book is also set. Some of the characters from earlier books make appearances in this one. And as usually happens with me, the characters introduced themselves to me first. I met Cassie Denton, the daughter of a pig farmer. Despite the way most of her peers made fun of her, she persevered and made her dream (and talent) of becoming a full-time baker a reality.

Then enter Pierce Spade, a native New Yorker and bestselling thriller author. He's somehow acquired a stalker, who has begun killing as a way to get Pierce's attention.

When Pierce buys Cassie's family pig farm, looking for a place to hide until his stalker is brought to justice, the unexpected sparks that blaze between the two are intense. Soon, Pierce realizes he has some decisions to make. But for now, not only must he make sure to keep Cassie safe but also protect his heart (and hers) from what seems to be inevitable.

I hope you enjoy reading this story as much as I enjoyed writing it!

Karen Whiddon

STALKED
IN WEST TEXAS

KAREN WHIDDON

ROMANTIC SUSPENSE

MIX
Paper | Supporting responsible forestry
FSC® C021394

Harlequin® ROMANTIC SUSPENSE™

Recycling programs for this product may not exist in your area.

ISBN-13: 978-1-335-47193-2

Stalked in West Texas

Copyright © 2026 by Karen Whiddon

Harlequin Enterprises ULC
22 Adelaide St. West, 41st Floor
Toronto, Ontario M5H 4E3, Canada
www.Harlequin.com

HarperCollins Publishers
Macken House, 39/40 Mayor Street Upper,
Dublin 1, D01 C9W8, Ireland
www.HarperCollins.com

Printed in Lithuania

Karen Whiddon started weaving fanciful tales for her younger brothers at the age of eleven. Amid the gorgeous Catskill Mountains, then the majestic Rocky Mountains, she fueled her imagination with the natural beauty surrounding her. Karen now lives in north Texas, writes full-time and volunteers for a boxer dog rescue. She shares her life with her hero of a husband and four to five dogs, depending on if she is fostering. You can email Karen at kwhiddon1@aol.com. Fans can also check out her website, karenwhiddon.com.

Books by Karen Whiddon

Harlequin Romantic Suspense

Texas Sheriff's Deadly Mission
Texas Rancher's Hidden Danger
Finding the Rancher's Son
The Spy Switch
Protected by the Texas Rancher
Secret Alaskan Hideaway
Saved by the Texas Cowboy
Missing in Texas
Murder at the Alaskan Lodge
Vanished in Texas
Alaskan Disappearance
Trouble In West Texas
Stalked in West Texas

The Coltons of Owl Creek

Colton Mountain Search

The Coltons of Alaska

Colton on Guard

Visit the Author Profile page
at Harlequin.com for more titles.

To my wonderful husband and daughter.
My family and my loves. Thank you for being you.

Chapter 1

Cassie Denton knew all about the five stages of grief, though she'd never personally experienced them. Denial, anger, bargaining, depression, and finally, acceptance. She'd thought she might feel at least some of them when her father died, but sadly all she'd felt had been relief.

But now, days after signing a contract with a Realtor to put the farm where she'd grown up on the market, she'd come to realize she'd already gone through the first two stages. Now she'd skipped ahead to the depression. Objectively, she knew she should look at this major life change differently. A fresh start, a new beginning. She'd sometimes thought she'd finally leave the small, West Texas town of Getaway and experience a new place, different people.

Even if she wasn't one hundred percent sure she wanted to. She'd grown up here and sometimes she thought she could still make a fresh start in the same place. Just because she'd needed seed money from the sale of her farm to open her own bakery didn't mean she had to leave Getaway.

Her cell phone rang, startling her out of her thoughts. As if her thoughts had magically conjured her, her real estate agent Trudi's number showed on the screen.

Cassie barely got out a *hello* before Trudi began excitedly speaking. "You're not going to believe this, but minutes after your farm's listing went live, you've already received an offer. It's over asking price, all cash, and looks absolutely amazing. I don't think you're going to find anything better."

Stunned, Cassie struggled to find the correct response. But all she could think about was the final stage of grief. Would her depression suddenly become acceptance?

When Cassie didn't immediately reply, Trudi talked faster. "I'll email you over the paperwork so you can read it. The buyer is also someone you might remember, though I've been asked not to disclose his name yet."

"Why not?"

"Because you might know of him." Trudi paused, sounding nervous. "And he wants to keep his identity a secret," she continued. "But for now, that's really all I can say. You also should be aware that you'll be asked to sign a nondisclosure agreement if you take this offer."

Which made zero sense. Only a celebrity would ask for an NDA, and what celebrity would want to buy a former pig farm in remote West Texas?

None. Either way, it didn't matter. She'd sell and move on. The only thing Cassie cared about was her pet pig, Albert, so unless the buyers were asking her to leave him, she doubted whatever they wanted would make much difference. If they wanted Albert, there wouldn't be a deal.

"I didn't expect this to happen so quickly," Cassie said. "I'll need to see if the buyer will be amenable to letting me live there a few weeks to a month until I find somewhere else to go."

"That's usually fine," Trudi replied. "They might expect you to pay some sort of rent. It all depends on when they want to occupy the house."

"That's fine," Cassie said. "Please make sure and work that into the contract if possible."

"That shouldn't be a problem. I'll keep you posted."

"If they agree, just send me all the paperwork," Cassie said.

After ending the call, Cassie dropped down onto a chair and put her head in her hands. Nope, still depression. She hadn't quite reached acceptance. Maybe this amazingly quick sale would turn out to be exactly the kick in the butt she needed.

Ten minutes later, Trudi texted that the buyer had agreed to let Cassie stay on for up to one month. The only caveat was that they would actually be cohabiting the property. Because of that, they wouldn't be asking her to pay any rent.

This gave Cassie pause. She wasn't sure how she felt about living in her house with total strangers. Even if Trudi had hinted she might know of them, they'd still be strangers. Part of her wanted to just turn down the offer so she wouldn't have to deal with it. But realistically, she knew how difficult selling a place like hers could be. She doubted an offer like this one would come along again anytime soon.

For that reason alone, she knew she had to accept. She'd just have to accelerate her search for a new place to live.

Her life was about to change. Hopefully for the better. When she texted Trudi the news, Trudi responded with a heart emoji and the words:

On it! I'll be sending over the NDA first. Once you sign that, we'll work on the contract.

Shaking her head, Cassie went and grabbed her laptop and powered it up. She located Trudi's email and downloaded the document.

It was a short, simple, nondisclosure agreement. If she

signed, she would be agreeing not to discuss the name of the buyer with anyone.

Using the electronic signature, Cassie signed and sent it back.

Got it, Trudi texted.

Will send contract shortly. I made your requested amendment. The buyer will have to sign first. I'll text you when they're sent.

Figuring it would be a few hours, maybe even tomorrow, Cassie went to the primary bedroom and began moving her personal belongings to one of the smaller guest bedrooms. Since she'd sold the house fully furnished, she didn't have to worry about packing up dishes or anything else.

She'd just be keeping her clothes and jewelry and personal grooming items. Her books, of course, and some framed photographs, but she didn't really have a lot. Most of the furniture had been there since she'd been a child. Her father had refused to change a thing when her mother had died in childbirth.

When Cassie's father had passed two years ago, she'd waited ten days before donating all his stuff. Like her, he hadn't had much. She'd cleaned out his room in an afternoon, only keeping his pocketknife and all of his guns. Now she'd move all that to the guest bedroom and eventually, to a new home. Whether in Getaway or someplace different.

Starting from scratch, she liked to think. A clean, new beginning would be better than dragging around a lot of useless clutter. Let the buyer dispose of what they didn't want.

Ninety minutes later, Trudi texted her to check her email. She had paperwork to sign.

Cassie read through the documents, finding them exactly

as Trudi had stated. When deciding to sell, she'd set a price for the farm slightly above its actual value, figuring any potential buyers would want to negotiate. Instead, this buyer agreed to pay full asking price *and* all of the closing costs, which surprised her. Heck yes, she'd agree.

When she saw the buyer's signature, she caught her breath. Now the NDA made sense. *Pierce Spade.* It couldn't be. Since she was an avid reader, she knew the name. Heck, most anyone who'd ever picked up a book would know the bestselling thriller author. She'd even heard one of his books was being made into a movie.

Cassie had read each and every one of his novels. They all occupied places of pride on her crowded bookshelf. She'd even promised herself if he ever went on book tour anywhere close, she'd take them all to get signed.

Looked like she wouldn't have to do that now. She could get his signature while staying with him in her house. Her *former* house, she reminded herself.

While she wasn't the fangirl type, the thought of actually meeting Pierce Spade made her heartrate accelerate. Except the idea that someone like him would want to buy her dusty old pig farm made zero sense. She doubted he planned to raise swine.

Puzzled, she read the documents again. With a cash influx this large, she could pay off all of her creditors and still have enough to buy her own house and start her new business. Whether in Getaway or somewhere else. Plus, staying here debt-free until she figured out her next move would help a lot. Any mild discomfort would be worth it.

It was a no-brainer. She signed electronically and sent the documents back. Then she got out her phone and called Trudi to let her know she'd done so.

Trudi squealed, a sound Cassie should have been used

to, considering where she'd grown up. "I'll let them know," Trudi said excitedly, no doubt thinking of the fat commission she'd receive.

"Good," Cassie replied. "Let's try to get the closing scheduled as soon as possible. I can't wait."

Trudi promised she would and ended the call.

After that, Cassie wandered into the kitchen, wishing she had champagne, or even wine, so she could properly mark the occasion. Even if, for whatever reason, she didn't feel at all like celebrating. Instead, the best she could do was pop open a can of Diet Dr Pepper. Carrying her favorite vice out to the back porch, she whistled for Albert. As usual, her pet pig came lumbering over, eager for attention.

She took a seat in the weathered rocking chair that had once belonged to her father, scratching Albert behind his ears with one hand, and sipped her drink.

Looking out over the farm, she sighed. No one would ever call this place beautiful. Dry and dusty, a mud pit when it rained, the family farm looked exactly like what it was. A pig farm, perfectly set up for raising swine. The various pens and shelters still stood, empty now since Cassie had long since sold off all the livestock.

If she half closed her eyes, she could still see it as it had been when her father had been alive, before alcohol made him not care about anything or anyone except his next drink.

There'd been all kinds of swine back then. Big and small, cute and…not so cute. Friendly, indifferent, and even mean. As a child, she'd been given the chore of helping feed them and had learned at an early age which ones to stay away from. They were all different, but they all, without exception, loved to eat.

One of the first things she'd been taught was not to give

them names. "You never name something you might be eating," her father had told her sternly.

For years, she'd followed those instructions. Even after her father's passing, when she'd struggled to keep the ranch going and a roof over her head, she'd made sure not to get too attached.

Until the night Albert had been born. After laboring for a few hours, the sow had a litter of ten. They were all healthy except the last one born. That little piglet had been sickly and small. Since the others pushed him out of the way when he tried to nurse, Cassie had kept him with her and bottle-fed him around the clock.

Somewhere during those first few weeks, Albert had gained not only his name but a huge chunk of Cassie's heart.

Now Albert had grown up. He was the only pig remaining. All the others had been sold. However, despite his size, he lived the life of a beloved pet. Cassie knew when she moved away from this farm that she'd need to find a place where Albert could live too. Because there was no way she'd ever leave him behind.

Sipping her cold beverage, Cassie tried to imagine what someone like Pierce Spade would want with a pig farm. She guessed she shouldn't worry too much about it. Just take the money, make the sale, and tell him thank you.

Then she would be free to make actual plans to start a new life.

Even thinking about how close she was filled her with both excitement and trepidation. Though starting her own bakery seemed kind of a pipe dream, she'd been supplementing her income for months, selling her cakes, pies, breads, and muffins to The Tumbleweed Café in town. They'd become so popular that customers had been placing preorders.

She truly believed she could make a living with her mad

baking skills. Luckily, since she had no other work experience to fall back on. Unlike her classmates in high school, she'd never worked at a fast food restaurant or in retail, working at a store. Which meant her experience doing anything besides working with livestock and baking cakes, pies, cookies, and bread amounted to zero.

Getaway currently didn't have a stand-alone bakery, so she figured the demand would be there to make hers a success. In addition, she'd taken a few online business courses and had a ton of common sense. After all, she'd been selling her baked goods to a couple of local eateries using her home kitchen to bake. She could do this. She knew she could.

Finishing her drink, she got up and took the glass into the kitchen, placing it in the sink. Then she went back outside, where Albert waited patiently, and took a stroll around the farm.

Just for old memories' sake. Once all the swine had been loaded up and transported away, she'd cleaned the barn for the last time. It felt weird when she'd finished, knowing it would stay clean.

She'd mucked out the outdoor pens, put down fresh sawdust, and done what she could to make the place look halfway appealing. When Trudi's photographer had arrived to take the listing photos, Cassie had felt satisfied that she'd done the best she could.

One thing she hadn't expected was for it to sell so fast. At full listing price and to a famous author like Pierce Spade, of all people.

The closing would be held in one hour. Ever since he'd arrived in the small town of Getaway, Pierce Spade had wondered if he was making the right decision. Unusual for him. He usually made a choice and then charged full steam ahead.

But then he'd never tried to hide from an admitted serial killer before. He had to guess the person was good, since he hadn't been caught. Even though he prided himself on the extensive research he did for his novels, he did a quick internet search looking for unsolved serial murders.

There were more than he would have guessed. Add to that the very distinct possibility that the police or the FBI might not have put together several murders that didn't appear to have anything in common, and his stalker could be anyone, anywhere.

And he should know. He'd written enough skilled, serial killer plots. They'd required a ton of research. It didn't surprise him that he'd apparently accidentally stumbled upon a real one's methods.

He'd hired a private security firm for a ridiculous amount of money. They took their job seriously, but when they'd wanted to whisk him away to an undisclosed "safe house," he'd decided to let them go.

The killer had continued to make threats, each one more and more unhinged. An innocent woman was killed, Pierce's name written in blood near the body, and the news media had gone berserk.

His agent and his editor had called an emergency meeting. Aware they were worried about him and hoping to ease their minds, he'd taken a cab to the publisher's office in midtown Manhattan. While he could have easily walked, with everything that had been going on, he'd decided to play it safe.

After an hour of both men working hard to convince Pierce to go into hiding, Pierce had finally, reluctantly agreed, even though he'd just fired his security firm for suggesting something similar.

At least this way it would be on his terms. He'd choose

where he went to stay, rather than going to some safe house set up by the security company.

Hearing this, both Michael, his agent, and Jamal, his editor, began offering suggestions for his consideration. Some of them were tropical paradises, other were known for the beautiful scenery.

Pierce had listened, smiling, and nodded. He told them he'd keep their ideas in mind and would make his choice in a few days. When the meeting ended, he caught another cab and traveled the few blocks to his apartment.

Now that he'd made a decision and agreed to take himself into hiding, he needed to figure out where he wanted to go. While tropical locales were great for a short vacation, he had no desire to stay at one long term.

An idea had been kicking around in the back of his mind for a few months now. Maybe all of this was the kick in the rear he needed to make his dream a reality. In order to accomplish that, he knew he wanted to buy rather than rent, paying with cash. He'd be using the place as an investment property. Possibly even a tax write-off, though he'd need to talk to his accountant. While hiding out there, he could take his time getting everything set up.

Once back home, he'd taken to scrolling several real estate apps, trying to figure out where this place would be. His agent had suggested the Rocky Mountains or maybe an island home in the Pacific Northwest. His editor had leaned more toward out of the country, like the Caribbean. All of these places had been tempting. But for whatever reason, Pierce had found himself remembering the untouched prairie he'd driven through on his way to Marfa, Texas, when researching one of his books.

Bleak, yet powerful, the rugged West Texas landscape appealed to him. When the thirty-acre farm had popped up on the outskirts of Getaway, something about the austerity of the place intrigued him. With all the land and the outbuildings, he could actually envision converting the farm into the type of place he wanted.

He did a bit more research. While he needed remote, he wanted to stay close enough to a town of some sort where he could get supplies. He even decided how he'd alter his appearance to make sure no one recognized him. Not that many in remote West Texas would, but better safe than sorry.

The more he dwelled on this farm, the more he liked it.

The name of the town also appealed. Getaway, Texas. He wasn't sure if it was meant to warn people off or to insinuate it was some sort of place to get away. Either one suited him. In fact, he couldn't imagine that anyone would ever think to look for him there. This place would be perfect.

He'd picked up the phone, called the real estate agent, and made an offer sight unseen. Now here he was, sitting in his Jeep outside the bank that apparently doubled as a title company, about to sign the paperwork to transfer ownership to him. His agent had made sure that everyone, from the Realtor to the title company people and the seller, had signed airtight NDAs. No one would be able to use his name or mention that he'd bought property in Getaway. Even if they had, he doubted anyone would believe it.

Before closing, he'd had his long, wavy hair cut short and had shaved off his beard and mustache. Eyeing his new look in the mirror, he hardly recognized himself. Since all of his author photos matched the long-haired, bearded version, he doubted anyone would give him a second look.

He should be safe here, for now. Hopefully just long enough for his stalker to be caught. Then he'd figure out what to do with the farm. Maybe he could turn it into some kind of writer's retreat.

Shaking off the thoughts, he took out the notebook he always kept with him and continued working on the outline for his next story. The one constant he could always depend on was his writing.

For the past few years, he'd lived life on his own terms. He wrote what he wanted to write, answering to no one but his editor. He'd considered himself relatively happy in his success. Soon, filming would begin of the movie version of his first book. He'd helped with the screenplay and had been looking forward to meeting the major movie stars who'd be playing the roles of his characters.

Life was good.

Until it wasn't. Sometimes, he felt like his feet had been knocked out from under him. He had worked his ass off to get where he was now. There'd been no overnight success for him. And he'd be damned if he'd let some mentally un-stable stalker take it all away from him.

One thing at a time, he reminded himself. First, he needed to get through this closing, take possession of his new farm, and meet the previous owner, who'd be staying on for a couple of weeks.

When he walked into the bank and asked for the title company, the very ordinariness of the small office helped settle his sudden bout of nerves even more. This would all work out. It had to. And if he was lucky, he'd get another bestselling novel out of it.

An older, portly man led him to a small conference room. A slender woman with long, dark hair waited there with her back to him, already seated at the table. When she turned her head to look at him, his world shifted on its axis. Long-lashed, green eyes the color of sea-foam met his. Her lips curled in a slight smile and she dipped her chin in a kind of greeting.

Beautiful, he thought, stunned. Was she the Realtor or the seller?

"Cassie!" a loud voice squealed. A robust woman wearing a bright red pantsuit barreled past him into the room, pulling the seated woman up and in for a hug.

The minute the second woman released the first, she turned toward him. She wore bright red lipstick, matching her clothes. "I'm Trudi Parsons, the Realtor. You must be Pierce Spade. Welcome to Getaway." And then she held out her perfectly manicured fingers, each one of them decorated with an ornate ring.

Bemused, he shook her hand.

"And this is Cassie Denton, the seller," Trudi continued, gesturing toward the first woman.

Instead of offering a handshake, Cassie simply nodded, her bright gaze wary. "Pleased to meet you," she said, her Southern drawl not at all what he'd expected. But then, they *were* in Texas.

"Why don't you both get seated. Everything is ready," Trudi said. "Shannon will be in shortly."

Another woman with short, gray hair and large, purple eyeglasses walked into the room carrying a large stack of papers. "Let's get started," she said. "Cassie will go first, and then Pierce."

Once the paperwork had been signed, Cassie slid the keys across the polished, oak table. "Congratulations," she said. "You're now the proud owner of a pig farm." She studied him, her expression grave. "I wish you nothing but the best of luck."

Confused, he accepted the keys. "Are you still planning to live there temporarily?" he asked. "If so, you might as well keep one of these for yourself."

Lifting her chin, she finally nodded. "Yes, Albert and I will be staying until I locate somewhere else to live."

Albert? Husband, boyfriend, or kid? About to ask, he decided not to.

"My pet," she elaborated, apparently correctly interpreting his expression. The twinkle in her beautiful green eyes distracted him, and he found himself simply nodding.

He liked pets, especially dogs. Since they'd be living in the same house for a few weeks, he'd be meeting Albert soon enough.

"Sounds good," he told her.

She rose, her movements graceful. He followed her from the room. They walked out side by side.

When she reached a large, battered, white pickup truck, she paused. "Do you mind if I ask you something? What does someone like you want with a pig farm in the middle of nowhere?"

Eyeing her, he figured she might as well know the truth up front. "I need a place to hide. Someone claiming to be a serial killer is stalking me."

Eyes wide, she stared at him, clearly not certain he was serious.

When he didn't elaborate, she slowly nodded. "I see," she said, even though she sounded as if she didn't. "Stalking you, how? Online or in person?"

"Both." He shrugged, as if he didn't think such a thing would be a big deal. "That's why I decided to go into hiding."

"If I stay with you, will I be in danger?" Blunt, yes. But something she truly needed to know.

He considered the question for a moment before answering. "Honestly, I don't know. But first off, this person seems solely focused on me, at least for now. Secondly, no one but my agent knows I'm here."

"If it makes you feel better, I think you should go ahead and move out. Find somewhere else to live."

"Which I've already been trying to do. There just aren't a lot of places in my price range for sale around here. And if I want to start a business, I need to do my best to keep my costs down. I don't think I can afford to buy both a house and a commercial space for my bakery. Every penny I have has to go into start-up costs.

"I'm looking," she said. "As soon as I find the right place, I'm gone. And knowing you have a stalker, I'll need to hurry up the search. Ideally, I hope to find a place where I can both live and operate the bakery."

"Suit yourself."

"Well, on the plus side," she said. "I have to say that no one would expect to find a famous author here."

"Exactly." Satisfied that he'd made his point, he glanced around. He'd placed his Corvette in storage, since the flashy vehicle stood out, and had purchased a brand-new Jeep Wrangler 4x4 to help him blend in. "I can't wait to see the place," he said, meaning it. "I've always wanted to own some land."

"I bet. Do you know how to find it?" she asked, her expression still guarded, though her voice sounded pleasant enough. "I know you declined to do any kind of walk-through before closing."

"I did. There was no need for a walk-through. I knew I'd buy it anyway." Then, realizing he hadn't answered her question, he replied that he didn't have the slightest idea how to get there. Even though he could easily put the address into his GPS, he asked her if he could follow her.

"Sure. I'll take it slow," she replied. "Which vehicle is yours?"

He pointed to his brand-new Jeep. "That one."

Again, she appraised him, her green gaze serious. "Follow me," she said, climbing into her ancient white truck and driving off slowly.

Bemused, he got into his Jeep and drove after her, curious to see his new home for the first time.

As he followed her, he thought about his visceral reaction to her. He didn't understand why the first sight of her made him feel as if he'd been punched in the gut.

After all, he'd known lots of beautiful women. Dated more than a few, though nothing had ever been serious. He liked to keep things light. Less distractions that way.

One look at Cassie Denton and he'd known she wasn't a casual kind of girl. Which meant he'd need to keep things strictly platonic between them. That shouldn't be too difficult, since she hadn't given him the slightest indication she might be interested.

A few weeks tops, he told himself. As long as he had his writing to distract him, he'd be fine.

Chapter 2

Turning onto the gravel road that led toward the farm, Cassie tried to picture Pierce Spade's reaction to the place once he actually saw it. While the professional real estate photos were untouched, the photographer had used favorable lighting to make parts of the place look better than they did to the naked eye. For someone not from this part of the country, she imagined her former family farm would look pretty bleak indeed.

If what Pierce had told her was accurate, she understood appearances wouldn't matter. If he truly had bought the farm only as a remote place to hide, she guessed he wouldn't care. After all, he could have gone someplace full of tropical beauty, accessible only by boat. Or bought himself a fortress high up in the rugged mountains, where any intruder would be seen miles before they reached him.

She knew what she would have chosen if she'd been in his shoes. It wouldn't have been her pig farm.

Technically, she knew she should count her blessings. What Pierce Slade did or didn't do wasn't any of her concern. She'd try her best to stay out of his way for the next couple of weeks while she figured out her path forward.

As she made the sharp right turn into her drive, she found herself assessing the little red ranch house with fresh eyes.

The paint had faded due to years of unrelenting sun, and some of the shingles on the roof appeared to need replacing.

Years ago, the pretty wood rails that fenced in the front of the place had been sturdy and strong. Over time, many of them had either fallen or rotted, and Cassie hadn't replaced them. She'd done her best to keep up with the more practical fencing that had kept the swine in, but the decorative ones she'd had to let go. She wondered if Pierce would bother to replace the broken ones.

The inside of the house had never been renovated or improved. Not only had she not had the funds to do anything like that, but she truly hadn't cared. She kept it clean, all the appliances worked, and that had been good enough for her.

Considering that the farm would be a temporary shelter for Pierce until the person threatening him had been caught, she doubted he would make any changes either. She didn't really blame him.

But to her surprise, it bothered her a little that she wouldn't have any say over what would become of the place once he was done with it. Hopefully, by the time he got ready to sell, she'd have moved on to her new and improved life. She couldn't allow herself to dwell on the past.

Parking in front of the two-car garage, she got out and waited for him to pull up beside her. Again, she thought how out of place his brand-new, shiny black Jeep seemed. That alone made her like it.

As he emerged from his vehicle, shading his eyes from the sun with one hand, she was struck again by what a handsome man the author actually was. He looked nothing like the photo on the inside jacket of his book covers. There, he'd had longish hair and a neatly trimmed beard and mustache.

Now he'd not only shaved but wore his hair much shorter. Surprisingly, she thought he looked better this way. But then what did she know? She'd never actually met him in person before.

Pierce made a slow circle, taking in not only the house but the outbuildings and fields. She'd mowed them herself shortly before the real estate photos had been taken, using the ancient tractor that miraculously still ran. They looked a lot better than they normally did, when the grass and weeds stood as tall as her hips.

"A lot of brown," he commented. "Just like the West Texas I remember."

Surprised, she eyed him. "Remember? You've been here before?"

"Driving through," he clarified. "I took a road trip to Marfa, doing research for a book. I found myself wandering all over West Texas." He grinned, taking her breath away. "There are a lot of wide-open roads and I also have a sports car."

That made more sense. Getaway wasn't a destination type of place. Most folks only stopped by on their way to somewhere else.

Albert, who always slept on the back patio when she left, must have heard them arrive. He came trotting around from the back of the house, making loud grunts of greeting.

"There's my boy," Cassie crooned, as Albert barreled toward her.

Pierce froze, eyeing the large pig warily. "I thought the listing said you said you sold all of your livestock."

She looked up from scratching behind Albert's ears, his favorite spot. "I did. This is Albert. He's not stock. He's my pet pig."

Albert grunted, looking from her to Pierce and back again, as if he understood. Then, with another series of grunts, he waddled over to Pierce to check him out.

Cassie watched closely. You could tell a lot about a man by the way he treated someone else's pet.

After giving Pierce's pant legs a thorough sniff, Albert tilted his head expectantly.

"He wants you to pet him," she explained.

"Okay." Then Pierce bent down and began petting Albert the way one would a much-loved dog, starting by scratching him all around his neck before moving on to his back, sides, and belly.

This put Albert in hog heaven. For a moment, Cassie swore her pet's eyes rolled back in his head.

When Pierce finished, Albert heaved a satisfied sigh before moving off, no doubt to take another nap in the sun.

"Do you think he likes me?" Pierce asked, watching the pig waddle away. "I wasn't sure how to pet a pig, so I just acted like he was a big dog."

The knowledge that he even cared what Albert thought of him touched her more than it should have. Clearly, she'd been a recluse for far too long. "I think so," she answered.

Since Pierce now had the keys, instead of leading the way into her former house, she had to wait for him. Unfortunately, he didn't seem to realize this. Hands jammed into his pockets, he stood as if he expected her to do something.

"Are we going to go inside?" she finally asked.

"Yes." He nodded. "I'd like that."

"You have the keys," she pointed out gently.

He laughed. "So I do. I still would like you to have a set for as long as you're here."

"Sounds good," she replied. "I didn't want to steal your thunder."

"Steal my…" Eyeing her as if he wasn't quite sure what to make of that, he finally shook his head.

Finally, he unlocked the door. "After you," he said, stepping aside so she could enter first. "Since, as you know, I actually bought this place sight unseen, I was hoping you could give me a tour."

"I see," she replied, even though she didn't. "Well, come on then. Let me show you around your new place."

It felt kind of weird, leading a world-famous author around the home she'd grown up in. He didn't comment or ask any questions, just took everything in quietly. The last of the four bedrooms had only a battered metal desk, an ancient computer, and a chair.

"This was where I tried to keep up with the records for the farm," she explained. She felt slightly embarrassed at how austere the area looked, but since she spent the smallest amount of time possible in here, she'd never bothered to decorate. Neither had her father before her, so the wood-paneled walls were bare. A cheap, old set of metal blinds hung at the window, and the threadbare carpet had seen much better days.

For the first time since the tour had begun, Pierce's eyes lit up. "It's perfect," he said, stepping into the small room and turning all the way around. "I did bring my own computer, but this desk and chair will work perfectly for now."

For his office, she realized. For whatever reason, she hadn't considered the idea he'd be writing once he moved in. Of course he would. That's what authors did. He likely had deadlines to meet.

If he turned out to be a decent person, she might even ask him to autograph all her hardcover copies of his books.

"I need to get a few things out of my Jeep," he said. "I didn't bring a lot with me, just some clothes and my computer. I figure I can buy anything else I might need in town."

Without waiting for her to respond, he strode away.

Bemused, she wandered back into the kitchen. She'd kind

of expected a moving truck to arrive at some point. Surely, he wanted his own furniture. But then she guessed since he'd gone into hiding, he hadn't wanted to do anything that might alert his stalker as to his whereabouts. Which would explain why he'd asked for all the furniture to come with the house.

A few minutes later, she heard the front door open and close. Pierce walked past, carrying a couple of duffel bags. He took them into the main bedroom that she'd recently vacated, closing the door behind him.

Standing alone in the familiar kitchen, she realized she felt awkward in the house that had once been hers and now wasn't. She didn't really know this man, other than being an avid fan of his books. She'd always pictured famous authors, especially bestselling ones, as living a life full of glamour, wanting for nothing. She'd sort of expected him to be arrogant and dismissive, which in turn would ensure she avoided him as much as possible.

This man, as handsome as he might be, seemed kind enough. Quiet, even. He clearly had a lot more baggage than she'd expected. The sooner she got out and into a place of her own, the better. Especially since he had someone wanting him dead.

A few minutes later, Pierce joined her. "It's been a long day," he said, meeting her gaze. "I appreciate you making things so welcoming for me."

Welcoming? Unsure how to respond, she sighed. "I should be the one thanking you for agreeing to let me stay. I'm guessing you didn't expect to have a houseguest with a pet pig for the first few weeks you're here."

"I didn't," he admitted, looking away toward the kitchen window. "But I think it'll be a good thing, having you here.

You can show me around and help me get used to living in this part of the country."

Now she allowed herself to study him. She liked his chiseled profile, admiring the way his rugged appearance seemed to go with this land. "Will you be able to leave the premises?" she asked quietly. "Since your goal is to stay hidden. If you were to go into town, there's always a chance someone might recognize you."

"I'm not that recognizable," he replied, still staring off into the distance outside the window. "Being a popular author isn't like being a movie star or something. People don't usually spot me from across a room and know instantly who I am."

He had a point.

"And just in case," he continued. "I cut my hair and shaved off my beard. With sunglasses and a baseball cap, I shouldn't be the slightest bit recognizable."

"Maybe not," she conceded. "But can you take that chance?"

Now he returned his attention to her. When his light blue gaze touched hers, she felt a shiver inside her bones.

"I have to be able to live," he said. "I'll need to buy groceries and other supplies." He flashed a brief smile, lighting up his face. "And if on the off chance that someone thinks they recognize me, I'll just deny, deny, deny."

Which would likely work. After all, she had no idea how many people in her small hometown would have actually read Pierce's books. The Bookstore in town had been struggling for years, even more so since the owner, Mr. Smith, had passed away. She wasn't sure how much longer they'd be able to stay open.

"How bad is it really?" she asked. "I'd like more of an explanation. When you say someone is trying to kill you, what exactly have they done so far?"

* * *

Following Cassie around the small house, Pierce had to remind himself to focus on his surroundings rather than Cassie's curvy figure. He hadn't truly thought this entire situation would feel so awkward. But then he hadn't realized he'd be sharing the space with a gorgeous woman.

When she asked him to elaborate on his stalker, he couldn't blame her. The only others who knew the entire story were his agent, his editor, and law enforcement. Since Cassie would be sharing space with him for a few weeks, she deserved to know what she was getting into.

"Someone—who actually claims to be a successful serial killer—thinks I took the plot for one of my books from their actual life. Apparently, they got away with multiple murders, but now they're convinced I'm trying to expose them. Which means they've vowed to permanently silence me."

"Really? What book?" she asked, her arms still crossed. Her defensive posture spoke of her skepticism.

"That's just it, they didn't say. Everything has been very cryptic, and the threats were made anonymously. At first, I didn't pay very much attention to them. I thought they were written by a person with mental health issues, which is still likely true." He swallowed hard. "They were vague and unspecific. Nothing concrete I could take to the police and say there'd been a threat."

"You've written more than one book about a serial killer," she pointed out.

Surprised, he nodded. "Yes, I have. You've read my work?"

"I read a lot," she told him. "So, yes, I've read your books. Reading is my main source of entertainment."

Which was exactly the reason he'd turned to writing.

"Okay, so you got threats. What finally made you start to take them seriously?" she asked.

He took a deep breath. Torn between not wanting to frighten her and feeling as if she deserved to know everything since she'd be staying with him for a little bit, he went with the truth.

"When someone blew up my car outside of my home in Manhattan." Luckily, he hadn't been in it, and it had been early enough in the morning that no innocent bystanders had been hurt. He could have been though. And the fire department had found evidence of a bomb that hadn't detonated placed underneath his bedroom window.

She blanched. "I seem to remember seeing something about that on the news. But they made it sound like some kind of accident. A malfunction of the engine or something."

"That was intentional. My publicist and my agent worked hard to make that happen. We didn't want the media to sensationalize any of this." He sighed, remembering how panicked local law enforcement had been. At least when they'd called in the ATF, those agents had been much more levelheaded and professional. One of them had actually been the one to suggest Pierce disappear for a while, at least until the perp had been caught. After all, Pierce did have the kind of job he could do anywhere.

"Do they have any leads?" she asked.

"Not yet. The investigation is ongoing. But my stalker was—is—very careful. Meanwhile, the threats kept coming. Emails, letters, and even phone calls from various burner phones. We got ATF involved after the bomb. So far, they haven't been able to find anything to suggest who this might be."

Eyes wide, she studied him. "That sounds like a nightmare. If they still haven't been able to find any viable leads, what did they suggest you do?"

"That I go into hiding until this person is caught." He took a deep breath. "I resisted at first. My agent and my editor both ganged up on me and convinced me. They even thought I should hire a bodyguard."

"A bodyguard? That sounds like one of your novels."

"It does," he conceded. "I decided against it. If I hide well enough, I don't see the need."

Studying him for a moment, she finally nodded. "That makes sense. And I seriously doubt anyone would look for you here."

Her statement made him smile. "Exactly why I bought this place. Plus, something about the terrain appeals to me."

She did a double take. "That's how I feel too," she said, her soft voice matching the look in her eyes. "Most of us who grew up here feel the same way."

Since he'd grown up in New Jersey, he had no explanation for his instant love of West Texas. If he'd been writing a character in one of his books, he might have hinted at the possibility of having lived there in another lifetime.

The notion amused him.

Touching his arm, Cassie drew his attention back to Earth. "Now that you've seen the house, do you want me to show you around the rest of the farm?"

"Sure," he replied. Even though he'd already viewed the photos and saved them to his album in the cloud, maybe the place looked a little less brown and dusty in real life.

"It's not much," she admitted. "But Albert really enjoys giving visitors a tour."

The idea of being shown around by a huge, black pig lightened the tension and made him smile. "I can't wait to see it," he said. To his surprise, he actually meant it.

Though he'd leveled with her about his reasons for buying, he still hadn't asked her why she'd decided to sell her family farm. No doubt the money would come in handy. But then what?

With Cassie leading the way and Pierce following, they stepped outside. Asleep on the back patio, Albert lifted his head, immediately spotting them. He let out a loud, delighted squeal as he trotted over.

After Cassie gave Albert the obligatory pets and scratches, the pig moved over to Pierce for more of the same. He laughingly obliged, realizing his mood felt lighter than it had been in weeks.

"Albert, can you show us around?" Cassie asked, once her pet had received his full share of attention.

Immediately, Albert tossed his head and began leading the way. They went first to the larger of the two barns, stopping long enough for Pierce to view several large, fenced enclosures.

"Those were the pig mud pens," Cassie explained. "Everything is in good condition and ready for whatever kind of livestock you might want to bring in."

"There won't be any," he responded immediately. "I don't intend to become a farmer."

She nodded as if his answer didn't surprise her. "We have another smaller barn and also a decent-sized storage building. There are several tractors in there. Not all of them are in working condition, but I've kept the one I use to mow running."

Mowing. Another basic chore he hadn't taken into consideration. Though judging by how brown everything looked, he had to wonder if it even grew.

"Weeds don't need water," she answered, wrinkling her

nose. "With it being so dry, it's best to keep everything cut low. It lessens the fire danger."

"Fires?" Clearly, he hadn't done enough research.

"Grass fires," she elaborated. "They can get out of control really fast, especially if the wind is blowing."

"I'll make sure to keep it mowed."

They toured the second barn and then the storage building. He had to admire the large, ancient red tractor.

"That's the one I use to pull the mower," she told him. "I'll show you how to use it before I leave."

"I appreciate that," he said.

Albert grunted again, clearly ready to head back to his spot in the sun on the back patio.

"All done," Cassie said, gesturing to her pet. "Let's go."

Needing no second urging, Albert turned and trotted toward the house without giving them a second glance.

"He's quite a character," Pierce mused. "I might work him into a book one of those days, if that's all right with you."

She beamed. "I'd love that. My boy would be famous."

When they reached the house, Pierce excused himself, telling Cassie he needed to make a phone call. Once in his new bedroom, he closed the door and got out one of the disposable phones he'd purchased. His private security firm claimed that the FBI always recommended using them, explaining how easy it would be to trace his cell phone. As a result, he'd left the latest iPhone model locked in the safe in his New York City home. He employed an assistant who handled all his social media, so he didn't have to worry about any of that.

First up, he called Michael as he'd promised, to let him know he'd arrived.

"Are you loving it?" His agent sounded decidedly upbeat. Out of an abundance of caution, Pierce had only let Michael and Jamal know where he'd decided to hide. After all, the three of them had worked together for so long that not only were they business partners but friends.

When Pierce had filled Michael in on his new location, he'd kept most of the details to himself. He'd only said he'd bought a farm in Texas. No doubt his agent pictured something along the lines of the ranch from the old TV show *Dallas*.

"We just closed, and I'm about to get settled in," Pierce replied. "The previous owner is going to be staying in one of the guest bedrooms until she can move in to her new place." He didn't mention that he wasn't sure she'd even started looking for another house.

"*She?*" Michael asked. "Let me guess. If I go by your usual luck with females, she's young, single, and gorgeous."

Pierce grinned. "She is all three of those things, but as you know, I'm not in the market for any kind of romantic relationship with all this going on."

"Relationship?" Michael snorted. "Who said anything about a relationship? You're no good at those anyways. Do what you usually do. Have a quick fling."

Since Pierce didn't want to tell his friend that he could tell Cassie wasn't the type who had casual flings, he simply changed the subject. He'd had all his fan mail forwarded to Michael's agency so they could keep on top of anything the stalker and self-admitted serial killer, who they'd taken to calling Joe, decided to send in. "Anything else from Joe?"

"Yes. He's amped up his game, almost like he knows you've gone into hiding. He's sent a letter daily for the last four days."

"The usual threats?" Pierce asked.

"Exactly. Except this time, he's gone into much grislier

detail. Very descriptive." Michael coughed. "You could learn something from him. He'd make quite a horror writer."

"I'll pass," Pierce replied, as no doubt Michael had known he would. While he wrote descriptive murder scenes in his novels, he tried to stay away from gratuitous bloodshed.

"I've turned everything over to the FBI. From what I understand, they're working with the ATF on this." Michael coughed again. "I think I've picked up a cold."

"Hope you feel better, man." Promising to check in often, Pierce ended the call. Turning his burner phone over in his hands, he shook his head before shoving the phone in his pocket out of pure habit. No one had this number, except for Michael, and once he'd used up all the prepaid minutes, he'd take a hammer to the phone. He missed his smartphone and the ease of accessing the internet, but figured he'd adjust. Hopefully, it wouldn't be too long until the person hunting for him was caught and he could resume his normal life.

He walked into the kitchen to find Cassie had placed a pie on the counter.

"Would you like to have a Diet Dr Pepper and a slice of my homemade peach pie?" Cassie asked. "I think it will make the perfect snack, since both of us have something to celebrate."

"That sounds great. Thank you," Pierce replied.

She made them both tall glasses of the soft drink on ice, placing those on the table before going back to slice the pie.

When she brought those over, Pierce stared.

Golden crust filled with glistening peaches. It almost looked too perfect to eat.

"Like something from a magazine," he mused out loud.

"Thanks." Finally appearing relaxed, Cassie grinned. "It's one of my specialties. Dig in."

Needing no second prompting, Pierce picked up his fork.

Peaches, cinnamon, vanilla, whatever Cassie had put into this pie, it was the best thing Pierce had ever tasted. It just melted in his mouth.

Sipping her drink, Cassie took a forkful of her own slice and ate it. She chewed deliberately, avoiding looking at Pierce.

"This is very good," Pierce said quietly. "Amazing, actually. It's restaurant quality."

Meeting his gaze, she smiled. "Well, since The Tumbleweed Café regularly sells out of it, I definitely hope so."

Pierce nodded. He took a long drink from his glass, clearly enjoying it. "It's been a long time since I had a Dr Pepper, even if it is diet."

"They're my favorite," she said. Then she lifted up her glass and held it out. "Let's make a toast. Congratulations on buying the farm."

He gently clinked his glass to hers. "And congratulations to you on selling it."

They both drank.

Gathering up the empty plates, she carried them over to the sink. When she returned, she dropped back into her chair and looked at him. "I hope you don't mind me asking, but have you given any thought to what you plan to do with this place once your stalker is caught and you can go back home?"

Since he'd only recently started fleshing out an idea, which might turn out unworkable, he didn't want to say. "I'm considering several options at the moment," he said. "Are you wanting to buy it back when I put it up for sale?"

Her eyes widened. "Oh, hell no. But I did grow up here, so I admit to being curious about what happens to the farm."

"I promise to keep you informed," he said. "If you don't mind me asking, why'd you decide to sell?"

Chapter 3

Cassie took a deep drink of her Diet Dr Pepper while she tried to think of a concise way to answer his question. In reality, she hadn't reached the decision to sell lightly. Or quickly, for that matter.

"I wanted a new start," she said, inwardly wincing at how glib that statement sounded. "Honestly, I didn't want to spend the rest of my life raising swine for slaughter."

This made him smile. "I get that. I wouldn't either. Especially if I had a pig like Albert."

Relieved, she nodded. "Technically, I could have kept this place and worked at something else. Which is likely what I'd have done if no one bought it."

"Then I guess you're glad I did," he said.

"Yes." She couldn't tell him she saw the ghosts of her past in every room of this house. The giant recliner would always be her father's chair, and even though he'd been gone five years, she still couldn't bring herself to sit in it. The material had faded and some of the seams had started to pull apart. A logical person would have simply tossed it. Not Cassie. Instead, she'd let the new buyer deal with it.

In this case, Pierce.

"What are your plans from here?" he asked.

"I'm going to look for another house," she replied, well

aware that he'd prefer her stay here to be as short as possible. If not for financial considerations, she'd have already moved. "I need to be able to bring Albert wherever I go. I've been trying to decide if I want to stay here in Getaway or venture out a little farther."

He finished his soft drink and pushed the glass away. "What will you do for a living?"

Taking a deep breath, she met his gaze. "Whether I stay here in Getaway or not, I'm going to look into the possibility of opening my own bakery. I want to call it Cassie's Creations."

Saying her idea out loud made it feel real. This filled her with a kind of excited optimism.

"That's amazing," he said, sounding as if he meant it. "Did you say you already sell your baked goods to the local café?"

"Yes. The Tumbleweed has a standing order, which they've recently increased since they regularly sell out." She took a deep breath and continued. "While I enjoy cooking, I'll never be a gourmet chef, except for baking. I've perfected my own recipes and I already have signature cakes, pies, and breads."

"Well if that peach pie is anything to go on, I believe you'll be a resounding success wherever you decide to go. Though if you already have a bit of a following here, it might make sense to stay local."

He had a point, and it was something she'd considered. While she hadn't had a super happy childhood, she knew this town and the people in it and they knew her. She was one of them, pig farmer's daughter notwithstanding. Realistically, she knew she'd have a better shot at making her bakery a success here in Getaway.

It tickled her to no end that the Tumbleweed sold out of her baked goods on a daily basis. They'd increased their standing order three times in as many weeks. And Serenity's niece Ella, who now ran the local metaphysical store Serenity owned, had opened her own café inside Serenity's store. She'd also begun placing orders for pies and cakes. All of this combined to help Cassie realize that yes, she really might be able to make a living with something that gave her so much joy.

Hope buoying her, she'd found the courage to finally take action, first by listing the farm. The fact that it had sold so soon might even be considered a sign from the heavens that she was on the right path.

Now she needed to do two things immediately. Find a new place to live. Then explore her options for opening her own bakery. Trudi had promised to help with both of them.

Like Cassie, Trudi had grown up here in Getaway. She'd moved away, attending college in Austin, where she'd also married and later, divorced. During that time, she'd gotten her real estate license. When she'd returned home, she'd gotten a job working for a real estate broker in Odessa who'd allowed her to open a small, satellite office in Getaway.

Surprisingly, Trudi had managed to do a decent amount of business. Judging by how well she'd done with listing Cassie's farm, Trudi was good at her job. Cassie knew she'd help her find the perfect place, both to live and to work.

Ideally, she'd like to find a building where she could live above the bakery. Of course, having a huge, pet pig complicated things. Albert would need his own yard. As long as he had dirt that could be made into mud and a small, grassy area, he'd be happy.

Cassie hadn't been sure how it would work out staying in her previous home with the new buyer, who also happened to be a famous writer. But so far, he seemed like a nice enough guy. The fact that he was easy on the eyes didn't hurt either.

"You're right," she said, meaning it. "That's exactly why I'm hoping to stay here in Getaway."

An alarm went off on her phone. Checking it, she realized she had to go. "I'm sorry," she told Pierce. "I've got to meet my Realtor. Wish me luck."

"Definitely," he said.

She met Trudi at the first property, a small ranch-style house listed as a fixer-upper. As she parked out front, Trudi came out the front door. "Welcome!" she chirped. "This one does need a lot of work, but I definitely think you'd get a lot back for your investment."

Though doing home renovations had never been something Cassie wanted, she'd agreed to take a look at this house due to the low price.

"It doesn't look too bad on the outside," Cassie said. "It just needs some landscaping."

"Right?" Trudi beamed. "Though maybe I'd paint the brick too."

Inside, the house looked as if it had sat empty and abandoned for years. "Did rodents make nests inside here?" Cassie asked, looking around in dismay. There were holes in the Sheetrock, droppings and nesting materials on the floor, and the stained and dirty carpet looked like someone had set a fire in the middle of the living room instead of using the fireplace.

The bathrooms both needed to be completely redone and when Cassie stepped into the kitchen, she let out an audible gasp.

"Someone started renovations here and then abandoned the attempt," Trudi guessed. "Too bad they didn't leave any of the appliances."

"It's all adding up to quite a bit of money," Cassie said.

"Not to mention how long it would take before this house is even livable. Let's go take a look at the next one."

"Okay. I think you'll like that one a lot better."

Following Trudi outside, Cassie waited while the other woman locked up. Then she got into her truck and followed Trudi's white Lexus.

The second house, a two-story colonial that had been built in the late 1980s, sat on the other side of town. While its price tag was significantly higher than the ranch, it was still squarely within Cassie's budget.

"This one is more move-in ready," Trudi said, as they walked up the sidewalk.

"I feel like we should be on an episode of *House Hunters*," Cassie mused, waiting while Trudi used the lockbox to extract the key and unlock the front door.

"That would have been nice," Trudi said, her trademark big smile back in place. "Come on inside. I think we're both going to like this one a lot better."

Stepping into the foyer, Cassie looked around. "This one is huge," she said, trying not to imagine the utility bills. "I'm not sure I need this much space."

"You'd be surprised," Trudi said. She checked her phone. "It's 3548 square feet, so it is quite large."

Cassie didn't say anything else as she followed Trudi around the home. It had four bedrooms and three and a half baths, two living areas, and a media room. "This is made for a large family," she finally said, once they'd made a complete circuit of the home.

"Which you might have someday," Trudi pointed out helpfully.

"Doubtful," Cassie replied. "I think I'll have to pass on this one too. Let's go look at the last house."

As she got into her truck, she realized she was glad she

wasn't on a TV show like *House Hunters* where she actually would have to make a decision. Right now, it wasn't looking too good for her finding a place to live in Getaway.

Hopefully, the third time would be the charm.

This house appeared to have been built in the late fifties. Its neighborhood sat just outside of where the commercial district began.

Parking in front of the cute little bungalow, Cassie felt her spirits lift. "I like that this is only a couple of blocks away from Main Street," she said. "I could definitely walk to town."

Trudi nodded. "Yes, you could. And this one has the best backyard for that pet of yours. There's an area under that huge live oak where grass won't grow. It's all dirt."

"Which would be perfect for Albert," Cassie said. Almost afraid to hope, she hung back while Trudi got the door open.

Once in, Trudi stopped so quickly that Cassie almost ran into her. "What is that smell?" Trudi asked, putting her hand over her nose.

A second later, Cassie smelled what seemed to be a mixture of urine and feces. She instinctively took a step back, covering her own mouth and nose. Her eyes started watering. "Is someone really living here with that?"

"I guess so." Trudi shook her head. "I'm sorry, I just can't." She stepped outside, Cassie right behind her.

"That's awful," Cassie said.

"Yes, it is. The Realtor ought to be ashamed of themselves." She got her phone out and pulled up the listing. "Oh. The owner is acting as his own real estate agent. Maybe he is so used to the smell that he doesn't realize how bad it is."

She glanced at Cassie. "I'll make sure and fill them in. I'm assuming you have no interest in seeing the rest of the house now, right?"

"Right." Cassie grimaced. "I don't have any idea what a buyer would have to do to get rid of that stench permanently. But I suspect it won't be an easy fix."

Trudi nodded. "That means I'm out of houses to show you today. I'm really glad you have a place to stay."

"Me too," Cassie answered, trying not to feel too discouraged. She'd looked at three houses. Or two, since she hadn't done more than walk in and walk out of the third. There weren't that many more for sale in such a small town.

"Do you want to expand your search to one of the nearby towns?" Trudi asked.

Immediately, Cassie vetoed that idea. "I'm either going to stay here or move far, far away," she said. "I was really hoping to find something in town. After I find a place to live, then I can start looking for space to open my bakery."

Expression serious, Trudi nodded. "I'll keep an eye out for anything new coming on the market, but right now I've showed you everything that's even close to your price range."

Since Cassie had also looked online, she knew the only other properties in Getaway were large ranches on the outskirts of town, with price tags well over a million dollars. In other words, unaffordable.

"If any new commercial buildings come on the market, let me know," Cassie said. "As you know, I'd love to find one with living space above what would be the bakery. It would have to have a small outdoor space as well. I'm aware that's a pretty tall order with my limited budget, but I'm putting it out there once more, just in case."

"I'll keep my eyes open," Trudi promised. "And let me know if you change your mind on any of the houses we saw today."

"I will," Cassie said, even though that was extremely

unlikely. Even if Pierce suddenly kicked her out. If she had to, she'd stay at The Landshark Motel. If she got one of the ground floor units around the back of the building, she doubted they'd even notice Albert. Not bad for a backup plan.

Trudi pulled her in for a hug and they said goodbye. As Cassie climbed back into her truck to drive home, she realized she could no longer consider the farm her home. It belonged to Pierce Spade, and the sooner she got out of there, the better.

Now that he'd taken possession of his newest property, Pierce hadn't expected to feel so restless. Unsettled, actually. What had previously seemed like an adventure now felt as if it might be a mistake. He couldn't shake the feeling that he'd overlooked something. Some small detail that might reveal his location to the person who wanted him dead.

Cassie pointing out that if he went into town, he'd run the risk of being recognized had made him think. While highly unlikely, since he doubted most readers studied the author's face on the book jacket, this still remained a possibility. The fact that he'd completely changed his appearance made this even less likely.

Initially, he'd had no intentions of holing up at the farm like some kind of recluse. He wanted to be able to check out the town itself. Trudi had given him a printout in his packet at closing. Clearly homemade, it had listed all the businesses in town and their locations. He'd been intrigued at the variety of eating places, both fast food and actual restaurants where you could sit down and enjoy a meal.

There were even two bars. The Rattlesnake Pub and a place called, interestingly enough, The Bar. Since he loved to people-watch, he fully intended to grab a beer or two in both places. Inspiration for his novels didn't come from a vacuum. He had to get out, experience the people and places around him.

There were several other places in Getaway that sounded intriguing. Rancher's Supply, which seemed to be a combination feedstore and hardware store. Serenity's, a metaphysical shop that also contained a small café inside that served breakfast and lunch.

But the place that Pierce most wanted to visit was the small-town bookstore. Once again, in what seemed to be a trend unique to Getaway, the owner had named it simply The Bookstore. Bookstores and libraries, which Getaway did not have, were Pierce's absolute most favorite places on earth.

Naturally, he planned to pay this one a visit. He'd take extra precautions when he went there, since if anyone in town could even begin to recognize him, it would be an avid reader. Yet he felt confident that the dramatic change he'd made to his appearance would deter even his biggest fan.

He should be safe for now. And like he'd planned, he'd consider this time here as a sabbatical of sorts. He'd write and work on the plans he had for turning the farm into something else. A few ideas had crossed his mind, but he really liked the idea of creating a kind of writer's retreat. A place where experienced authors could mentor beginners. A way for people like him to give back.

Cassie had left a few hours ago, explaining she was meeting up with Trudi to look at a few houses. He'd nodded, wished her luck, and sent her off with a wave.

Once she'd driven away, he wandered the small house and thought about all the renovations he'd do if he truly planned to live here.

After a few minutes, he kept feeling like something was missing. And then he realized. The silence felt deafening.

He'd spent the past several years living in Manhattan, at first paying outrageous prices to share a tiny apartment with two other guys. He'd moved there from upstate as soon as he could. He'd wanted to become a published author and in his mind, NYC was just where a serious writer needed to live.

He'd grown to love the constant sounds of the city; the traffic, the horns, the buzz of conversation in crowded coffee shops, the press of seriously busy people on the street.

When he'd sold his first book, he'd celebrated. To his surprise, this sale didn't make him instantly rich. Nor did that book—or the one after it—become instant bestsellers. However he had managed to earn out his advance, which meant the publisher had offered him a second contract.

By then, he'd hired Michael Huffstetler as his agent. And when his third book had garnered a huge, word-of-mouth buzz that had catapulted it onto the bestseller lists, Michael had been ready.

Pierce had done well enough that he'd been able to buy his own apartment in a beautiful building close to 100th Street on the East Side. While he had lived alone for the first time then, he'd had a constant stream of friends and employees, including his personal assistant, who often worked at his place for eight hours a day. In addition to her, he employed an editorial service to do basic proofreading and editing of his rough drafts.

Then he'd had to go off the map and leave everything and everyone behind. While this should have been great for his writing, he wasn't really sure how he'd deal with so much solitude.

He'd ended up here on this pig farm by choice, he reminded himself. He'd figure out what to do with the farm when all this was over.

But for now, he realized that he didn't want to live at this remote location all alone. He thought about turning on the TV, but during the day he usually listened to music. Since he didn't see any kind of stereo or even a smart speaker, that would have to be one of his first purchases in town.

The sound of tires on gravel made him realize Cassie had returned. He felt an uncharacteristic jolt of relief.

She opened the front door and came barreling in, stopping short when she first saw him.

"Well, that was a huge waste of time," she said. Shaking her head, she bustled past him toward the kitchen, truck keys still in hand. "None of the places I looked at with Trudi were even remotely acceptable."

"You know you're welcome to stay as long as you like," he heard himself say as he followed her.

When she spun to stare at him in disbelief, he felt he needed to elaborate. "I mean it."

Gaze appraising him, she finally dipped her chin. "I really appreciate that, more than you know. It's a very kind offer." She took a deep breath. "But I can't help feeling like I'm in your way. You bought this place to be alone. Not to have the former owner underfoot."

"How about I offer you a job?" he said, coming up with what he had to admit might be a brilliant solution to both of their problems. "You stay here, work as my editorial assistant, and I'll pay you."

He named what he considered a fair salary, noting how her eyes widened. "Mostly I'd need you to do some proofreading, maybe help me brainstorm or work out some sticky parts of my plot."

"On your books?" she asked, her voice full of disbelief.

The question made him smile. "Yes, on my books. I'm just fleshing out the next one. I haven't even finished writing the synopsis yet."

She thought for a moment, clearly not entirely convinced. "Don't you already have someone to do that?"

"Back in New York," he replied. "She's on vacation right now. I couldn't tell even her where I went, for her own safety as well as mine."

She studied him, her expression considering. "What are the hours?" she asked.

"You can work part-time," he replied. "That would mean you can spend as much time as you need getting your bakery set up."

"That sounds too good to be true."

"Does it?" He carefully kept his tone casual. "I need the help. And I honestly think it might be easier getting everything in place for a new business without having to worry about setting up a new place to live."

"True."

"I could really use your help," he said. "And when all this is over, I'll name you in the dedication."

"The dedication?" Making a face, she shook her head. "Maybe most people might jump at something like that, but I'm not sure I'd want my name put out there for no good reason. Unless you were advertising my baked goods."

Her quick smile lit up her face, making him inhale sharply. He'd never met a beautiful woman who wasn't aware of the power of her looks until now. Cassie seemed down-to-earth and completely unaware of how her appearance affected him.

"Let me think about it," she finally said. "Right now, I'm out of options. Trudi has promised to let me know if anything else comes available."

"Please do. I really could use the help."

They spent the rest of the day managing to avoid each other. Cassie made a simple meal of spaghetti with meat sauce for the evening meal. Since she'd cooked, he cleaned up, amused when she acted surprised at his help.

She disappeared into her room shortly after they'd eaten, and only briefly resurfaced when she went into the main bathroom to wash up before bed.

The unfamiliar bed gave him pause, but the sheets were clean and the mattress comfy.

The next morning, he rose shortly after sunrise. Mornings were his favorite time of the day. He dressed comfortably and headed toward the kitchen for his necessary cup of coffee, figuring he'd shower later.

The instant he turned the corner, his mouth started watering. He smelled bread or cake or muffins. Maybe all three. Vanilla and cinnamon and hints of chocolate.

To his surprise, he found Cassie already seated at the table, mug in hand. Clearly, she'd already started baking. And then he remembered she'd said she made regular deliveries to a couple of cafés in town.

She looked up when he entered. "You're up early," she said, unsmiling.

"So are you."

"Old habits die hard." She shrugged. "Such is the life of a former farmer, now professional baker. I have to get these baked goods delivered before the breakfast rush happens. The fresher, the better. I usually start around 3:30 a.m."

"Three thirty," he repeated. "Respect."

Her smile lit up her face. Trying not to stare, he found himself looking wildly around the room.

A grunt from the other side of the table made him realize she'd brought Albert into the kitchen. The large pig lay on his side, clearly enjoying the feel of the cool tile floor.

"Is he house-trained?" Pierce wondered out loud.

Still smiling, she nodded. "Believe it or not, he is. It's one of the first things I taught him."

Weird, but Pierce realized he didn't really mind. In fact, he might actually use this scenario in one of his books someday.

After getting his coffee, he joined Cassie at the table.

"You didn't ever say what you're doing up at the crack of dawn," she said, eyeing him over her cup. "Aren't you supposed to be on vacation?"

"Vacation? No. This is probably the furthest thing from a vacation that I can imagine."

"Touché," she acknowledged. "But even if it's not, you never did say why you're up so early."

"I'm a morning person," he explained. "By choice. I find I think better earlier in the day, so I save all the physical tasks for the afternoon."

"Which, I'm guessing, means if I decided to take the job as your assistant, I could choose my own time to work."

Surprised, he nodded. "I'm flexible about a schedule. As long as you get the task done, I'm good."

"I see." Sipping her coffee, she went quiet, appearing to be lost in her own thoughts.

Since he didn't want to rush her, he contented himself with watching Albert, in case the pig did something amusing. Instead, Albert continued to doze, his large sides rising and falling in rhythm with each breath.

"Are you sure you want to hire me?" Cassie asked, breaking the silence. "I have zero experience with the type of work you're wanting me to do."

He met her gaze. "I saw your book collection," he said. "You're an avid reader. I also couldn't help but notice you have every single one of my novels in hardcover." He smiled. "I think you might be much more experienced than you think."

With a sigh, she slowly nodded. "I'll take the job. It's not looking like I'm going to find another place to live anytime soon. And as long as you don't mind me using the kitchen to continue baking, I think we'll get along just fine."

More relieved than he wanted to reveal, he leaned across the table and held out his hand. "Then we have a deal."

They shook. He fought the urge to hold on to her a bit longer than necessary.

His phone rang, announcing a call. Michael's number showed on the screen. Even though it was an hour later on the East Coast, it was still early. Since Michael could only reach him on whatever burner phone he was using at the moment, Pierce knew his agent would only call if it was urgent.

"What's up?" Pierce asked instead of saying hello.

"He set your place on fire." Michael sounded agitated and out of breath. "It was bad. One firefighter was killed along with several residents. Three more people were seriously injured. The building is destroyed."

Speechless, Pierce struggled to find words.

"I wanted to let you know before you see it on the news. They're calling your building a total loss."

"Are they saying it's arson?" Pierce asked, hoping Michael would say the fire had been caused by something else—a faulty circuit or someone who'd left something on the stove when they'd gone out.

"They're still investigating, but they're calling it suspected arson," Michael confirmed. "And while your stalker hasn't attempted contact to gloat, you and I both know this was likely his handiwork."

Still grappling with the news, Pierce swallowed hard. "But people have died. Lost their homes, their possessions. Because of me."

Cassie got up and squeezed his shoulder, clearly hearing the anguish in his voice.

"Not because of you," Michael said fiercely. "This is not your fault. You have no control over anything this murderous killer does. Hopefully, he made some sort of mistake when he set this fire. Maybe someone got him on camera."

"They need to catch him." Before, when he'd been the only target, Pierce had felt righteous anger and admittedly, annoyance for the disruption of his life. Now the stalker had gone a step further. Total strangers had died and were actively suffering because of his actions.

"I feel confident they will," Michael replied. "I hope you took with you whatever belongings meant the most, because it's looking like everything you left there is gone."

"Things can be replaced. People cannot. Thanks for letting me know."

"The authorities want to speak with you," Michael continued. "I didn't want to give out your number, but you need to contact them. I'll text you Detective Rodriguez's information."

"Thanks. I'm sure they're going to have a lot of questions. Did you put them with the ATF people?" Pierce asked.

"I did. But they still need to take your statement."

"That makes sense." Pierce sighed. "I hate this."

"I know you do. I'll be in touch as soon as I hear anything more," Michael said. "Or if the stalker reaches out. Just make sure and let me know when you switch phones."

Pierce promised he would and ended the call.

Chapter 4

The instant Pierce finished his call, Cassie hurriedly moved away from him. She'd acted instinctively, sensing his need for comfort. But then she'd realized she definitely didn't want to give him the wrong message.

"Bad news?" she asked, deliberately keeping her voice light.

Gaze bleak, he nodded. When he told her what his agent had said, she realized his situation had just gotten a million times worse than it had been before.

His life had been completely turned upside down. Nothing, not even being famous, could insulate someone from something like that. She barely knew the man, but damned if she didn't feel bad for him. Anyone with an ounce of empathy would. She just didn't want him thinking she meant something else. He seemed like a nice guy, but she knew it paid to be careful. Especially since she'd just agreed to work for him and they'd be living together to boot.

Still, his deer-in-the-headlights expression tugged at her heart. He looked like he'd just been run over by a truck. For a quick second, she thought she'd do almost anything to make him feel better.

Chiding herself for her foolishness, she looked down at her mug. Since she'd finished her first coffee, she went and got another cup. When she'd finished filling her cup and turned around, Pierce was sitting absolutely still, staring at nothing, a look of shock still on his handsome face.

"I'm sorry," she offered.

He blinked, his gaze coming back into focus. "Me too. I don't know why, but I somehow thought that by my going into hiding, this stalker would have to stop. Even if temporarily, until he regained his bearings."

"You're pretty sure it's a *he*?" she asked, genuinely curious.

"Statistically speaking, most serial killers are male. While there's always a remote possibility that this one is female, it's unlikely. That's why I tend to use the masculine pronoun when referring to him."

She could sense the tension leaving him the more he talked. Good. She'd keep him talking then.

"That makes sense." She took another drink of her coffee. "I'm guessing you had to do a lot of research on the subject, considering what you write."

"I did." Hands curved around his own mug, he almost seemed contemplative. "I never would have guessed that the type of things I wrote about would actually become my own life."

Then, while she was struggling to figure out something to say, he shook his head. "I'll just have to work harder and try to figure out which serial killer this person is."

Now she gaped at him. "I thought the police were working on that."

"They are. But I know my books better than anyone else. I made folders full of research for each one. And I brought those folders with me. I'm going to look through them. Maybe some similarities will jump out at me. It's worth a try."

Confused, she studied him. "Am I assisting you with your writing or with your research?"

"Both." He dragged a hand through his hair, his briefly startled expression revealing that he'd forgotten he'd cut it. "I definitely have a shortage of time."

She couldn't tell if he was being pragmatic or self-pitying. In the end, it didn't matter. She had been asked to do a job and she'd agreed.

"When do you want me to start?" she asked.

The blank look he gave her made her realize his thoughts were still somewhere else.

"Work," she elaborated. "Acting as your PA. I'm a big fan of routines, so I need to set up my schedule."

One of her timers went off. She got up and carefully removed four pies from the oven, placing them on cooling racks.

"Those smell amazing," Pierce said, inhaling deeply.

"Thanks. Muffins go in next. I can't wait until I have an actual commercial kitchen so I don't have to bake things in stages."

He looked around at the counter. She had two large, electric mixers out, multiple mixing bowls, all kinds of measuring cups, and a rolling pin. "Looks like you already have most of the other equipment," he said.

His comment made her laugh. "Not even close," she told him. "I have a running list of things I need to purchase. What I'm working with here isn't nearly enough for the kind of volume I plan to have. Thank goodness there's a discount restaurant supply company in Midland."

"I'd like to go with you some time," he said, surprising her.

"Why?" she asked, genuinely curious.

His expression a combination of amused and sheepish,

he shrugged. "I'm always interested in learning new things. I know next to nothing about bakeries. Who knows, the information might come in handy someday."

"As in, you could use it in a book?" she asked.

"Guilty as charged," he replied.

"Speaking of books, have you decided yet when you'd like me to start working for you?"

He eyed her, considering. "I'm not ready yet, but as soon as I have enough material, I'll let you know. That way, I can take a little time to get settled before I get back to work."

She hid her surprise. For whatever reason, she'd assumed he wanted her to start immediately. "Sure, that will work," she agreed. "By the way, since I'm a fan, isn't your next book coming out in June?"

"It is," he answered, making a face. "It's a continuation of *Too Broke to Die*, called *Too Dead to Be Broke*."

Interest piqued, she eyed him. "I'd heard that, but wasn't sure I believed it. Since you wrapped everything up in *Too Broke to Die*, how is it a continuation?" Then, before he could answer, she held up her hand. "Never mind. Don't tell me. I don't like spoilers. Since I'll be buying it, I'll read it myself and find out."

"No need to buy it," he said. "I can give you an ARC— advance reading copy—right now. I've got several of them."

She wanted to jump up and down but managed to contain herself. He'd think she was a fool if she let him see her glee. "I'd like that a lot," she said. "In fact, I can't wait."

"Let me go see if I can find them," he said. "I'm pretty sure I brought a few copies with me."

A timer went off. Which meant the muffins were done baking. After she got them out, she needed to check on the rising bread dough.

Turning, she tended to all that, humming quietly while

she did. She'd always loved this time of the day, the quiet hours she spent mixing ingredients and baking up her own creations. Pierce had quietly left the room, no doubt to look for the book he'd said he'd give her. Which she considered a very kind offer, especially since his books came out in hardcover. Other authors, she'd either download an e-copy or wait a year for the paperback to come out. For a Pierce Spade thriller, she allowed herself to indulge in hardcover copies. After all, he was her favorite author.

Despite all of the drama surrounding him, her first impression was a quiet, kind man who appeared completely unaware of his own masculine beauty. Or, she amended, if he knew, he didn't play games or try to use that to get what he wanted.

So far. After all, she barely knew him. She supposed time would tell.

Hearing what had happened to his apartment building had come as a shock. Partly because she'd supposed a famous author as popular as Pierce would live in a mansion somewhere rather than an apartment. Though she guessed if one liked living right in the middle of the hustle and bustle of the city, his choice of living spaces would seem more understandable.

All of it seemed—luckily—very distant. Faraway. Which was a good thing, as far as she was concerned. The last thing she wanted to deal with was a serial killer who clearly didn't care who got in the way. Hopefully, the magnitude of this latest act would compel law enforcement to step up their efforts to catch him.

She'd try to remember to turn on the news later. She'd bet that would be one story they'd definitely feature.

Since the bread took a bit longer to bake, she hurried off to take a quick shower. It felt weird using the guest bathroom and locking the door, but she'd just have to get used to it. Just like she'd grown accustomed to living alone. Sharing the house with a man so attractive that every time she looked at him her toes curled would also require a bit of an adjustment.

Emerging from her shower with her hair still damp, she arrived just in time to take the bread out so it could cool.

Pierce had left the book on the table for her. She picked it up, thrilled even though it wasn't hardcover. It also had the words *Advance Reading Copy* stamped on the front.

The title made her smile. *Too Dead to Be Broke*. Definitely a continuation of his previous novel.

When she opened it, the inscription inside made her catch her breath. *To my new friend and assistant, Cassie. I'm looking forward to working with you! Pierce Spade.*

Autographed even. Clutching the book to her chest like a starstruck teenager, she carried it into her room and placed it on her dresser. Then she blow-dried her hair, put on a little mascara and lip gloss, and went back to the kitchen.

Now that she'd finished baking, she loaded everything into plastic tubs and secured those in the bed of her truck. She'd wished a hundred times for an SUV, but that type of expenditure wouldn't be in the budget for a long, long time. She had more important things to spend her money on.

She'd just packed up the last tub and placed it into her truck when Pierce returned, his dark hair still damp from the shower.

"Where'd it all go?" he asked, looking around the kitchen.

"I've got it all loaded up to take into town. I've got to get it to the Tumbleweed before the breakfast rush starts."

"About those pies," he said, expression serious. "Can I just buy one now, before you even deliver it?"

"No," she told him. "They're all part of the Tumbleweed's order. But I can make an extra one later."

"I'd be happy to pay you for it."

"No need." She waved his words away. "Consider it a trade for the advance copy of your book."

"I'm guessing you haven't had time to even glance at it, have you?"

His grin made her stomach somersault. "No, not yet. I'll take a look at it later," she said, keeping her tone brisk. "I need to get these into town."

After Cassie left, Pierce found himself wandering the small house, alone with his thoughts. Part of him regretted not asking her to let him accompany her, but he hadn't wanted to be too pushy. He would have plenty of time to spend with her later on down the road.

Alone in the small house, he quickly realized he wasn't sure how to deal with the quiet. There weren't any sounds at all, not even distant traffic or sirens. While intellectually, he'd known a farm by its very definition would be out in the country, he hadn't realized how much the absolute silence would affect him.

That wasn't the only problem either.

He'd never felt as restless as he did right now. Like his skin no longer fit. Out of his normal environment, out of sorts, he'd been shocked to realize how much of a distraction he found Cassie Denton.

He loved her down-to-earth nature and the way she seemed completely oblivious of her own sensual beauty. He suspected she didn't take any BS from anyone, and the pride she took in her craft reminded him of the way he felt when he finished writing a book.

Everything in him wanted to get to know her better. But

why? He certainly had no plans to stay here once his stalker had been caught. And he'd never been the type to start something he couldn't finish.

Going into hiding went against everything in his nature. Like the protagonists in his books, he preferred to take action and influence the outcome rather than passively wait for things to happen to him.

Right now, he felt particularly impotent. Way out here in West Texas, he was helpless to do anything about the wreckage the stalker/alleged serial killer had left in his wake. Pierce's name would be forever linked to what had happened. And he knew no matter what it took, he'd somehow figure out a way to make it right for all those who'd suffered.

He'd loved his apartment. But more than the building and its contents, he'd loved his neighbors. Some of them had been living in the building for decades, even before the extensive renovations some of the units had undergone. He hated to think of them out on the streets with nothing but the clothes on their backs.

No one and nothing was safe with Pierce around. Even his fleeing New York hadn't kept his neighbors safe.

Then his thoughts returned to Cassie. With her cheerful optimism and innocent smile. The idea of her suffering even the slightest bit because of him made his stomach swirl and nausea rise in his throat.

Maybe it would be better if she found another place to live sooner rather than later. Most likely, he shouldn't have offered her a job, no matter how badly he might need the help and the companionship.

Once he'd had the thought, it wouldn't leave. One of the downfalls about being an author was his vivid imagination. Unfortunately, he could actually envision in great detail what would happen if the stalker made his way to Getaway. Clearly. Way too clearly.

The thought of someone attacking Cassie brought the kind of impotent rage that made him want to punch something. A punching bag, preferably. His building had a state-of-the-art gym, of which Pierce had made good use. Here, he had nothing. He'd seen a woodpile out back. Maybe chopping some logs would have the same kind of effect.

Instead, he continued to pace the house. Kitchen to living room, hallway to primary bedroom, and repeat. While small, this house was bigger than his first Manhattan apartment, though it wasn't nearly as big as his last.

He felt trapped. Like a sitting duck.

As a man who'd always trusted his instincts, everything inside him screamed *run*. But where and for how long? He didn't want to spend his life running away from a madman. No. He wanted to meet the threat head-on and take it out.

Like some hero in an action movie. Shaking his head at himself, Pierce knew that, while physically he was in good shape for a fight, this was not the way. This stalker had made it clear that the threat wasn't the kind that could be settled using hand-to-hand combat. Like the plots of the books Pierce wrote, this had become a game of psychological warfare that would culminate in one or the other being killed.

Pierce did not intend for that to be him.

The only consolation was that maybe the fire would cause the Fed's investigation to go into overdrive.

Because the sooner this lunatic was caught, the better. For everyone.

Finally, Pierce grabbed his favorite pen and a notebook and dealt with his stress the way he always did. By writing.

By the time Cassie's beast of a truck rumbled down the long driveway, he'd filled several pages with handwritten notes. With his life in turmoil, he'd been struggling to flesh out a synopsis for his next book.

Now he'd managed to find a glimmer of an idea, and the more he fleshed it out, the more he liked it. Even better, he realized he felt human again.

Cassie breezed through the back door. She stopped short when she spotted him at the kitchen table. "Hi," she said, her voice sounding shy. "I hope I'm not interrupting anything."

Realizing she meant his notes, he shook his head. "You're not." Standing, he stretched. "Sometimes writing is the only way I can clear my head."

"I get that. Baking does that for me."

Another flash of an idea. He hadn't realized until that moment that there'd be someone who baked in this next book. Whether the character would be male or female, he didn't yet know.

"Excuse me a second," he said, jotting that information down so he didn't forget it. He'd learned a long time ago never to trust anything related to writing to memory. Especially ideas that blew up in his mind overnight, waking him from a sound sleep. Those plot twists were never as brilliant in the morning as they'd seemed at 3:00 a.m., but he'd surprisingly gleaned a few gems from his nocturnal notes.

When he looked up again, she still stood motionless, watching him. He couldn't interpret the expression on her beautiful face. Intrigued or amused or interested. Perhaps a combination of all three. For the first time, he realized he might be as much of an oddity to her as she was to him.

His phone rang before he could comment. Since no one but Michael had this phone number, he braced himself for more bad news as he answered.

"What's happened now?" he asked, by way of greeting.

"You can run but you cannot hide," a guttural, clearly

altered voice said. "I will find you. And you will pay with your life."

Pierce's heartrate kicked into overdrive. "How'd you get this number?" he demanded.

But the caller had gone. Pierce didn't receive a response.

"Michael!" Pierce gasped, trying not to panic. He dialed his agent's number from memory. As it rang, he willed the other man to pick up.

When the call went to voicemail, Pierce left a short message asking for a call back.

"What happened?" Cassie asked, her eyes wide.

He relayed what the caller had said. "The only person who has this number is my agent." He cursed. "If this creep has harmed one single hair on Michael's head…"

"I don't think your agent would be careless enough to let this stalker close to him," Cassie pointed out, clearly trying to reassure him.

"Maybe not," he admitted. "But until I speak to him, I'm going to worry. I can't see any other way this guy could have gotten my number."

"Maybe he's a hacker. Just because it's a burner phone, doesn't mean the actual phone number wouldn't show up in a database somewhere. Maybe he just looked into phone calls Michael made."

Begrudgingly, he had to admit she could be right. "That's a very good possibility. I actually wrote a situation where the bad guy did exactly that."

"I know." She smiled. "It's entirely possible that your stalker is simply using your novels as a playbook."

"Probably. But it's hard to know what he'll use. He's already burned down almost an entire apartment building with no regard for how many people he might hurt or kill.

Someone like that wouldn't hesitate to hurt someone I care about just to get to me."

Her smile faltered, then faded away. "All I can say is that I hope not. I have to think your agent, being fully aware of what's going on, wouldn't let his guard down."

Slowly he nodded, willing to let himself be reassured in the moment.

"Plus," she continued. "Didn't you say law enforcement was involved? Surely, they've assigned someone to watch over him."

Another good point. He swore he could feel some of the tension leaving his shoulders. "Maybe you're right. If Michael doesn't call me back, I'll try again to reach him later."

Her clear green gaze appraised him. "That sounds like a plan. Now how about I show you how to make one of those peach pies you asked for?"

Willing to be distracted, he agreed.

After Cassie assembled all the ingredients, she motioned him over. "I make my piecrusts in bulk ahead of time and I freeze them," she said. "If I had a larger freezer, I'd do that with whole pies, but this is what I have to work with for now."

As she showed him how to make the filling, which turned out to be something else she made in advance, they stood hip to hip. Though Cassie didn't appear to be affected in the slightest, he found himself noticing every little thing about her. She smelled like vanilla, which he hadn't expected. Her delicate wrists and capable hands had him longing to have them touching his skin. Her high cheekbones, those emerald eyes framed by long lashes, and a lush mouth that seemed made for kissing, all were part of her appeal. How had he never noticed the way she moved like a dancer, sensual and confident?

Everything about this woman, a former pig farmer in a dusty, West Texas town, attracted him the way a moth felt drawn to a flame. The simple analogy made him smile, since he knew if he'd been writing this in one of his own books he'd have to find a better choice of words.

Knowing that did not negate the effect she had on him. He knew it was something he'd have to get over, the sooner the better.

"Are you okay?" she asked, breaking into his thoughts.

"Just imagining how good that pie is going to taste," he said, only partly lying.

Her grin made her eyes sparkle. Entranced, he had to force himself to look away.

The sound of his phone startled him. He pulled it from his pocket and answered.

"What's going on?" Michael asked. "I got your message. I have a meeting in ten, so I can't talk long."

Pierce quickly filled him in on the unexpected and unwelcome phone call. He ended with telling his agent that he had no idea how the stalker had gotten his number since Michael was the only one Pierce had given it to.

"Which is why you sounded so frantic," Michael said. "You thought maybe that stalker got to me."

"Exactly. And since he hasn't, now seems like a good time to warn you to take precautions."

"Thanks." Tone wry, Michael continued. "Still, this begs the question. Since it's a burner phone, how did he get the number?"

Pierce gave him Cassie's theory. Michael promised to see if he could look into that and then said he had to go or he'd be late for his meeting.

Once Pierce had shoved his phone back into his pocket, he looked up to find Cassie watching him.

"I got the gist of the conversation from listening to your end," she said. "I'm glad your agent is all right."

"Me too," he replied. Then, aware he sounded far too glum for such good news, he grabbed his notes and excused himself, heading outside. To his relief, Cassie didn't follow him. She must have realized he wanted to be alone.

Settling into one of the wooden rockers, he gazed out over the brown, dusty landscape. Maybe he should get a horse. With all the barns and sheds, he definitely had room for any livestock he might buy. Though he didn't really know how to ride, he figured he could always learn.

But then he'd have to figure out what to do with the animal when all this was over and he went back home. Or at least back to New York. He wasn't sure where he'd live once he returned.

Shaking his head at his own foolish thoughts, he returned his attention to his notebook and reread what he'd last written. As often was the case, his next novel revealed itself to him in fits and starts, little by little, often with excruciating slowness. When he finally had the entire picture, he wrote a synopsis, purposely leaving parts of it vague, since the characters always managed to surprise him.

Sometimes, scenes from his book played in his head like a movie. Others, he had to coax the words out from the dark recesses of his mind in bits and pieces, which sometimes seemed to take forever. Most days, the writing was somewhere in-between.

He liked writing the most when he lost himself in the story. Lately, with all that he had going on, he considered it a rare gift from the universe.

Sketching out some possibilities for several future scenes, he found himself distracted, thinking of Cassie. Her sensual beauty appealed to him in a way that rocked his world.

Bad timing, wrong location, and all in all the worst possible idea, but knowing this didn't make him want her less. Instead, the lure of the forbidden had her occupying his every waking thought.

Good thing he didn't affect her the same way. They'd both be in for a world of trouble if he did.

Chapter 5

Cassie watched through the window as Pierce settled into her father's old rocking chair. When Pierce had ended the call with his agent, instead of relief, his gaze had darkened, his expression shuttered and distant. He'd been lost in his own thoughts for a moment or two, almost as if he'd forgotten her presence.

She hadn't been surprised when he'd pushed to his feet, grabbed his notebook and pen, and excused himself. Clearly, he'd needed to be alone. She didn't know him well enough to even imagine what kind of thoughts might be going through his head, but her heart ached for him just the same.

Realizing this, she shook her head. A man like Pierce didn't need her sympathy. Nor did she have the time or energy to waste mooning over a drop-dead, gorgeous man who happened to be one of her favorite authors. She wasn't a groupie nor would she ever be.

Though she had to admit Pierce made her feel way out of her league.

Living on an isolated farm, Cassie hadn't spent a lot of time alone with members of the opposite sex. She'd barely dated in high school. Her status as a socially unacceptable outcast had made the only boys interested in her the kind who had a one-track mind. And every time she'd turned one down, they retaliated by telling more and more false stories about her.

There'd been her friends of course. The girls who rallied around her, walked through the hallways with her, and defended her against all the nonsense that a couple boys and their group of friends had tried to spread.

When graduation had finally rolled around, she'd managed to walk across the auditorium stage with her shoulders back and her head held high. She'd heard the whispers, noticed the knowing smiles, the leers, the cruel digs some of the other girls had lobbed her way.

Her friends, the ones that mattered, had stayed by her side. They'd celebrated the end of high school.

While some had gone off to college, attending Texas Tech, A&M, or UT, others had been like Cassie and stayed in town. They'd worked at their family business or had taken jobs in town.

They'd been kids, they'd been young. Most of those boys had gone on to other things. They'd grown up, moved away, and started families.

And she'd survived. Despite the stories they'd spread about her, Cassie hadn't experienced lovemaking until she'd turned twenty-four—last year. She'd had a whirlwind romance with a cowboy named Morgan, who'd come to work at one of the neighboring cattle ranches.

Passion had burned hot and fierce between them. She'd even thought, for a hot minute or two, that she'd been in love. They'd been together for three months, until one day he'd told her the time had come for him to move on. Then he'd up and left without a backward glance or a promise to stay in touch.

Devastated, but definitely wiser for the experience, she'd picked herself up and worked hard to heal. As the months had passed, she realized she hadn't loved Morgan nor he her. It had been sexual chemistry, pure and simple, nothing more. Looking back, she could understand it had been a learning experience. No regrets, no remorse.

Now the time had finally come for her to move forward with her own life. She was strong, she was capable, and she was smart. People loved her baked goods, and she couldn't imagine a better career than making money doing what she loved.

Again, she found herself looking out the window at Pierce. He'd gotten back to work, writing in his notebook. While she found him fascinating, she didn't have the time or the energy for another fling like she'd had with Morgan.

For the first time ever in her twenty-five years, she needed to focus on herself.

She'd assist Pierce Spade, earn her salary, which she desperately needed, and find, not only a new home in which to live, but more importantly, a building to open her bakery. She felt quite sure things would fall into place once she got started.

At least she no longer had to worry about maintaining the farm. She figured Pierce would learn about that soon enough. Keeping the pastures mowed took several days, but had to be done to keep the fire risk low.

Meanwhile, she still had the ARC—advanced reading copy—of Pierce's next book to read. She'd been purposely avoiding it, wanting to savor the anticipation. Hopefully, she could get started tonight.

Her cell rang, startling her out of her thoughts. It was her best friend, Kate.

"What's up?" Cassie asked.

Kate giggled. "I should be the one asking you that. I heard you're living with the guy who bought your farm. I want the tea. Is he young, is he hot, and how long before you two are—"

"We're not," Cassie interrupted. "I asked to have it written into the sales contract that I could stay here and pay rent until I found a new place to live. That's all."

"Seriously? I'm disappointed."

"Don't be," Cassie said. "This is all temporary. You know that."

"I do, but a girl can dream. You, of all people, could use a little romance in your life."

Since Kate had recently gotten engaged to her boyfriend, Jeremy, an RN who worked for Dr. Westmoreland, the local physician, she wanted the same thing for her best friend.

"I'll pass," Cassie said firmly. "The timing isn't right. I'll just sit back and bask in your glow."

This made Kate laugh again. "I'll let you too. I don't know when I've ever been happier. Do you want to meet up for a drink tonight?"

"At The Rattlesnake Pub?" Cassie asked.

"No, I want to go to The Bar. Have you been there?"

Since Cassie rarely went out drinking, she had to admit she hadn't.

"Oh, you'll love it," Kate promised. "Though Jeremy said he isn't a fan. He likes The Rattlesnake Pub better."

Since Jeremy looked more like a cowboy than a nurse, Cassie could understand that. The Rattlesnake Pub was where almost everyone in town congregated. They had live bands and trivia night, plus anytime Getaway had a meeting, they held it there. It was loud, it was rowdy, and it was fun.

"I've heard The Bar is kind of upscale," Cassie said. "Is there a dress code?"

Kate snorted. "In Getaway? No. It's quiet and classy, I'll

give it that. They have a ton of exotic cocktails, the waitstaff is friendly, and you can hear yourself talk."

"Do they have food?"

"They do," Kate replied. "Appetizer stuff, mostly. They have an entire menu called Small Plates. It's good too. And not all that expensive."

Her description made Cassie smile. "When do you want to meet up?"

"How about tonight? Seven?"

Cassie agreed. "Sounds good. I'll meet you there."

As she ended the call, she looked up and realized Pierce had left his seat. He hadn't come inside, so she guessed he must be wandering the property.

Though she knew technically where he went or what he did was absolutely none of her business, she stepped outside, hoping to see where he'd gone. She caught sight of him about to enter the barn, the sunlight turning his dark brown hair to gold.

For a moment, her entire world shifted. Then he disappeared inside and she blinked, chiding herself for her own foolishness.

She didn't see him again until she'd turned on the TV to watch the five-thirty news. He came in the back door, still carrying his notebook, whistling.

Which stopped when he saw her. "Hi," he said.

"Hi, yourself," she responded, hating both how she felt out of place in what had once been her childhood home and the ease with which he drew her to him without even trying.

"I got some good work done," he continued, holding up the notebook. "And I looked around and sketched out some ideas for converting the barn."

Interested despite herself, she eyed him. "Converting it into what?"

He gave her a sheepish smile. "I'm not sure yet. Just ideas at this point."

The nightly news came on. As she turned her attention to the anchorman, Pierce came around and took a seat on the opposite end of the couch. Even though a good four feet separated them, Cassie again felt that prickle of attraction.

Then a video of a raging fire in Manhattan came on the screen. "Arson is being blamed for a fire that completely destroyed a luxury apartment building in New York City," the anchor said. "Several residents have been hospitalized and there are at least four fatalities that we know of. One of these was a New York City firefighter."

Horrified, Cassie couldn't look away. Even though Pierce had told her exactly what had happened, seeing video of it actually happening felt like a punch in the gut.

Next to her, Pierce made a sound low in his throat. She turned to look at him, but he pushed to his feet. The bleakness in his expression made her ache.

"I'm sorry," she began.

He dragged his hand across his jaw. "Thanks," he said. He looked away for a moment and then returned his gaze to her. "Do you want to go into town and have a drink? I'm pretty sure no one would recognize me, but I can wear a baseball cap and maybe a pair of old eyeglasses just in case."

Inwardly, she felt a twinge of guilt, though she had no idea why. "Maybe another time? I have plans tonight."

Gaze locked on hers, he slowly nodded. "Okay. We'll do that."

Though she couldn't tell if he believed her or not, it didn't matter. Or shouldn't. He dropped back onto the couch and they watched the rest of the news in silence.

When it ended, he asked her if she wanted something to eat.

"I think I'm going to get something when I'm in town," she replied, even though she wasn't sure. After all, Kate had mentioned an appetizer menu. She could make a meal of those.

After the news, she left him still sitting on the couch and popped the peach pie she'd made into the oven, before she went into her room to get ready for her evening out.

Since she didn't go out much and had no idea what to wear, she'd settled on her best pair of skinny jeans, a new pair of dressy boots, and a loose-fitting top that showed her shoulders. She wore her hair curled and loose down her back, her only accessory her favorite pair of large, gold, dangly earrings.

Unaccountably nervous, she figured if she looked too out of place, she'd have one drink and talk Kate into going somewhere else.

When she emerged from her room, Pierce was nowhere in sight. Though she knew she shouldn't feel disappointed, she did. Shaking her head at her own foolishness, she grabbed her car keys and her purse and headed out the door.

Pulling up to the low-slung, modern-looking building with a blue neon sign that simply said The Bar, Cassie sat in her truck for a moment, looking around at the other vehicles in the parking lot. Her beat-up old truck looked out of place.

Judging by the brand-new pickup trucks, expensive sedans, and shiny sports cars, this place served an entirely different sort of clientele than The Rattlesnake Pub. She'd guessed that would be the case, considering what she'd heard about it. Now, after talking to Kate, she couldn't wait to see the inside and try one of the exotic cocktails her friend had mentioned.

Her door creaked as she opened it. She got out of her truck and manually locked it before slamming the heavy door closed. As she turned to go in, she heard someone calling her name.

"Cassie!" Kate cruised up in what looked like a brand-new Ford Explorer, her window down. "Let me park and we can go in together."

More relieved than she wanted to admit, Cassie nodded. She waited while Kate parked her SUV.

"Wow, you look great," Kate said, smiling. She wore similar jeans and boots, but had chosen a silky, long-sleeved top with a lacy half camisole.

"So do you." Cassie grinned back. "I'm really excited to try this place."

As they stepped inside, she saw they'd carried the understated look to the interior as well. Luxurious, dark wood paneling and strategically placed lighting gave the place a luxurious feel. The modern, stainless and red furniture provided an interesting contrast. Yet somehow, it all pulled together.

"It's not too busy," Cassie observed.

"Not yet," Kate agreed. "This place really gets hopping around nine. That's why I wanted to come earlier. At least now, we can hear ourselves talk."

Though Pierce had initially planned on going into town for a drink by himself, he didn't really want to. In a town this small, a stranger would not only be noticed but remarked upon. At least if he went with Cassie, he might have better luck blending in to the surroundings.

Seeing his apartment burn on the news had shaken him almost as much as the phone call from Michael had. He hated hiding out while his stalker wreaked havoc on people who'd been minding their own business and been guilty of nothing except the fact that they'd lived in the same building as Pierce.

Not for the first time, he wondered if he'd made the wrong choice agreeing to leave town until this deranged person had been caught.

The irony that he, unlike those poor innocent others, still had a place to live wasn't lost on him.

Despite constantly imagining that he smelled a pie baking, he'd been once again trying to lose himself in his writing when he'd heard the front door close. A moment later, Cassie's old truck engine rumbled to life.

Once the sound faded into the distance, he put the notebook down and wandered into the kitchen. Even if Cassie hadn't asked to stay here, he knew he'd still feel like he was staying in someone else's house. If this place were to really become his home, he'd do extensive renovations, starting with getting rid of the old, outdated furniture.

But since he had no plans to stay, he'd leave it as is and put it back on the market exactly as he'd found it. Hopefully, Cassie would have moved on and found her next home as well as opened up the bakery.

Then he noticed the perfectly baked pie sitting on the counter. Cassie had propped up a folded piece of paper next to it. *Here you are, as promised. Enjoy!*

Grinning, he rummaged around the cabinets, located a small plate, fork, and knife, and cut himself a large slice. As he ate, he found himself making sounds of pleasure. If all of her baked goods tasted as wonderful as this peach pie, her bakery would be more than successful.

Once he finished his piece, he briefly considered going for a second but talked himself out of it. The simple combination of fruit, sugar, and flour made him feel better, optimistic even.

He retrieved his notebook and pen. Turning the TV on for background noise, he continued fleshing out his earlier notes. His excitement grew as he realized what had started as a glimmer of an idea had begun to take shape as a synopsis for a full-length novel.

Finally.

Michael would be so happy. With everything that had been going on, neither Pierce nor his agent had held out much hope of the synopsis getting done in time to meet his deadline. For the first time in over ten bestselling thrillers, inspiration had eluded him. With a deranged stalker after him, Pierce had lost his writing mojo. He'd continued trying, especially since he wasn't a believer in writer's block. But his certainty that he'd find the words had begun to erode over time.

"Your mojo will come back," Michael had insisted. "Just give it time."

Pierce had agreed, even though he wasn't entirely sure he believed he'd recapture that smidgen of magic that gave him the ability to tell his stories.

Who knew he'd manage to locate it here?

Like many other writers he was acquainted with, he got superstitious. Even though logically he knew his sudden burst of creativity had nothing to do with Cassie's perfect peach pie, he went back and got a second slice. He ate this quickly, giving himself just enough time to enjoy the rich burst of flavor before putting the empty plate aside and picking up his pen. He'd always loved the feel of his pen gliding over paper, finding it freeing. Many of his story ideas were fleshed out this way, and he often wrote parts of his first drafts by hand before typing them into his computer.

Today, his pen couldn't keep up with his mind.

He wrote furiously, almost afraid that at some point the

words would slip away and he'd be once again left with nothing but a blank page. As he wrote, he made notes in the margins, just in case he needed a reminder of the thread he wanted to tie each scene to.

By the time he heard the sound of Cassie's truck outside, he'd managed to sketch out a bare-bones outline. From that, he should have no problem developing a detailed synopsis.

Standing, he stretched, glancing at the wall clock. Surprised to see it showed barely after 10:00 p.m., he guessed Cassie's date or whatever it had been, hadn't gone well. He hoped she wouldn't be too bummed out about it.

But when she came strolling in through the kitchen door, she appeared upbeat. Happy, even. She smiled when she saw him, her eyes sparkling. With her luxurious dark hair curling around her bare shoulders, she looked even more beautiful than usual, if such a thing were possible.

For a moment, he couldn't even find the words to greet her.

"I'm glad you're still up," she said, clearly oblivious of her effect on him. She headed to the fridge to grab a bottle of water before joining him. "Two pieces of pie?" she asked, her smile widening. "It always makes me happy when someone truly enjoys my baked goods."

"That pie is an inspiration," he said, meaning it. He held up his notebook. "I got a lot done."

"I'm glad to hear it. I hope I didn't interrupt you."

Unsure how to respond to that, he simply shrugged. "You're back early," he said.

"Am I?" Tone mild, she shrugged. "My friend Kate and I had a lot of catching up to do. We ate and had a drink or two. But The Bar got really crowded and when we couldn't hear each other talk over the noise, we decided to call it a night."

Trying not to stare at the smooth skin revealed by the shoulder cutouts in her shirt, he nodded. "When I first arrived in New York, I wasn't a big fan of crowds. But since there's no avoiding them there, they grew on me." He thought for a moment. "Crowds carry their own kind of energy."

She tilted her head, considering. "Maybe they do. But the kind of people packed into a bar on a Friday night have partying in mind. Since I was only there to catch up with a good friend, it made sense to leave."

"Good point," he replied.

Still standing, she took a drink of her water and eyed him. "My friend Kate wanted to know all about you."

Slightly alarmed, he met her gaze. "What did you tell her?"

Her grin both captivated and alarmed him. "Are you sure you want to know?"

Despite her teasing tone, he went instantly on alert. "I do," he said. "Spill."

"I told Kate that you were a city guy who'd decided to try his hand at farming. She seems to think that's pretty darn funny."

Not sure if he should feel relieved or put off, he decided as long as Cassie hadn't told her friend the truth, everything would be fine.

"She also wanted to know if you are easy on the eyes," Cassie continued in the same teasing voice.

He decided to play along. "What did you tell her?" he said again, this time much more curious about her answer.

His question made her laugh. The sound, light and feminine and full of joy, sent a dart of desire straight through him.

"I like you," he said slowly, and then immediately realized he'd spoken his thoughts out loud.

Instead of appearing surprised, Cassie gave him a considering look. "Thank you. I think I like you too, though to be honest, it's a bit too soon to tell. I mean, we barely know each other. But you seem like a nice enough guy."

"Nice enough guy." He shook his head as he pushed to his feet. "Those are the ones I always kill off first in my books,"

Gathering his empty dessert plate from the coffee table, he carried it into the kitchen, where he rinsed it off before placing it in the sink.

When he turned around to rejoin her, to his surprise she was right there. So close he nearly bumped into her.

In that instant, the entire world shifted on its axis.

Their gazes locked.

His heart hammered against his ribs.

He put his hand to her slender waist and gently drew her close. Dizzy with the scent of her—peaches? Vanilla?—he inhaled and tried to clear his head. Futile. Instead, he took another deep breath before he covered her soft lips with his.

She welcomed him, mouth open, drawing him deeper, making him reel.

Though he'd intended the kiss to be slow and thoughtful, the instant his lips made contact with hers, desire flamed to life. A slow burn he thought maybe he could control, if he was careful.

Raising his mouth from hers, he met her gaze. Her pupils were huge and dark, the desire swirling inside him reflected right back. "Yes," she whispered, tilting her face up to him. "Kiss me again."

And so he did. This time, he didn't hold back. To his amazed delight, neither did Cassie.

Tongues danced, heartbeats quickened. Her soft body pressed into his.

Hunger sang in his veins, demanding more. He drank her in, and she met him halfway.

Not enough. He ached for more. His aroused body needed to be inside of her.

The instant he realized where his thoughts were headed, he yanked himself back to reality. Gently setting her away from him, he took several deep, shuddering breaths as he tried to regain his composure. They stood staring at each other in silence, five, maybe six feet apart. Judging by the rise and fall of her chest, she was breathing as hard as he.

He wasn't sure what was worse—his remorse or the painful look of betrayal he saw on her face.

"I'm…sorry," he finally said, his voice tight. He dragged his shaking hand through his hair. "That really shouldn't have happened."

When she lifted her chin, for a moment he thought she might challenge his statement. Instead, she gave a slow nod. "You're right."

"I'll make sure it never happens again," he promised, even as he still yearned to press his mouth against hers once more.

Appearing to collect herself, she straightened. Head held high, whatever composure she might have lost earlier, she seemed to have found. "It's okay," she murmured. "It was only a kiss. No need to beat yourself up."

Only a kiss. Only. A. Kiss.

"Right," he said. "But you don't need to worry that I'll try to take advantage of you or something. Because I won't. Ever."

Expression bemused, she nodded. "I know you won't. I wanted that kiss just as much as you did."

A bolt of instant lust shot through him at her words. Half turning to hide his arousal, he swallowed hard.

"Are you okay?" she asked, one wavy strand of her long dark hair falling down over her eye.

Despite everything, he couldn't stop himself from reaching for her to smooth it back.

She froze and then tucked it behind her ear. "Look, we're both out of our element and trying to navigate an unfamiliar situation. I get it."

What that had to do with them kissing, he didn't know, but he nodded.

"What I'm trying to say is if you want to kiss me again," she said with a shy smile, "it'll be all right."

A groan escaped him. "Since we're going to be working together, I don't think that would be a good idea."

"Maybe not," she agreed, still grinning. "But nothing fun ever is."

Every nerve ending on fire, he could only stare. She clearly had no idea how she affected him or what her kiss had made him want. Guileless or truly innocent, it didn't matter. She wasn't aware that she was playing with fire.

"It wasn't that much fun," he drawled, telling the lie with a straight face. "All in all, not an experience I'd like to repeat."

The instant of hurt that flashed across her face filled him with regret. Still, since resisting the temptation she presented, he knew he had to discourage her.

"I see," she said tightly. "Then I'll make sure it never happens again."

"Good."

And then, before he said anything else he might regret, he slipped past her and left the room. It wasn't until he'd closed his bedroom door that he realized he'd left his notebook and pen behind.

Chapter 6

•

Cassie wasn't sure who'd made the first move, but she damn sure knew who'd been the one to pull back. Pierce, his expression troubled, had physically removed himself from her immediate vicinity. Almost as if looking at her made him feel ill.

And then he'd flat out told her he hadn't enjoyed it. He obviously had no clue how badly his words hurt her.

She'd kept her head up and managed to agree with him that, not only should the kiss never have happened, but it couldn't ever happen again.

While she knew that technically he was right, and she hated that he hadn't enjoyed the experience as much as she had, she couldn't find it in her to regret kissing him.

The kiss had rocked her world. She'd seen fireworks, heard harps, and all that other romantic stuff. Her entire body had been set ablaze, and she'd darn near melted into a puddle of desire while he'd held her in his strong arms.

Clearly, it hadn't done the same for him. Likely a good thing, even if it stung.

She'd wanted more. He hadn't been able to get away from her fast enough. Knowing this made her want to cry.

But she shouldn't have been surprised. It was just another repeat of every date she'd ever gone on. Rejection could have been her middle name. She'd always wanted more, wanted too much. No one wanted to have a relationship with a pig farmer's daughter. They'd all made it clear they only wanted one thing, nothing more. When she'd refused to give that, the insults and false rumors had started.

At least in that respect, Pierce had been different. He hadn't wanted her at all. Or so he'd claimed.

Except she'd felt his body quicken as she pressed up against him. He'd kissed her the way a man kisses a woman he finds desirable, not out of some obligation or duty or whatever.

Why lie? Did he think if he admitted he wanted her too that she'd somehow take advantage of *him*?

She'd probably dodged a bullet.

Even so, none of the jumbled thoughts running through her head changed one underlying fact. She still wanted him. More than she'd ever desired a man in her entire life.

What was wrong with her? He'd made it clear he didn't intend to stick around, he made excuses for what had been a perfectly natural kiss between two healthy, young adults.

Sheesh. Shaking her head at herself, she looked around the room, trying to focus. She didn't need this kind of complication in her life right now, and neither did he.

When she spotted his notebook, still on the couch, she caught her breath. Tempted, she glanced back toward the short hallway that led to the bedrooms. Should she dare? While she knew she really shouldn't, that didn't negate how badly she wanted to take a look. Just one quick peek, to get a rough idea of what his next, still unwritten book would be.

Against her better judgment, she edged herself closer to the coffee table while continually checking to see if Pierce would return. She could just imagine her embarrassment if he were to catch her red-handed looking at his work before she'd asked.

No. This wasn't her. She'd never been sneaky or underhanded. Slowly, she backed away. Pierce had been nothing but kind to her, allowing her to stay after she'd sold the place and even offering her a part-time job. She wouldn't do anything to exploit his goodwill.

Since she'd be working for him, she'd likely see it at some point anyway.

Her phone pinged, indicating a text. Glad of the distraction, she pulled it out and looked at it. It was Kate, letting her know that instead of going home, she'd decided to meet her boyfriend at The Rattlesnake Pub. You're welcome to join us, the text said. Bring your new roommate, the city rancher guy. This was followed by laughing emojis.

Again, Cassie found herself glancing toward the hallway. As if. She suspected that right now, Pierce didn't want to be anywhere in the same vicinity as her. Which should be fine with her, even if it wasn't.

Full of restless frustration, Cassie decided she might as well join her friend. After all, the night was still young, and she didn't see the need to stay trapped in this house with a man who clearly found her repulsive.

On my way, she texted back. After stopping off in the bathroom to freshen her lip gloss, she grabbed her purse and her car keys off the entryway table.

"Where are you going?" Pierce asked just as she reached for the door, startling her.

Immediately, she stiffened. Then, deciding that acting all offended would be ridiculous, she turned. "Kate texted me. After she and I met up, she decided to go to The Rattlesnake Pub for a couple of drinks with her boyfriend. She invited me to meet them there."

Then, deciding she had nothing to lose, she told him the rest of it. "She wanted me to bring you too."

He stared at her. "She did?"

"Yep." Then she waited to hear what he would say.

"Would you mind terribly if I went with you?" he asked, his expression remote despite the plea in his voice. "I'm going a little stir-crazy here in this house. A bit of local nightlife might help me feel better."

She said the first thing that came to mind. "What if someone recognizes you?"

"That's doubtful. I'm an author, not a movie star. Most regular people have no idea what I look like."

He had a point. And she could definitely sympathize with the cabin fever.

Still, his clothing practically screamed *City Dweller*. Men's skinny jeans, high-top sneakers, and a logo T-shirt.

"Do you have anything else you could wear?" she asked, gesturing at him.

Clearly taken aback, he looked down at himself. "What's wrong with my clothes? This is the kind of thing I wear every single day."

"In the city," she elaborated, feeling slightly guilty. But then again, he didn't want people noticing him. "I stacked a pile of my dad's old clothes on the floor in the main bedroom closet," she said. "You look like you might be about the same size. It's all clean. Why don't you go and see if anything fits you?"

He didn't move. "How old is this stuff?"

Feeling even worse, she shrugged. "A few years. I've been meaning to donate it, but kept forgetting. The only reason I thought of it now is because I know you want to blend in."

"I do," he agreed. "But would you mind clarifying what kind of clothes would do that?"

"The ones on the closet floor." His obvious confusion made her sigh. "You need Wrangler or Levi brand jeans. Boots. And either a snap button Western shirt or a plain T-shirt. If you dress like that, no one will give you a second glance."

"I don't know," he began.

"Anonymity over pride," she pointed out.

Since she was right, he nodded. "Would you mind showing me what you think would work best?"

"Sure."

She led the way back into his bedroom. Opening his closet door, she gestured at the several stacks of neatly folded men's clothing on the closet floor. "They're all clean," she repeated. "I meant to donate them, but quite honestly I completely forgot about them. Now, let's see."

She grabbed a pair of Wrangler jeans and handed them to him, along with a snap front, Western shirt. "I'm pretty sure those will fit. I'll wait here while you change into them."

Accepting them, he disappeared into the bathroom.

A moment later, he emerged. Eyeing him in her father's shirt and jeans, she did a double take. After slowly looking him up and down, she nodded.

"Much better," she finally said. "Though I have to say, it feels kind of weird to see you wearing his clothes."

The jeans were a bit too big in the waist, but she grabbed a belt with a large, Western buckle to take care of that. Handing that to him, she waited while he put it on.

"There you go," she said brightly. Too brightly, because for some reason all of this felt too intimate.

"This shirt…" He gestured at the snaps that closed it instead of buttons. "I've never seen anyone wear something like this, never mind put one on myself. Are you sure?"

"I am," she said, her voice firm. "Now, just change your sneakers for motorcycle boots, and we'll be good to go."

Once he'd completed the outfit, she watched as he checked himself out in the mirror. "You know, I think I could walk into my publisher's office right now and no one would recognize me."

"Since that's kind of the point, you're welcome," she replied, unable to resist grinning at him.

"Just to make extra sure, I'll wear a baseball cap." He turned and began rummaging through his dresser drawers. When he turned, he had placed a Yankees baseball cap on his head.

"That's not going to work," she pointed out, trying not to grimace.

"Why not? People out here don't like baseball?"

Laughing, she shook her head. "Oh, they like baseball. Just not that team. Do you have something else?"

"No," he admitted. "I don't."

She thought for a moment and then went to the front coat closet. She'd washed and kept several of her father's old caps, figuring they might come in handy one day.

Selecting one emblazoned with the logo of a popular local trucking company, she handed it to him. "Wear this. You'll blend right in."

Though he grimaced, he removed his cap and put her father's old one on. "There. What do you think?"

Swallowing hard, she tried not to share. All her life, she'd grown up surrounded by boys and men who wore caps just like that. While she suspected he'd blend right in and no one would take a second glance at him, she found the contrast between his normal, sophisticated appearance and this one irresistible.

"Well?" he asked, making her realize she hadn't responded.

"That'll work," she said, trying for nonchalance. She jingled her keys. "Let's go."

"Since I'm not a big drinker, do you want me to drive?" he asked. "You'd have to give me directions, but that way you could have a couple of drinks with your friends."

Keys in hand, she considered. "You know what? I'd like that. Plus, I'm sure your Jeep is way more comfortable than my truck."

Outside, once he'd unlocked the doors, she climbed in. The interior still had that new vehicle smell, something she'd never personally experienced except in friends' vehicles.

Dark leather seats, real or not, she couldn't tell, complemented the wood-grain look on the dash and doors. "Does this come standard?" she asked, looking around in disbelief. "I didn't think Wranglers were so luxurious."

"No," he answered, smiling as he buckled his seat belt. "I had some custom work done on it after I bought it. These things are supposed to be rugged, but I like to have the best of both worlds. I also had dual exhaust put in, among other things."

Impressed despite herself, she nodded. When he started the engine and shifted into Drive, she sat back in her seat, ready to enjoy the ride.

As they drove down the long driveway that led to the road, he gestured at the radio. "I haven't learned the stations here yet. If there's one you like, please go ahead and put it on."

"Out here, there aren't many choices other than country music," she told him. "Which is perfect since we're going to The Rattlesnake Pub and that's what they play."

"I like country," he said, surprising her.

"I didn't know they played that kind of music in New York City."

This made him laugh. "Have you ever been?"

"No," she admitted. "To be honest, I've never traveled out of Texas."

Aside from a quick, disbelieving glance, he didn't comment.

To avoid any potential awkward silence, she put the country music station she liked best on the radio. When one of her favorite songs came on almost immediately, she sang along. To her surprise, Pierce knew a lot of the lyrics, which he proved by joining her. He sang too, quietly at first. But as she let her voice grow louder, he did as well. He sang in a clear baritone, definitely different from his speaking voice. It sent shivers through her entire body.

Pretty dang good, she thought. And sexy too. No. She immediately shut that thought down.

Following her directions, he turned into The Rattlesnake Pub's parking lot.

"Wow, this place is busy," he said, finally locating a spot near the back row.

"It is," she agreed. "It's popular. Plus, this is one of only two bars in Getaway. It's been here the longest and is largely considered the meeting place in town."

"I'm looking forward to this," he told her. They got out of the Jeep, Cassie pretending not to notice the way he'd hurried around to her side to open her door.

Together, they walked toward the bar. Even outside, they could hear the thump, thump of the bass.

"Live music?" he asked.

She shrugged. "Sometimes. I'm not sure about tonight."

Opening the door, he stepped aside to allow her to enter first.

Inside, they squeezed through the press of people, Cassie searching for Kate. When Pierce reached out and took her arm, she briefly froze, but then realized he likely didn't want to take a chance of losing her in the crowd.

A local band played Willie Nelson cover songs up on the stage. Several couples swirled around the small dance floor, clearly enjoying the evening.

She spotted Kate across the room, standing and waving. Her fiancé Jeremy sat next to her. By luck or chance, they'd managed to grab a four-top close to the stage.

"This way," she said, speaking loudly to be heard over the noise. When Pierce looked blankly at her, she took his arm and steered him toward her friend.

Eyes huge, Kate looked from Cassie to Pierce and back again. "You brought him," she said, grinning.

Cassie nodded and then performed introductions all the way around. Since Kate and Jeremy already had drinks, Pierce asked Cassie what she wanted and then headed up to the busy bar to get it.

"Come here," Kate said, the instant Pierce left. "Scoot your chair over. Your new roommate is handsome. I want more details. Spill."

Next to her, Jeremy snorted.

"There's nothing to tell," Cassie began. "He just wanted to get out of the house."

Before Kate could ask more, Pierce reappeared, carrying Cassie's vodka cranberry and a beer. This last surprised her, since Pierce had said he wasn't much of a drinker. But then she supposed he could make that one beer last all night. Since he was driving, she sure hoped so.

This thought underscored how little she really knew about Pierce Spade. While she might have read all of his books, personally they were total strangers.

His good looks and sexy vibe—who knew she found intelligence so sexy?—were just distractions she needed to avoid. Time to rein herself in, enjoy getting to know him, and when the time came, go on her way.

Decision made, she took a sip of her drink. Pierce tried to make conversation with Jeremy, but the band had started up again and this proved impossible. Grimacing, Jeremy shrugged and turned his attention to scrolling his phone.

Though briefly tempted to do the same, Cassie took another drink and tried to be social. As an introvert, she found crowds and noise jarring, but she wanted to try to do better.

Looking up, she met Pierce's gaze. He nodded, almost as if he understood, before turning his attention on the band.

Taking a cue from him, Cassie did the same.

Pierce felt it the instant Cassie stopped looking at him. Sometimes, her gaze felt like a caress. Which was something he might have written in a book but had never experienced in real life.

Across from Cassie, Kate be-bopped in time to the music. Jeremy continued scrolling. Pierce briefly envied him, but since he currently still had a burner and couldn't access any of his social media, he didn't have anything to scroll anyway. Plus, he'd wanted to get a feel for the town and its people. He couldn't do that by being oblivious to his surroundings.

The band did well, playing the Willie Nelson standards faithfully. The dance floor remained crowded, and he saw people having a good time everywhere he looked.

Little by little, Pierce began to relax. He took a small drink of his beer, tried to ignore the beautiful, sensual woman he now shared a home with, and watched the band play.

His phone vibrating in his pocket startled him. This indicated an incoming call, definitely from Michael, but he decided to ignore it. There was no way he'd be able to hold a conversation in here with all the noise. Though it was late—and even later in New York—he felt certain Michael would leave a message. With the hours his agent kept, late-night phone calls were the norm rather than the exception. Pierce figured he'd simply call him back on the drive home.

Except his phone immediately began vibrating again, which meant Michael wasn't giving up until Pierce answered. Whatever he needed to tell Pierce must be urgent.

He glanced at his companions. Cassie and her friend Kate now had their heads together, apparently having an animated discussion. Jeremy seemed to be playing a game on his phone rather than scrolling.

Pierce excused himself and stood. Even though he felt pretty sure no one heard him, he attempted to at least catch Cassie's eye before he walked away.

When she noticed him, she smiled and continued her conversation with her friend.

The phone had stopped vibrating by the time Pierce stepped outside. He pulled it from his pocket, intending to check the call log, but it immediately started ringing again. Sure enough, Michael's number showed on the Caller ID.

"Hey, Michael. What's up?"

"Have you seen the news?" The urgency in Michael's voice made Pierce freeze.

"No. I'm out at a local bar. I had to step outside to talk to you." He braced himself. "What's going on?"

The long pause told him Michael was trying to figure out the right thing to say. "Do you remember researching some unsolved murders committed upstate by a murderer they were calling the Catskill Killer?"

An ominous shiver of foreboding snaked down Pierce's spine. "I do. He cut off each of his victim's left ear."

"That's the one."

"The murders stopped a couple of months ago." Pierce paused a moment to think before continuing. "I did some research on it, intending to use it in a future book, especially since it's still unsolved. The police kept saying they had no leads. The whole thing seemed destined to become a cold case."

"Not anymore." Michael's voice sounded grim. "He's killed again. And this time, he left a note for the police."

"What did it say?" Pierce asked, though part of him suspected he didn't really want to know.

"Brace yourself." Michael cleared his throat. "I'll read it verbatim. 'Until Pierce Spade makes his whereabouts known, a different woman will die a painful death each week. They will suffer greatly and each one will know before they die, that they can thank Pierce Spade for what has happened to them.'"

Stomach churning, Pierce swallowed his revulsion.

"All the major news outlets have picked up the story," Michael continued. "This is your stalker's way of turning the screws to get you to reveal your location to him."

Now Pierce began to pace the sidewalk in front of The Rattlesnake Pub. "I have to," he said. "I don't see that he's left me any choice."

"The Feds disagree. In fact, they want to put you in the Witness Protection Program."

"No." Pierce didn't even have to think about that. "I'm fine where I am. You haven't told them where, have you?"

"No, I have not." Clearly offended, Michael sighed. "You asked me not to."

"Good. They don't need to know. It's safer that way."

"I don't know about that," Michael replied. "But I'm guessing they're either tracking my phone calls or have subpoenaed the records. I'm sure they'll have your phone number soon."

"Probably so," Pierce agreed. "Which means it's time to switch phones. That's the whole purpose of having burner phones."

"I agree. And I'm thinking maybe you shouldn't call me for a while."

Though Pierce hated the idea, he knew it made sense. "I won't," he replied. "At least, not until I finish that synopsis."

"Always joking."

Since he'd been serious, Pierce wasn't sure what to say to that. "You be careful, Michael. He knows you're my agent."

"I've got that covered," Michael replied. "You just need to look after yourself. Since you mentioned it, is going out to a bar really a wise option? What if someone recognizes you and posts your photo to social media?"

Since Pierce didn't want to give specifics over the phone, he simply told his agent that he'd changed his appearance and looked nothing like the photo on his book jackets. "Plus, authors aren't that recognizable, unless you're Stephen King."

Michael laughed. "Get rid of that phone. Now," he ordered, and then ended the call.

Staring at his cheap, disposable phone, Pierce slammed it into the concrete sidewalk and then crushed it under his boot. Doing this felt oddly satisfying, though he had no idea why.

Likely because it gave him an outlet for his frustration.

Never in his wildest dreams had he imagined something like this happening. His books were fiction, the stories created in his head. Sure, he'd done a ton of research on serial killers, and yes, he'd incorporated some real-life scenarios into his thrillers.

But for a serial killer to not only read one of his books but to take offense and believe that Pierce was telling a tale that belonged only to him? And then to carry this a step further and determine to make the author of said story pay?

If he'd written something like that into one of his proposals, he suspected his editor would have culled it as unrealistic.

Now innocent people would die because of a fictional character in a fictional book. All due to someone's misguided vendetta on the author.

Pierce wanted to do more than stomp on his phone again. If he'd been in his apartment building at home, he would have gone down to the well-equipped gym and had a few rounds with the punching bag. But now even that refuge, his home, had been destroyed. All because of one freaking book.

It was almost enough to make him want to quit writing.

Instead, he felt a burning hunger to find this real-life villain and bring him to justice. The man needed to pay for what he'd done.

Inside, the music briefly stopped. He could hear the lead singer talking to the crowd, but he couldn't make out the words.

Though the last thing Pierce felt like doing was going back inside to rejoin all the partying people intent on having fun, he had no choice. He'd driven Cassie here and, more importantly, had promised to be her sober driver home.

At least he didn't have to worry about anyone here seeing the breaking story on the news. It would be morning before anyone learned about what had happened. He guessed to most of these people, New York seemed like a long way away.

By the time he stepped back inside, the band had switched

to playing George Strait instead of Willie. More people got up and stepped onto the dance floor. To his surprise, Pierce spotted Cassie, accompanied by her friend Kate dancing across from each other, both their faces glowing with happiness.

As always when he looked at Cassie, Pierce had to drag his gaze away. In the dim light of the bar, she looked even more alluring, if such a thing was possible.

Turning his back on the dance floor, Pierce made his way to his seat.

Kate's boyfriend Jeremy remained seated at the table, still intent on his phone. He didn't even look up when Pierce dropped into the chair across from him. Good. Because Pierce wasn't in the mood to make small talk with anyone.

He took another sip of his beer, trying to get his mind away from the stark, awful truth.

Some deranged madman was out there killing women— no, *torturing* women—and blaming it all on Pierce.

In all honestly, he didn't think he could continue to stay here, hiding out like a coward. If he did, he'd be allowing this to continue to happen.

But then, considering what they were dealing with, even if Pierce offered himself up as some sort of sacrificial lamb, there was no guarantee that the killings would stop. The guy *was* a serial killer after all.

The band announced a break, and the dance floor emptied out. Cassie and her friend came back to the table, flushed and out of breath.

Smiling happily, Cassie dropped into the chair next to Pierce. Her smile instantly disappeared the moment she saw his face.

"What's wrong?" she asked. Since the music had stopped, he could actually hear her.

"Michael called," he replied, hoping he managed to sound neutral. "I can't talk about it here."

Cassie glanced over at her friend, now busy making out with Jeremy. He'd apparently found something he liked better than his phone. "We can go. Are you still okay to drive?"

Grateful, he nodded. "Yes. All I've had to drink is part of this beer."

She pushed to her feet. A second later, he did the same.

"We're leaving," she announced to her friend. Instead of stopping what she was doing, Kate simply lifted her hand and wiggled her fingers in a goodbye wave.

Cassie took Pierce's arm as they soldiered through the crowd. If anything, the bar had gotten even more packed. Pierce wouldn't have imagined that a town as small and remote as Getaway could have enough patrons to fill up a place of this size. Clearly, he was wrong.

Outside, he sucked in deep breaths of fresh air as they walked to his Jeep. Hand still on his arm, Cassie didn't ask any questions.

Once inside the Jeep, he locked the doors and turned to face her. Speaking carefully, he relayed everything that Michael had told him.

Her expression went from quietly watchful to outraged.

"I don't know what to do," he admitted, giving vent to his anguish. "It's wrong for me to stay here hidden when this is all my fault."

"This is *not* your fault," she said, touching his arm. "Don't even think that. You cannot hold yourself accountable for something a madman does. This is a killer. He's killed before and he'll kill again, whether you're here or not."

"Technically, all true. I agree with everything you've said." Still miserable, he shook his head.

"You feel like you could somehow stop him?" she asked.

Surprised, he nodded. "Yes. I know that doesn't make much sense. But if I could show up, the Feds could set some kind of a trap, and he'd be arrested."

"Or he'd kill you," she pointed out. "And continue torturing innocent women. Has anyone in law enforcement approached you with this idea?"

"No. No one but Michael has my phone number. Or had," he elaborated. "I destroyed that burner phone and I need to activate another one."

She acknowledged this statement with a dip of her chin. "Okay, but if the FBI wanted you to act as some sort of decoy, Michael would tell you, right?"

"Right." He pushed the button to start the engine, but made no move to shift into Reverse and back out of the parking space. "I don't know what to do," he admitted for the second time.

Her quick inhale almost sounded like a gasp. Half turning to make sure she was all right, he couldn't hide his surprise when she cupped his face in her hands.

"I know we agreed we shouldn't," she said. "But I'm going to anyway."

And then she kissed him again.

Chapter 7

A low thrum of desire had been buzzing inside Cassie all night. Ever since their first kiss, to be honest. Even though she'd had a few drinks, she wasn't drunk, just buzzed enough to let her inhibitions slip.

Hearing the dejection in Pierce's voice had made her chest ache. At first, she only wanted to comfort him, maybe distract him.

But when he turned that rugged profile toward her, his pain palpable, she acted solely on instinct.

The instant their mouths met, fire consumed her. She whimpered low in her throat, resisting the urge to breach the console and climb into his lap.

Sensation overwhelmed her. Nothing existed but him. One hand tangled in her hair, he met her passion with his own, his tongue mating with hers.

Inside, she swooned, melting into a puddle of desire right there in his passenger seat. But this time, she somehow retained awareness of their surroundings. They were sitting in a parked vehicle in the Rattlesnake parking lot, for Pete's sake!

She managed to break this kiss, despite every fiber of her body urging her not to. Sitting back, she stared, taking in his dazed expression. "We'd better go home," she managed to say, breathless and not trying to hide it.

"Yes. We'd better." But he made no move to shift into Reverse. They sat there a moment, staring at each other, the light from the streetlamp making shadows of their features.

"Why did you do that?" he finally asked, his quiet voice husky.

"Do you really want to talk about this now?" she countered, her gaze imploring him to say no. If he continued to press, she wasn't sure she could vocalize an answer. She'd kissed him because she wanted to. She hadn't been able to stop thinking about their first kiss and she'd figured he needed a distraction. Or she had. Didn't they deserve a simple instant of pleasure?

All rationalizations that she would never mention. Hopefully.

After another moment, he finally shook his head. "I guess not," he replied, and finally backed from the parking space.

Neither spoke during the drive home. But as they pulled into the long drive that led to the farm, she sighed.

"I'm sorry," she said. "I know you've got a lot on your plate and me complicating things is the last thing you need."

Instead of immediately responding, he waited until he'd pulled in front of the garage and parked before turning to face her. He opened his mouth and started to speak, but then shook his head and got out of the Jeep.

A moment later, she did the same, following him inside. As she did, she couldn't help admire his broad-shouldered, slim-hipped body.

Still silent, he went straight to his room, leaving her standing alone in the foyer. Feeling foolish and still way too aroused, she made her way into the kitchen. She grabbed a bottle of water and drank half of it in one long gulp.

One thing seemed crystal clear. She needed to find somewhere else to live and quickly. Staying here with Pierce felt like sitting on a powder keg, waiting for it to explode. The man had enough trouble. He didn't need her making any more problems. His life had already become something like a plot from one of his thrillers.

Trying not to feel melancholy, she sat by herself at the kitchen table and finished her water. Then she took herself off to bed, hoping things would look better in the morning.

The sunlight streaming through her window woke her. She lifted her head, her first instinct to burrow under her covers. It took all of three seconds for her to realize she must have overslept. She hadn't even begun baking anything to take to the Tumbleweed. The small clock on her nightstand read 8:05 a.m. She'd overslept!

Heart pounding, she jumped out of bed, threw on some clothes, and raced to the kitchen. Grateful not to see Pierce, she started grabbing ingredients, trying to shake the cobwebs from her mind.

Then she realized all this rushing would be pointless. The breakfast rush would have already started. She could make her pies and cakes for the lunch and dinner service, but…

Wait. What day was this? Yesterday had been Friday. She'd made extra yesterday morning. That, combined with the fact that the café had actually frozen a couple of pies for later use, had made Gertie at the Tumbleweed tell her to take Saturday off. Gertie had promised to let Cassie know if they needed anything else, but she'd thought they'd be good until Sunday.

Which meant that today was her day off. And she was meeting Trudi at nine at Serenity's. Which meant she'd better hurry.

She hurried off to the bathroom to wash her face and brush her teeth. Once she'd taken care of this, she put her hair into a ponytail and went back for a quick cup of coffee, stepping over a sleeping Albert on her way to make it.

Still no sign of Pierce. She went to the window. His Jeep was gone, which meant he'd left.

She didn't like this feeling of awkwardness. Nor the way she couldn't stop thinking about kissing him and, quite honestly, wanting more. If they were going to work together—and that was a very big *if* at this moment—she needed to be able to get past this infatuation or whatever it was.

Though she'd already apologized, she'd likely apologize again. Except she couldn't shake the feeling that he owed her an explanation too. She'd like to know why he said and did what he did. Maybe she should call him out on it, especially since he had been a willing and enthusiastic participant in the kiss.

Or maybe she should follow his lead, avoid the subject, and pretend it had never happened. Honestly, she had no idea what had gotten into her lately. She definitely wasn't acting like herself.

Picking up her phone, she scrolled through social media. The serial killer's actions plus his announcement were posted on several mainstream news pages and were being talked about on every platform. She read one article posted by a national news outlet that only confirmed everything Pierce had said.

She couldn't even imagine how he felt. She'd heard the anguish in his voice when he'd admitted he didn't know what to do. And then she'd kissed him.

The kiss could have been construed as a distraction, or a misguided attempt to offer comfort. Only she knew that her intentions hadn't been the slightest bit pure or altruistic.

She hadn't been able to think much past the haze of desire that clouded her judgment whenever she got close to him.

Intellect apparently now had become an aphrodisiac to her. Combine that with Pierce's chiseled features and lean body, and she couldn't resist.

One of the things Cassie had always valued about herself was her resolve and determination. No matter the obstacle, once she'd chosen a path, she stuck to it. She did whatever it took, without hurting anyone, to reach her goals.

She'd decided to open a bakery so she'd sold the farm, intending to use the proceeds to fund her business as well as another place to live. Instead of sitting around mooning over a man who'd bring nothing but heartbreak, she needed to redirect herself and put her focus where it belonged.

Picking up her phone, she texted Trudi.

When you have time, I'd like to look at commercial rentals also.

Immediately, the Realtor texted back.

Let me put together a list. Maybe we can do that this morning. If not, we'll have to meet up later, like this afternoon.

Amazing how much better she felt after taking definitive action. She'd steer clear of Pierce physically and make sure all interactions were pleasant and professional. She could do this. And the sooner she got out of his hair, the better for both of them.

At least now that he'd gone somewhere, she didn't have to worry about running into him in her childhood home.

Making a quick circle around the empty house, Cassie sighed. Before she'd listed the place for sale, she'd looked for anything she might want to bring with her. Some sentimental memento, a knickknack, something to remind her of her childhood. But her father hadn't been a sentimental man, nor an affectionate one. No good memories had been made in this house.

In the end, she'd decided to leave everything. And making the rounds of the interior today, she knew she'd made the right call. Pierce was welcome to everything, even if he discarded it when he was ready to move on.

Right now, she'd better get going if she wanted to meet Trudi on time.

Her old truck cranked right up. Since she'd be meeting Trudi there in a few minutes, she decided to go ahead to Serenity's. The little metaphysical shop on Main Street had always been one of Cassie's favorites, since it represented the polar opposite of her stodgy, grounded life. The store had once also contained a florist but now had a thriving café inside. The original proprietor, a beloved older woman named Serenity, had become ill and her niece Ella Lindie had taken over. Though Cassie—along with just about everyone else in town—adored Serenity, Cassie and Ella had forged an instant friendship. Not only were they close in age, but Cassie loved hearing Ella's stories about her life in Fort Worth before she'd moved to Getaway permanently. Her whirlwind romance with Mac Sennett, a local who'd moved away and then returned, had been the talk of the town. Now Mac operated a law office in town and he and Ella had recently become engaged.

Cassie loved the way Ella's entire face lit up anytime she mentioned Mac's name.

Even though Cassie delivered baked goods to her daily, Cassie figured the other woman wouldn't mind if she dropped in to browse the store and chat. The café would be busy for the morning rush, but she bet she and Ella could squeeze in a few minutes before Trudi arrived at nine.

When she pulled up to the store, she found a parking space right in front, which she considered a good omen. She hopped out and hurried into the store.

Ellie looked up from her seat behind the counter in the back. "Hey," she said, smiling. "Did you want something to eat?"

"I'm good. I'm meeting Trudi here to look at some properties for my bakery," Cassie replied, strolling through the store. "Looks like you got in a new shipment of crystals. I've always had a soft spot for those."

"We did. Take a look. You never know when you might find one you like."

"I will later," Cassie said, approaching the counter.

"I heard you have a cute new roommate," Ella teased. "I want details. Tell me all about him."

Though she felt her face flush, Cassie tried to keep her expression neutral. "There's nothing to tell," she said. "He's from the East Coast and decided he wanted to try his hand farming in West Texas."

Ella's expression ranged from incredulous to shocked. "But why?" she asked. "Why would any rational person want to do that?"

The question made Cassie laugh. "I don't know. I was just too happy to sell the farm. I didn't ask too many questions."

Ella glanced around the packed room. "All my tables are taken care of for now. Sit. Talk to me a minute."

Cassie took a seat at the breakfast bar. "I remember your aunt used to make me tea and cookies when I visited her," she mused. "How's Serenity doing?"

"She's getting stronger every day," Ella replied. "She's even resumed taking yoga classes next door. I've been letting her work here a few times a week, as long as I can keep an eye on her."

"That's wonderful. I'll have to try and stop in one day when she's here and say hi."

"She'd love that." Ella leaned her elbows on the counter and eyed Cassie. "You sure haven't had much to say about your handsome roommate."

This comment had Cassie rolling her eyes. "Is that the way the gossip is going? Because there's absolutely nothing going on." If she didn't count the two kisses they'd shared.

"Really? Then why are you blushing?"

Since Cassie's face had heated at the thought of those kisses, she didn't even try to deny it. "He *is* hot," she admitted. "But I need to focus on opening my bakery and he…"

"He what?" Ella asked, making Cassie realize she hadn't finished her thought. Nor could she.

"He's got a lot to learn about starting up a farm or ranch," she finally said. "But enough about me. How's your business going?"

"Awesomely," Ella replied. "Initially, I was a little worried that I'd be competing with the Tumbleweed, which as you know is an institution. But I'm not, not really. It's a different kind of clientele. While a few men come in with their wives or family, it's mostly women. I see a lot of friends wanting a quiet place to have a healthy lunch or breakfast. Extended families come too. Sunday after church lets out is the busiest time. I guess people don't want to wait at the Tumbleweed. You know how busy they get on Sunday."

Cassie nodded. "I'm so glad for you," she said.

Just then, Trudi sauntered in, looking around the packed shop with an air of satisfaction. "Cassie?" she called out, making her way to the back counter. "Are you ready to go?"

"I am," Cassie called, jumping up. Ella came around the counter and the two of them hugged.

"Good luck on your real estate search," Ella said, smiling.

In the morning, Pierce rose early and headed to the kitchen for his coffee, despite knowing Cassie would be there baking. His first clue that she wasn't should have been the utter absence of the aroma of delicious things baking. Since the kitchen was still dark, he flicked on the lights and started the coffee maker.

Briefly, he wondered if Cassie had decided to skip her daily deliveries today. But since that was none of his business, and he really wanted to avoid her until he got his head on straight, he decided to leave it alone. Since her bedroom door was still closed, he guessed she'd decided to sleep in.

Since mornings were the best time of the day in Texas—anywhere, really—he carried his coffee outside to drink on the back patio. At least he could watch the sunrise. The sky had already started to lighten and the sun should peek over the horizon any moment now.

Three months ago, he would never have imagined the dramatic turn his life had taken. Then, he'd been happy, living his best life. The ideas and the writing had flowed, he'd explored the city with his friends, and had toyed with the idea of getting a pet. Luckily, he'd never gotten around to acting on that. Who would have guessed he'd be sharing space with a pet pig.

As if his thought had summoned him, Albert came waddling around the corner, grunting when he spotted Pierce. Smiling, Pierce waited for the pig to reach him. Albert settled down near the leg of the chair, looking up at Pierce while waiting for his pets and scratches.

Obliging, Pierce couldn't help but smile. As he scratched

behind Albert's ears, the pig made little grunts, clearly enjoying the attention.

Then, apparently deciding he'd had enough, Albert got to his feet and lumbered away without a backward glance.

Watching him go, Pierce took another sip of his coffee. He found himself constantly waiting for the back door to open and Cassie to appear.

The sun had now cleared the horizon, lighting up the sky with brilliant shades of orange and pink. Pierce took it all in, trying to find the sense of peace he remembered from sitting on his terrace in New York. So far, it had been elusive.

Today was no exception. His thoughts switched between the awful murders his stalker kept committing to the intense kisses he and Cassie had shared.

He'd never considered himself romantic or given to flights of fancy. In fact, the main fault readers found with his novels was the lack of romance woven through the story. Sure, Pierce always made sure to give his protagonist friends and family, sometimes even a girlfriend. But he always steered clear of adding another thread to the others already in play. He purposely avoided developing a romance or anything close.

Once, his editor had asked him why. He'd commented to Pierce that doing so might take his novel to the next level. Instead, Pierce had resisted, making a joke about how he'd already come up with enough ways to ruin his character's lives.

After teasing Pierce for being anti romance, his editor had eventually let it pass. Pierce had forgotten about it until now.

Now he had to wonder if he might be doing his readers a disservice. He'd always told himself people read his books for the thriller aspect and knew to go elsewhere if they wanted to read a romance.

That didn't make him anti romance, did it?

In NYC, he'd dated plenty, but took care not to let anything get too serious. He'd never wanted to be part of a couple and had managed to find partners who felt the same way. This lifestyle suited him well. He shuddered to think about the effect of his stalker's actions on anyone who might have been attached to him.

Bad enough that the killer was committing murders in Pierce's name. He couldn't imagine the pain of having someone he cared about suffer just for being in a relationship with him.

Again, he found himself thinking of Cassie and those kisses. They'd just about sent him to his knees. Luckily, he'd managed to collect himself and break away.

He couldn't figure out why she affected him so strongly.

Though stunningly gorgeous, she wasn't his usual type. Cassie Denton wasn't the type of girl who indulged in casual relationships.

Or was she? After all, she'd kissed him the second time. Even after he'd told her that doing so would be a bad idea. Maybe that had been her way of expressing her desire to have a fun fling before moving on.

Except he'd seen the stars in her green eyes when she looked at him.

No. He wouldn't do it, couldn't. No matter how tempting. He already carried a ton of guilt over having a serial killer use his name as a reason for torturing and murdering people.

Decision made, he should have been able to rest easy. Should have, but his body clearly had other ideas. Even thinking about the kisses he and Cassie had shared aroused him.

He needed to focus on something else. Anything else. So he pulled out his phone.

After destroying his old phone, Pierce had activated another one. He'd loaded the prepaid minutes into the thing and shoved it into his pocket. After all, he didn't have anyone to call. Since he kind of missed social media, he'd decided he'd open a new account with the platform he'd used most and post under another name. He'd use an avatar as his profile picture and carefully avoid all things Pierce Spade related.

It wasn't like his writing accounts would suffer. He had an entire team who handled posting to his author profile, posting promo about his books. All that was taken care of.

He just missed the everyday interactions, seeing what his friends were up to. But then he realized with a new profile, none of those people would still be his friends.

Despite this, he decided to make one anyway. At least he'd feel like less of a Luddite. He managed to do this in less than fifteen minutes. By now, the sun had cleared the horizon and beamed bright and warm, promising a hot, autumn day. Even though his sports watch showed seven thirty, the dry heat in the air already felt oppressive for this time of the year.

Still restless, and constantly looking back over his shoulder toward the house in case Cassie made an appearance, he decided to grab his keys and go for a drive. He needed to familiarize himself with the downtown area anyway.

After the twenty-minute drive to the city limits, he made a circle around town, noticing most of the shops were still closed. The Tumbleweed Café parking lot looked full, since they served breakfast. And there was a store on Main called Serenity's that apparently also had a café inside, also with quite a few customers.

Nothing else appeared to be open.

Instead of continuing to aimlessly drive, he decided to stop at Serenity's and check the place out. Since it seemed less crowded, he figured it'd be less likely someone might recognize him. Plus, Cassie had mentioned them as one of her customers.

When he stepped inside, the small eating area was surprisingly packed. In fact, there were no open tables. A small eating counter had one empty seat, and he made a beeline for that.

"Coffee?" A smiling woman appeared, carrying a glass carafe. When Pierce nodded, she grabbed a chunky glass mug and filled it.

"Here you go. Did you want something to eat?"

He'd already spotted one of Cassie's pies under a dome on the opposite counter. "I'd like a slice of that pie. Is it peach?"

"It is." Her smile widened. "The baker is a local who hopes to soon open her own bakery. Her stuff is amazing."

When she brought over his pie and set it down before him, instead of rushing off to her next customer, she stood watching him expectantly.

To oblige, he grabbed his fork and took a bite. The flaky crust was perfection, and the peach filling managed to be both tart and sweet.

He rolled his eyes. "That's amazing," he said.

"I told you." Someone called out to her and she dipped her chin at him. "I'm Ella. Let me know if you need anything else."

Sipping his coffee, he took his time eating the pie. While he wasn't sure what time the rest of the town's shops opened, he figured he had a lot of time to kill if they opened at ten.

The instant he finished his plate, Ella reappeared. "More coffee?"

As soon as he nodded, she refilled his cup.

"What time does the rest of Main Street open?" he asked.

"Ten, mostly. Rancher's Supply is earlier, like seven." She eyed him knowingly. "You're welcome to hang out here if you want. Or you can browse my shop. Technically, that part isn't open yet, but if you find something you can't live without, I can definitely ring you up."

After settling the check, he left her a five for a tip and went to do as she'd suggested. The shop was definitely eclectic, to say the least. Bookshelves made up one entire wall that ran the length of the store. He pulled several of them out to look at. Every single one dealt with metaphysical subjects, like spirit animals and reincarnation.

The rest of the place had small sculptures and rocks. Lots of rocks, both polished and in the natural state. He picked up a large geode, admiring the colors, before setting it back down carefully. It would, he thought, make an excellent paperweight.

After making a complete circuit of the space, he went back to the café, waved at Ella, and headed outside.

He got into his Jeep and debated whether or not to return to the farm. Since it was only eight thirty, he still had ninety minutes to kill if he wanted to shop in town. He really wanted to check out the bookstore, but wasn't sure that would be wise. If anyone were to actually recognize him, it would be there. For now, he decided to head over to Rancher's Supply.

Pulling up, he drove around back to park. His Jeep stuck out among dozens of pickup trucks.

Hoping to look unremarkable, he made his way inside. A small crowd stood near the back counter, all ranchers or farmers from the looks of them.

Since he had plenty of time, he grabbed a shopping cart and made his way slowly up every aisle. To his surprise, he found quite a few things he couldn't live without, from decorative solar path lights he'd put around the back patio, to an ornate set of ballpoint pens. He liked the way they felt in his hand.

By the time he reached the back counter, the crowd had thinned. Glad he carried quite a bit of cash, he unloaded his purchases and paid. The teenage clerk who rang him up barely made eye contact, which suited Pierce fine.

Outside, he stowed his new purchases in the back seat of his Jeep and checked his watch. Nine thirty. He could either find something else to do for thirty minutes or he could go home.

Restless, he decided to go back to the farm.

Still, as he drove down Main Street, when he spotted The Bookstore, as the sign stated, he slowed. From the outside, he couldn't tell much about the place, other than the fact that it didn't appear to be busy, likely due to the fact that it hadn't yet opened. Even so, most independent bookstores weren't busy these days, which saddened him.

After cruising Main, he turned off at Second and explored some of the other commercial areas. Here he saw a barbershop, an attorney's office, an auto body shop, and several empty buildings with For Sale or Rent signs on them. Several of those would make a nice location for Cassie's bakery, he thought. Some of them even appeared to have living spaces above, though that might be challenging since she lived with a large pet pig.

Not his problem, he told himself. He didn't need to let boredom cause him to get involved in Cassie's life. Especially since he doubted he'd ever see her again once all this was over.

Funny how that thought made his chest ache.

Turning on the next street, he got back on Main and headed toward the farm. He couldn't yet bring himself to call the place home.

When he got there, the absence of Cassie's truck in the drive surprised him. He, who'd always valued his solitude, felt a sudden jolt of loneliness. He missed her, he realized.

Bracing himself, he went in through the front door. Once again, the absence of the scent of delicious baked goods struck him. Funny how quickly he'd come to take some things for granted.

Briefly, he paused. The empty house—*his* house—felt weird. Shaking his head at himself, he continued toward his own room. Once inside, he grabbed his other notebook and pen. Then he climbed up onto his bed to do some journaling. The quiet might be good for that.

Early on in his writing journey, he'd taken up the practice of writing morning journal pages. He thought of it as stream-of-consciousness, freestyle writing. Since no one but him would ever see it, he gave himself the freedom to write whatever he wanted.

Today, he decided to write about his impressions of Getaway. What he'd seen so far, the atmosphere and vibe and the people—admittedly few—he'd met. Anything and everything to take his mind off the gut-wrenching knowledge that someone was torturing and killing women and using Pierce's name as the reason.

If he spent too much time dwelling on that, he suspected he'd lose his mind.

Chapter 8

Since Trudi always insisted they go in her vehicle, Cassie left her truck parked outside of Serenity's and climbed into Trudi's white Lexus. The buttery soft leather seats were way more comfortable than the well-worn vinyl of Cassie's old beater. And don't get her started on the suspension. The SUV's smooth ride was like night and day compared to Cassie's ancient truck.

Someday, Cassie thought. Someday she'd purchase a new vehicle, though not until her bakery had become profitable. While she currently had the funds to pay cash for one, she didn't want to touch the proceeds from the sale of the farm. Those were earmarked for her new business as well as her new home.

Hopefully, she'd find a location for Cassie's Creations—as well as somewhere to live—today. Since Getaway was booming with new businesses, there were quite a few empty buildings for sale or rent. She just wasn't sure how many of them she could afford, especially since she'd prefer to buy rather than throwing money away on rent.

"I have two for rent on the same street," Trudi said. "And I'm sure the owner would be open to selling instead, if you'd rather buy. They're both owned by Bob Dudley, the guy who owns that big cutting horse outfit north of here."

Cassie nodded. She'd heard stories about Bob Dudley most of her life.

"He's a good guy," Trudi continued. "A bit full of himself, but he has a kind heart. Have you ever met him?"

"I have not," Cassie answered. "Though I guess if I like one of his buildings, I will."

"Probably so." They turned off Main onto Third, then took a right on Bowman. "Here we are." She parked in front of a two-story, older, brick building. "This just came on the market. There's street parking and even a small lot in the back."

Getting out of the Lexus, Cassie looked up at the building. "All the windows are sparkling clean."

"The inside is too," Trudi said, putting the code into the lockbox on the door and extracting the key. Once she'd unlocked it, she opened the door and stepped inside. "He's kept the electricity and water on too. Come take a look."

Cassie followed the Realtor. "What did this place used to be?" she asked. They were in a large, open room. Here, she could easily envision a counter with refrigerated display cases for her cakes, cookies, etc. A single doorway led to another room.

"A few years ago, someone planned to run a catering business out of here," Trudi said. "They installed a commercial kitchen, but the husband became ill before they could get everything up and running. Bob let them out of their lease without penalty, and the place has been empty ever since."

"A commercial kitchen?" Cassie breathed. "Do you know how many ovens?"

"I don't. But you can see for yourself." Trudi gestured toward the doorway. "It's right through here."

Telling herself not to get her hopes up, Cassie moved

past Trudi into the kitchen. Someone had spent a lot of money here, she thought. Taking in the stainless steel appliances, the huge grill area, and four large ovens, along with a huge island where she could do prep work, she realized she couldn't have picked a better place for her bakery if she tried. "I can't believe this," Cassie said, turning a slow circle. "If I rent this place, it will save me thousands of dollars in renovation."

"I know." Trudi beamed. "Since Bob just put this place back on the market, that's why I haven't shown it to you until now. I have no idea why he waited so long but he kept it clean and in great shape. You'd just have to renovate the customer area, but otherwise it would be perfect for you."

Cassie thought so too and said so. "What's upstairs?"

Already beaming, Trudi gestured toward a closed door. "It's been used for storage, but if you wanted, I bet you could use it for temporary living quarters until you find someplace better. There is a full bathroom, but no kitchen."

"Interesting. I like that idea." Cassie followed Trudi.

But her hopes for using this building to live in, even if temporarily, crashed as soon as she stepped through the doorway. The stairs going up were unusually steep. There was no way Cassie could see herself getting Albert up and down those. Not to mention the complete lack of a yard. Upstairs, while basic plywood flooring had been done, the rest of the space was unfinished. She could see the pink insulation through the framing.

"That needs a lot of work," Cassie said.

"It just needs drywall and some paint," Trudi pointed out. "And carpet or some other sort of flooring and it would make a perfectly good living space for you to get started."

While living above her bakery would be ideal, since she had to start baking at the crack of dawn, Cassie had Albert to consider. And there wasn't any way she could live somewhere like this with her pet pig.

Unless… She thought for a moment. Albert might be perfectly happy living in the downstairs portion, if she made him an area away from all the food. She'd need to take a look at the parking lot out back and see if there was any sort of area where she could make a fenced-in space for Albert to get his sun and mud fix.

"What do you think?" Trudi asked, noting Cassie's silence.

"It has a lot of potential," Cassie replied. She explained her reservations. "I'd like to see what else you have to show me."

Unable to hide her disappointment, Trudi nodded. "Let's go check out the back first, just in case there's a space that might work for Albert."

The parking lot wasn't very large. Cassie guessed it would fit twelve cars max, which would be more than enough. It wasn't like her place would have sit-down dining or anything. Customers would only be coming to the shop to pick up baked goods they'd ordered ahead of time or wanted to purchase from what she had on display.

Best of all, a small strip of grass under a large live oak tree sat between one side of the lot and next door.

"See?" Trudi pointed. "You could put up a small fence and Albert could have his outdoor space."

"It might work," Cassie agreed, though she wasn't really comfortable having her pet out back with the public coming and going and where she couldn't see him. "I can't decide. Sometimes I think I'd rather have two separate places. One for the bakery and another for my home. Then I think it would be better to live and work in the same space."

"Something like this would do for short term," Trudi said.

"Maybe," Cassie conceded. "I just don't know about this one."

"Well, you saw all the residential offerings I have in your price range," Trudi pointed out, leading the way back to her Lexus. "Let's go take a look at the other commercial properties."

The second building, a few blocks north, had the kind of exterior charm Cassie had been hoping for. Someone had renovated the storefront to make it look Victorian. The pale blue paint with white trim almost had a beachy feel, odd in landlocked West Texas, but still cute. Cassie could picture displaying her cakes and pies in the large bay window. This one had a slightly larger parking area since it sat on the corner of Pine and Eighth.

"Easier traffic flow off Main," Trudi commented as she parked. "From what I can tell on the MLS listing, this one has been renovated too, but I'm not sure it's going to have the kind of kitchen the last one did."

Cassie nodded. "Does it have a kitchen at all? From what I remember growing up, this used to be a dog grooming place."

"Right. After that, it was several things. Most recently, a coffee shop. I thought they had really good coffee, but I don't think Getaway has a lot of people who grab coffee to go. They were only open a couple of months."

"I didn't even know they were here," Cassie admitted. "I might have tried them if I'd known."

"Well, too late now." Trudi hopped out, leading the way to the front door. "They probably should have done some advertising."

Stepping inside, Cassie looked around with interest. The large front window brought in natural light. A long counter over glassed-in display cases divided the room. The cases would be perfect for displaying her baked goods.

She could tell where the coffee machines and the cash register had been. "This setup would work perfectly for a bakery," she said. "Is there any kind of kitchen in the back?"

Trudi grimaced. "It's a converted residence, and I believe they left part of the original kitchen. I don't think it would be anywhere near what you'd want for a bakery, so you'd have to do renovations. There's a half bathroom for the employees and guests to use, but no shower or tub."

"Which means I couldn't live here then."

Trudi frowned. "Not immediately, no. You couldn't even operate the bakery right away. I don't know how long it would take to get all the equipment you'd need."

"Fair point. Let's go ahead and take a look."

Despite the exterior charm and the airy feel to the public area, the rest of the building seemed dark and cramped. There was only one section that could be used as a living area, and the small storage room could be turned into a bedroom. But that would leave no space for storage.

Correctly interpreting Cassie's expression, Trudi suggested they move on. "I still have one more place to show you. It's not owned by Bob Dudley. Let's go take a look at that. It's actually on Main, which will give you more foot traffic."

"On Main? Wouldn't the rent be more expensive?"

Trudi shrugged. "Surprisingly, the last time they had it listed for rent, it wasn't that much more. Probably because it's on the south end of Main. The building on the left of it is boarded up."

Trying to place it, Cassie followed Trudi back to her SUV and got inside. When they reached Main, Trudi turned left, the opposite way from Serenity's.

"Here we are." They pulled up in front of an unassuming brick storefront with a large For Sale sign displayed in the front window. As Trudi had mentioned, the building next door had the windows boarded up. It wasn't a good thing, but Cassie decided to focus on the actual space and try to ignore the neighbor.

This time, Trudi unlocked the door in silence, stepping aside so Cassie could precede her.

Inside, a thick layer of dust covered everything. Still, it seemed a good-sized space. "Do you know what was here before?" she asked.

Trudi checked something on her phone. "It's been empty for years, but the last business to operate in this place made jerky and shipped it around the country."

"Jerky? Like beef?"

"And chicken, turkey, as well as other specialty meats. Apparently, they had a large following and were doing really well back in the early 2000s. Both of the owners were killed in a small plane crash near Dallas and their adult children had no interest in running the business."

She consulted her notes again. "It says they tried to rent or sell it, but couldn't find any takers. The place has been for sale for a long time. I'm guessing since most of the downtown revitalization took place on the north side of Main Street, not too many people were willing to look this far south."

"If they made jerky, they had to have some kind of kitchen set up," Cassie pointed out, trying not to get too excited. A place right on Main Street, even if at the less busy end, with the kind of setup she needed, would be a dream come true.

Though the air smelled musty and the power wasn't on,

the counter and display cases appeared to be in perfect condition. All they needed was a deep cleaning.

"This is almost exactly the way I wanted to set up the front room of my bakery," she said, unable to shake the feeling of familiarity. Though she'd never been inside this building before, she'd seen this space numerous times in her dreams.

Trudi smiled. "I like it too. There aren't a whole lot of photos in the MLS listing, so I'm pleasantly surprised."

"Me too," Cassie said. "I'm almost afraid to look at the kitchen." She wasn't sure how to make jerky, but knew it needed to be cured and then dried. Whether or not they'd used ovens to dehydrate the meat remained to be seen.

Since Cassie hesitated, Trudi stepped through the door into the kitchen area. "I think you'll want to come see this," she said, nearly giggling.

Taking a deep breath, Cassie followed her. "Ovens," she breathed, scarcely able to believe her good luck. While they weren't brand-new stainless steel like the first place, they were large, looked functional, and there were six of them.

"I wonder if these all work," she mused.

"We'd need to have the power turned on to find out," Trudi said. "But since the place has been locked up tight for years, I see no reason why they shouldn't."

Cassie nodded. "This place is perfect. How much is the rent exactly?"

"Right now, they have it for sale, not for rent," Trudi replied. "But previously they were trying to rent it out." She named a figure that seemed fair, considering the condition of the place. "I'll talk to them and see if they're willing to rent instead of sell."

Cassie thought for a moment. She wasn't sure she could afford to purchase both a business space and a residential property. For now, she was staying at the farm. But she didn't know how long that would last. If she could rent one and purchase the other, or even better, rent both, it would definitely help her cash flow.

Time to make a decision. She decided to take a leap of faith and go for her dream. "Please do. I think I'd like to try and get this one. Renting, for now. I'd like to have you ask if the owner would be open to selling eventually, if Cassie's Creations takes off."

"*If?*" Trudi scoffed. "Your baked goods are already super popular. There's no doubt in my mind that your bakery will be successful."

This made Cassie smile. "Thanks for the vote of confidence. Right now though, I'd like to see if they're open to renting to me, but if not, purchasing is another possibility."

"Noted," Trudi replied. "I get it. Right now, renting carries much less risk."

"It does. But I also want to have faith in myself and my abilities. If I have to, if they aren't open to renting, I'll buy the place. Especially since I wouldn't have to do too much interior work at all." She took a deep breath, bracing herself. "How much should I offer if they only want to sell?"

Trudi named a figure much lower than Cassie had been expecting. "They've lowered the price several times," she said. "I'm thinking at this point they might be willing to take any offer."

Maybe the time had come to take a giant leap of faith. Deep breath.

"I want to buy it," Cassie said. "On the condition that those are working ovens." Heck, she'd probably still take it even if she had to replace the ovens, though if that were the case, she'd have Trudi negotiate on the selling price.

"I'll get to work on it right away." Beaming, Trudi led the way out, locking up behind them.

The sound of tires on gravel alerted Pierce to Cassie's arrival. Her giant truck, very similar to the ones he'd seen in the parking lot at Rancher's Supply, pulled up and parked.

"Pierce?" She came bounding inside. When she caught sight of his face, she frowned. "Is everything okay?"

"Yes, sorry. I just got worried when you weren't up doing your baking this morning. All good with you?"

Her smile made his insides hum. "Yes. I took the day off and met with my Realtor in town. You were already gone when I got up."

Feeling oddly tongue-tied, he nodded. "I drove down Main Street, visited a place called Serenity's, and then shopped at the Rancher's Supply."

"You ate at Serenity's? I was there too. We must have just missed each other."

"I left about eight thirty," he said. "When were you there?"

She laughed. "Eight forty-five. I met my Realtor at nine." Her mild tone contrasted with the spark in her eyes. She turned and headed toward the kitchen. Even though she'd clearly dismissed him, he followed.

"Tell me about the bookstore," he said. "Does it have any other name? When I drove past it, the sign just said The Bookstore."

Barely glancing at him as she fixed herself a glass of ice water, she replied, "That is its name. The Bookstore. The owner, Mr. Smith, was a big fan of simplicity. Plus, he always said no one wanted to say Smith's store." A ghost of a smile touched her face. "The entire town misses him."

"What happened to him?" he asked.

"He was murdered." She spoke so matter-of-factly that at

first he wasn't sure he'd heard correctly. "For whatever reason, Getaway has had more than its share of killers. Luckily, we have a very competent sheriff who's skilled at capturing them."

This intrigued him. He itched to go grab his notebook and ask more questions so he could take notes.

"Tell me about your sheriff," he prompted. "What's he like?"

"*She*," Cassie responded. "Her name is Rayna Coombs. Everyone loves her. You'll have to meet her, though I have to warn you, she might figure out you have something to hide. She's really good at her job."

Now he knew he had to get his paper and pen. "Hold that thought," he said. Hurrying to his room, he retrieved his supplies. "Sorry. I never know when something might come in handy for a book."

Finally, she looked up and met his gaze. Expression serious, she sighed. "Your computer would probably be better. Just google 'Getaway, Texas, serial killer.' A couple of different stories should pop up and you can read all the details there."

He nodded. "Fair point. And I'll do that. But I'd still like to hear your perspective."

"I don't really have any. I was never directly involved with any of that. All of my info came secondhand."

Intrigued, he nodded. "Who passed the information on to you?"

This question elicited a laugh. "Like most small towns, Getaway has an active gossip grapevine. Someone tells someone else, who passes it on to three or four others. Things often get a little distorted, but the basic truth is still there. You just have to know how to weed through the nonsense to get to it."

Though he wasn't sure why, he wrote all this down. "I've never lived in a small town," he admitted. "New York City born and raised."

"I'm not sure whether to envy you or pity you," she said. "I'm the opposite. I've never lived in a big city. In fact, I've never lived anywhere but here."

Now he definitely jotted a note. Character inspiration rarely came all at once. Instead, he put together little pieces until he had a whole person. And even then, every single time he'd learn something new about them as he wrote.

"I think I found the building I want for my bakery," Cassie announced, her voice catching.

"That's fantastic," he said, meaning it.

"It is," she agreed, and then proceeded to tell him all about the place. "I'm going to have my Realtor put in an offer to buy it."

He nodded. "Still no luck finding a new place to live?" The instant the words left his mouth, he inwardly winced. He hadn't meant to sound so much like he couldn't wait for her to go.

Instead of immediately answering, she studied him. "I had hoped to find a place where I could both work and live," she finally said. "But while there were a couple of possibilities, none of them would have worked for Albert."

"I see," he replied, keeping his tone neutral.

"I plan to keep looking though." She lifted her chin. "I'm confident I'll find something soon. If you need me out of here earlier, just say so."

"I don't." He winced. "I didn't mean for that to sound the way it did."

"It's all good," Cassie said, "I promise I'll keep you posted. Check out the information about Getaway on the internet if you're really interested."

Thanking her, he watched as she hurried away toward her room. For whatever reason, he once again had to stop himself from calling after her and asking if she'd like to eat lunch with him in a bit. He wasn't sure if the prospect of being left alone again bothered him or if he simply wanted her company.

Either way, aware he needed to get himself under control, he kept his mouth shut. Taking a deep breath, he went back to his notebook and sat down. He reread his notes and sighed. Then he got up and fetched his computer. Might as well comb the internet as Cassie had suggested. Sometimes tidbits like this provided inspiration for his writing—whether current work in progress or something in the future. Judging by Cassie's statements, it sounded like Getaway just might be a much more interesting town than he'd originally thought. Serial killers? Murders? And an astute female sheriff, who'd managed to successfully make arrests? Right up his alley.

As usual, once he got started on research, Pierce lost track of time. He read stories and made notes, learning how the owner of The Bookstore had been murdered. Some of the stories were even more fantastical than they'd sounded. There'd been a cultlike group, and the DEA had been involved. Considering there had also been a serial killer or two, he had to wonder what it was about a small town like Getaway that attracted that type of person.

Fascinating.

When he finally looked up from his research, over an hour had passed. He got up and stretched, looking out the window at the bleak landscape. Until he'd arrived at his new place in Getaway, Pierce had never felt so restless. Living in Manhattan, he'd always been able to find somewhere to go, something to do. Even if he just went roaming the streets or took himself to Central Park to commune with nature.

Out here in the flatlands, the open sky felt oppressive, somehow. The lack of buildings and trees combined with the monotony of the landscape had him feeling…exposed. While he felt sure he'd eventually get used to it, he couldn't help but hope he wouldn't have to. He found himself checking the news media online constantly, hoping to learn the serial killer had been caught.

No such luck. And, since he had a new phone and new number, Michael couldn't reach out to him if there happened to be anything new to share. Not wanting to take the risk of endangering him, Pierce didn't dare contact his agent or his publicist or any of his social media team. It was a bit disconcerting how everything moved like a well-oiled machine without him.

It all made Pierce feel as if he'd ceased to exist, at least as far as his writer persona. He didn't know what to do with this new Pierce, the one who owned a pig farm in rural West Texas and lusted after the beautiful former farmer. And, he reminded himself grimly, hid like a coward from a serial killer.

This, more than anything, unsettled him.

He couldn't shake the conviction that there had to be something he could do. Both Michael and the FBI had reminded him that he might write thrillers, but this was real life and not fiction. He'd only get in the way of the investigation or manage to get himself killed.

Which infuriated him even though he suspected they were right. What he hadn't expected was for all of this inaction to send him spiraling.

Currently being in between books didn't help. He had the one releasing in June. He'd just finished the final edits on a book already slated to release in October next year and needed to come up with a more detailed synopsis for his next one. So far, while he'd had some major breakthroughs lately, he hadn't yet put everything together into a cohesive story.

All his life, Pierce had been able to immerse himself in his writing. Doing so often felt akin to stepping into a parallel universe, as if he existed in the same place and time as his fictional characters.

Not now. Not since he'd left New York. And springtime in the city was one of his favorite times of the year.

Frustrated, he threw the notebook down on the couch and pushed to his feet. He'd agreed to go into hiding but on his own terms. He'd been the one to choose this farm, this town, this state.

Since apparently the police and the FBI hadn't been able to garner any leads on the killer, maybe Pierce could figure out a way to trap him. Doing so while remaining hidden might be tricky, but if he treated all of this like one of his novels, he felt confident he could come up with some sort of plan.

The sound of Cassie calling to her pet pig made him turn. His heart took an unexpected leap inside his chest. Hurrying to the front window, he watched as Cassie and Albert strolled toward the house, the sun putting golden streaks in her dark hair.

Damn. He wondered when she'd gone outside. He must have been lost in his research. Transfixed, he stood watching. Only the realization that she'd see him gawking at her made him turn away and head to the kitchen.

"Hey there!" The lilt in her voice matched her smile. "Did you have a good rest of your afternoon?"

Since there was no way in hell he'd tell her he'd spent a

good portion of it feeling sorry for his whiny ass self, he shrugged and muttered that it hadn't been bad.

"Good." After grabbing a glass of water, she scooped some food into Albert's bowl. While she did that, he couldn't help staring at her, transfixed with longing.

What on earth was wrong with him? All up in his head, full of self-doubt. This wasn't the person he'd worked so hard to become.

"Do you want to have lunch?" he asked. "I know it's kind of late but I'm actually really hungry."

"Sure." She shrugged. "What do you have in mind?"

The carnal images that flashed in his head had nothing to do with food. Composing himself, he told her he'd make them sandwiches.

He put together a couple of thick ham and cheese slices, along with crisp lettuce and thinly sliced tomatoes. Carrying those to the table, he grabbed a bag of corn chips and put that in the center. "Lunch is served."

Chapter 9

Biting into the sandwich, Cassie realized she'd been hungrier than she realized. She made quick work of her meal, looking up to realize Pierce had done the same.

This felt homey, she thought, amazed at how well she liked the unfamiliar sensation. Her next thought—that she'd better not get used to it—had her restless.

"Let's watch the early news," she said, getting up and going into the living room. "Maybe they'll have something on about your serial killer."

She turned just in time to catch him wincing at her choice of words. Still, he followed her.

Grabbing the remote, she turned on the TV. The early news had just started. While it mostly covered local stories, sometimes they'd mention national news if a big story broke.

The words *Breaking News* appeared on the screen.

Pierce glanced at her. He appeared to be bracing himself, clearly hoping that this had nothing to do with him or his situation.

"The Thriller Writer Serial Killer has written a declaration to the press," the reporter intoned. *"In addition to ramping up his or her murders, this unknown and deadly killer has asked for the public's help. The killing of inno-*

*cent women will stop if the public helps find the person he
or she really wants. The writer Pierce Spade."*

A picture of Pierce came up on the screen. Luckily, it
was his stock publicity photo, the one where he wore his
hair long and sported a beard.

"At least that doesn't look anything like you now," Cassie
observed.

*"Special Agent in Charge Denotello of the FBI has de-
nounced this letter."* The SAC appeared on the screen, expression furious. "This is a dangerous and mentally unstable
individual," he said, his voice tight. "No one in the public
should even consider making any sort of deal with him. To
do so will not only put yourself in danger but could definitely endanger law enforcement as well."

He took a deep breath before continuing. "We are asking
the public to help *us* find this killer and bring this person to
justice. Crime Stoppers has offered a reward for information leading to the arrest of this serial killer. If you know
something, please call this number."

After the phone number flashed across the screen, the
news anchor went to another story.

Expression dumbfounded, Pierce stared at Cassie. "I have
no words," he said.

"Hey, they're trying," she replied. "Though I hate to say
it seems really obvious they have no leads."

"I want to figure out a way to help them." He shook his
head. "I didn't mean to say that. But now that I have, I actually feel a little better. It's driving me up a wall not being
able to do anything to help. Especially since all of this is
indirectly my fault."

"Not even close." She touched his arm, letting the fierce-
ness she felt show in her voice. "You have no control over
what this deranged killer does. Heck, you don't really even

know which one of your books set him off. He needs to understand they're all fiction."

"I told him that. Back in the beginning, when the emails started coming. They were full of vitriol, claiming I'd put his life in one of my books. He never said which one. And when I said they were all fiction, he claimed they were fact and based on him. I wasn't sure if he wanted some sort of credit, or even a cut of my royalties, at first. It wasn't until several more, increasingly unhinged emails later that I realized what he wanted. *Me*."

The news anchor continued to drone on in the background. Cassie used the remote to turn the television off. "I can't believe the FBI or police don't have any concrete leads."

"Me neither. But this guy is good at what he does."

"And you still don't know which of your books he's claiming mirrors his life?" she asked.

"They're all fiction," he answered, his frustration showing in his voice. "I do a lot of research, and then I base my own fictional cases on a combination of actual ones. None of my bad guys were based on any particular killer. And based on what this guy has done so far—and blaming it on me—I can't think of anything he does that fits the profile of one of the cases I researched. And definitely not anyone I created."

"Has anyone tried asking him?" She gave an apologetic smile. "I mean, people like that crave notoriety. I'm sure he'd be happy to brag about what he's done and the similarities to whatever character in whichever book."

"If he was willing to talk to someone and answer questions, that'd be a great thing to ask," he said. "Unfortunately, there hasn't been any way to get him to talk."

"I can think of a way that might work," she told him.

"Have your social media or PR people issue a statement basically calling him a liar. There's no book based on him, and you have no idea why he's targeting you. I guarantee someone with narcissistic personality traits won't be able to resist."

Cassie wasn't sure whether Pierce would take her suggestion seriously. She didn't even know why she'd thought to give him advice. After all, he was the bestselling thriller writer. He likely knew more about how a serial killer would think than she did.

After considering for a moment, Pierce smiled, excitement lighting up his blue eyes. "You know what? That's an excellent idea. I'd send my PR team an email, but the Feds told me to stay off the internet, since that kind of thing can be traced."

"But I've seen postings on your social media," she said, then blushed. Now he knew that she followed him on socials. But then again, she guessed that wasn't unusual. She'd told him she was a fan of his work.

"I have a team of people who handle my socials. Honestly, I just created another account under an assumed name and using an avatar as a profile pic. I just won't post anything related to my real self."

"But who would you interact with? None of your friends would even know it was you."

"I know." He shrugged. "Actually, I don't see why I can't use my normal personal profile. As long as I don't post any photos, I fail to see how doing that would endanger me."

"Agreed," she said. "But the authorities think it would?"

"I hired a private protection detail," he said. "They worked with some people in law enforcement. But I let them go when they wanted to put me in a safe house." He grimaced. "Talk about going to extremes."

"Private security? You didn't mention that."

"They didn't last long. I fired them less than a week after I hired them."

"Because they couldn't keep you safe?" she asked, genuinely confused.

He stared at her for a moment. "I found the measures they wanted to take a little too extreme."

"What, like making you relocate to the middle of nowhere? Use burner phones and stay off all social media?" She crossed her arms. "All the things you're currently doing?"

Acknowledging the truth of her statement with a quick nod, he smiled. "I promise you, I'm only doing a third of the things they suggested. By hiring them, they wanted me to cede all control over my life to them. I couldn't do that. When I refused, we mutually agreed it was best to part ways."

"I see," she said, though she didn't. Celebrities and private security were all things way outside of her realm of experience.

"All these precautions, while annoying, are not only to keep myself safe but my agent, Michael, too. I'm worried my stalker might go after him."

"That makes sense."

Apparently encouraged by her agreement, Pierce continued.

"After the last time Michael and I talked, I destroyed my old burner phone and activated this one. If I call him again, I'll likely have to do the same with this one. We're being very cautious."

"I'll say." Eyeing him, she debated for a second before speaking. While she knew it'd probably be better to keep her mouth shut, she just couldn't. "Honestly, do you really think this stalker guy is all-seeing and all knowing? The amount of effort it would take to monitor not only your phone calls but your internet usage seems to be beyond what just one person could manage. The time alone…" She shook her head. "He'd be so busy with all of that, he wouldn't have time to kill."

When she'd finished, Pierce stared at her. She couldn't guess his thoughts. While she hated to burst his bubble, someone had to. And if she was wrong, then she'd welcome hearing how and why.

"Fair point," Pierce said, once again surprising her. "Now that I think of it, the security team who came up with the initial suggestions might have just been following protocol for a high-ranking government official or something. Though to be fair, in some of the books I've written, I had a villain with IT skills who could track and find anyone, no matter what precautions they took."

"But that was fiction," she pointed out. "I don't know. Better safe than sorry, I guess. I just think maybe you can give yourself a tiny bit of leeway."

Again, he went silent, appearing to consider her words. "Maybe so. I think I'm going to call Michael and run all this by him."

"You are?" She didn't even try to hide her surprise.

He grinned. "I am. All of what you've said makes sense. Everyone, from law enforcement to Michael, has been acting like this stalker is all knowing. Myself included."

Now she felt like she needed to offer up a few restraints, in case Pierce decided to completely throw caution to the wind. "I mean, you definitely should stay hidden," she said. "And it makes sense not to post any photos or tag your location. Just be careful, that's all. Commonsense stuff."

If anything, his grin widened. "Commonsense stuff," he

agreed, echoing her words. "You're right, you know. While using burner phones is sort of logical, and even that seems iffy, the rest of it isn't. Most of all, I love your idea about baiting him." He took a deep breath, his eyes sparkling. "For the first time since I left New York, I feel like I'm actually doing something that might help capture him."

Then, before she had time to even formulate a response, he leaned over and kissed her.

Stunned, she froze. Though her heart leaped and everything inside of her ached to kiss him back, she managed to keep herself still. After all, he'd pulled away from their last kiss and made it clear he hadn't felt anything.

Instantly, he moved away. Clearly, he'd meant the quick press of his lips on hers as a celebratory moment, nothing more. If he noticed her lack of response, he didn't comment. To her secret disappointment, he didn't try to prolong the kiss, or tempt her into something more.

To cover her misplaced desire, she turned away and strolled into the other room as if she didn't have a care in the world, willing her racing heartbeat to slow.

Clearly clueless, he followed. When she turned to look at him, something in her expression must have made him realize.

"I want you, Cassie," he said, his deep voice thrumming emotion. "I know I acted like I didn't want to kiss you, that I felt nothing." He swallowed hard, his throat moving. "In fact, the truth is the opposite of that. I felt too much."

Unsure how to react, she simply nodded. "Understood."

"Good." He smiled. "Changing the subject. Do you mind if I tell Michael that this plan is your idea?" he asked. "I want to give credit where credit is due."

She managed to collect herself to nod. "Sure, that's fine. Unless he thinks it's a horrible idea. Then it's all on you."

His short bark of laughter made her feel warm all over.

"You're a treasure, Cassie Denton," he said. "Let me go and call him and see what he thinks."

A treasure? No one had ever called her that before. Another warm glow inside, no doubt misplaced as well.

Watching him go, she wasn't sure what to think. In the end, she decided not to overthink things. He was grateful for her idea, that's all. Nothing more.

Since he'd closed the door to his bedroom, she couldn't hear more than a few snippets of his phone conversation. Obviously, he'd wanted privacy, so she'd give it to him.

Her phone pinged, signaling she'd received a text message. It was Trudi.

I've emailed the seller your offer. I'll let you know as soon as I hear back.

Excited, Cassie texted back her thanks. She stuck her phone into her back pocket and found herself with way too much energy. In the past, she'd put that energy to good use by baking or cleaning or exercising, or even taking care of the livestock. Now, with all the swine gone, and the house belonging to someone else, and today being her day off from baking, that left exercising. Even with the overcast sky and the threat of rain later, the temperature seemed mild enough for her to enjoy a nice, long walk.

Since Pierce still hadn't emerged, she debated whether or not to leave him a note. In the end, she decided letting him know her comings and goings wasn't necessary.

Outside, she looked around the familiar landscape with a pang of nostalgia. She'd taken her first steps here, celebrated numerous holidays and first days of school.

This farm had been her home for her entire life. Now

that it had been sold, she found herself wondering what Pierce planned to do with it once he was able to return to New York.

Albert came lumbering around the corner. When he spotted her, he squealed. Moving as fast as his little legs would carry him, he hurried over to her.

"Hey there." Greeting her pet with a thorough scratching around his neck and ears, she straightened. "Do you want to go for a walk with me?"

There were only a few words her pet pig understood. *Walk* was one of them. Albert grunted his agreement, and the two of them set off on the path that led past the main barn toward the open pasture.

Like most of the area, the flatness of the land enabled her to see great distances. There were very few trees and those that had managed to take hold were short and hunched over, leaning as a result of the perpetual wind.

Some might find the view desolate or even ugly. She wasn't sure what Pierce thought of it or if he regretted buying her farm. Not her problem, she told herself fiercely. Albert nudged her with his snout, almost as if he understood her thoughts.

When they reached the old barn, she stopped. It felt like the barometric pressure had changed. She'd always been sensitive to the weather, except for dust storms. Those dang things just seemed to pop up out of nowhere.

Now she felt that familiar electric sort of tingling that meant a storm would soon be here. Slowly, she turned. To the northwest, the sky had notably darkened. Was that a hint of moisture in the wind?

Pulling out her phone, she checked the radar in her weather app. *Severe Thunderstorm Warning, Tornado Watch* popped up on her screen. The radar timeline showed she'd better hightail it back to the house. And, since Pierce wasn't from around these parts, she'd need to fill him in on what to expect. Not to mention get her usual storm anxiety under control.

She took off at a slow jog, so Albert could keep pace. Bless his sweet little heart, he trudged along next to her.

By the time they reached the side yard, the wind had picked up, gusting at times and sending mist mixed with dust to coat every surface. As she grabbed for the door, a particularly strong blast of wind snatched it from her hand, slamming it into the outside wall.

Albert took advantage of the open door to go inside. Cassie grabbed the door and wrestled it closed behind her.

"Looks rough out there," Pierce commented, eyeing her and Albert, who'd gone for his favorite spot on the kitchen floor.

"It's going to be," she replied. Outside, the wind began to howl, making her shiver. "Looks like a bad storm is about to hit."

He nodded, clearly unconcerned. "I talked to Michael. He seemed to like your idea, but wants to run it past the FBI before implementing it."

A boom of thunder shook the house. Though it startled her, Albert had begun to snore. *Spoiled beast*, she thought affectionately. She couldn't help but remember when she'd had livestock hogs and how she'd have to rush outside to make sure the gentle creatures were secure and protected in their pens when it stormed.

When she looked up from her pet, intending on warning Pierce how bad it might get, she realized he'd left the room. Evidently storms didn't bother him. Unlike her. She always felt a mixture of alarm and excitement at the prospect of severe weather. The combination kicked her anxiety up a few notches.

By the time the heavy rain began to pound the roof, she'd already turned on the television for the local weather, as well as pulled up the weather app on her phone.

"Watching the news?" Pierce asked, emerging from his room, dragging a hand through his already rumpled hair. He glanced at the TV and frowned when he realized it was all about the weather.

"It's tornado season," she pointed out. "Storms tend to be severe. We've been under a Severe Thunderstorm Warning and a Tornado Watch all day. Just making sure the Tornado Watch doesn't get updated to a Warning."

"What's the difference?"

At her incredulous look, he shrugged. "I'm not from around here, remember?"

"*Watch* means conditions are ripe for a tornado to form," she replied. "*Warning* means one has been spotted on the ground. That's when the siren goes off in town."

He appeared slightly alarmed at her comment. "Siren?"

"Not out here," she replied. "But in Getaway city limits. There is one, centrally located. They let everyone know it's time to take shelter."

Eyeing the TV, he processed this news. "I guess I should ask. Do you get a lot of tornados out here?"

"We are in what's considered Tornado Alley." Then she took pity on him. "I've lived in this house my entire life and never had one touch down on the farm."

"That's good, right?" he asked. "Or is it? Does that mean there's a higher possibility one will take out the house and us with it?"

This made her laugh. "I guess that's one way of looking at it. But most Texans prefer to take a more optimistic approach."

"I'm not sure I can do that," he said, voice serious. "I'm a New Yorker. We tend to be realistic."

She laughed again. A moment later, he joined her. The warm, masculine sound of him made her entire body tingle. Dang it, this guy made her want him without even trying.

Which meant of course that she needed to jump to her feet and get away from him. Because she didn't want to take a chance of doing something she might regret.

A boom of thunder shook the house. A moment later, the power flickered.

"I'd better get candles out just in case," she said, hurrying off to grab her stash.

"Let me help you." Clearly unaware of her lustful thoughts, he followed her.

As she dug out the candles and found her long lighter, she hoped he didn't notice her flushed skin and rapid pulse. With luck, he wouldn't get close enough to notice anything.

"Let me help with that," he said, reaching for a candle. His elbow accidently brushed her breast, which sent a sizzle of sparks through her.

She hissed through her teeth, and then, instead of moving away, caught herself about to lean closer. "I've got it," she said, her voice tight.

Something in her tone must have reached him. He took a step back and eyed her quizzically. "Are you all right?"

"Excuse me," she muttered, instead of answering. She hurried off to the bathroom, phone in hand in case she needed to use the flashlight.

As he watched Cassie run away from him, a sound from the yard made Pierce glance at the window. Outside, it had gotten so dark that he couldn't tell what the weather might be doing out there.

Rain, check. Thunder and lightning, ditto. And wind. As long as it didn't get any worse, he figured they'd be okay. He'd never experienced a tornado, not up close, and he didn't really want to start now. The fact that this little ranch house didn't have a basement wasn't lost on him, and when Cassie came back, he planned to ask her why not.

Albert let out a loud snore, coaxing a reluctant smile from Pierce. He'd always heard animals knew when the weather was about to get bad. The pig didn't seem all that worried, despite Cassie's seeming panic. Pierce still had no idea why she'd rushed off, unless it had been his accidental brush against her. He'd thought he'd hidden his body's fierce, instant reaction. But maybe she'd noticed, and that's why she'd run.

Either way, her idea of taunting his stalker had been brilliant. Since it was like something he'd have the protagonist do in one of his books, he didn't get why the thought hadn't occurred to him first.

Even Michael had been on board. Maybe, just maybe, insulting a serial killer might infuriate him enough to cause him to make a mistake. Hopefully, one large enough to catch him.

Thunder boomed, loud enough to shake the house. Almost immediately after, lightning flashed. The steady thrum of the rain became a roar. And Albert continued to snooze.

Since Cassie hadn't emerged, he went to fetch his notebook. Rainstorms had always inspired him and this time was no exception. He began to jot notes and then, full-fledged scenes as they appeared like a movie playing inside his head.

As he hurried to get everything down, he wished he'd gotten his laptop since he could type faster than he could write. But he knew from past experience he couldn't get up and switch. Every time he'd tried that, he'd been unable to get back to where he'd left off. Which he knew would sound weird to anyone who wasn't a writer.

"Earth to Pierce." Cassie's voice. He looked up, blinking. Momentarily confused, it took him a few seconds to focus. By the time he did, the rest of the scene had gone. Poof, just like someone had turned off the movie.

"Sorry," he muttered, going back to trying to get the rest of it down from memory before he'd lost it entirely. "Just need a couple seconds."

A siren filled the room, startling him into swearing. "What the...?"

"It's my phone app," Cassie said, tapping her screen to turn off the wailing sound. "Alerting us to a tornado. We need to take shelter immediately."

Alarmed, he pushed to his feet. "Take shelter where? Why doesn't this house have a basement?"

Instead of answering, she grabbed his hand and called for Albert. "Come with me."

As she tugged him along, he managed to hang on to his notebook and pen. Down the hallway they went, Albert lumbering after, into the primary bedroom's walk-in closet.

"No exterior walls and no windows," Cassie explained. "Growing up, this was where we always went when there was a tornado warning."

Bemused, he made way for Albert. The pig went to the back wall and settled under a row of pants on hangers.

"That's his spot," Cassie pointed out, lowering herself to the floor. "He knows the drill."

"The drill?" He sat down cross-legged opposite her. "How often do you get tornado warnings?"

Looking at her phone, she shrugged. "A couple times each spring. Sometimes late summer, early fall. And once or twice in the winter if it's a weird weather year."

"Seriously?"

At her nod, he groaned. "You never did tell me why this house doesn't have a basement."

"Most houses in Texas don't. It's a combination of the clay soil, which expands and contracts, and the fact that the bedrock is really close to the surface, making digging difficult. Folks here aren't used to basements anyways, so no one really expects to have one. Though they would come in handy when there's a tornado."

As if on cue, the lights flickered. But they stayed on. And the roar of the storm seemed muted in this small space, almost as if one could pretend nothing was happening.

"I'll say." He eyed her glumly. "How do you know when it's safe to come out?"

"I continually check the weather app." She held up her phone. "Plus I pull up one of the local news station's social media pages. They usually have a running commentary going when there's this type of weather."

"This feels like I've moved to another country," he commented.

Her laugh sparked a warmth low in his belly.

"Is it really so different in New York?" she asked. "I'm guessing you don't have tornadoes there?"

"No, we don't."

"Tell me what it's like living there," she asked, her gaze intent, though she periodically checked her phone.

There were two things Pierce could talk about endlessly. His writing and his life in New York City. So he told her about his favorite corner bodega, the newspaper stand he frequented every morning, the way the city lights looked at night from his living room windows.

Fondness coloring his voice, he spoke of the near-constant noise that felt like a thrum of life and how he felt lost without it. "The silence is heavy," he explained. "I love how I can walk almost everywhere, and if I can't walk there, I can ride the subway or call a cab. The variety of the restaurants, the easy access to seeing the shows on Broadway. Central Park, where you feel as if you're out in the woods somewhere far from the city, but you're not. I could go on and on, but you get the general idea."

Her wistful expression surprised him. "I can't even imagine," she said. "But to be honest, I think all of that might terrify me."

Right then and there he knew if he ever got a chance, he'd take her to New York and show her around. When he told her this, she tilted her head and studied him.

"You really mean that, don't you?" she asked, a note of wonder in her voice.

The soft glow in her eyes made it difficult to catch his breath. He caught himself focusing on her kissable mouth, glad they were sitting across from each other instead of side by side.

A huge boom of thunder rattled the house. Cassie jumped, clearly startled. Unfazed, Albert continued to snore.

"Are you okay?" Pierce asked quietly. "Aren't you used to this kind of thing? Should I be more worried?"

This last question coaxed a smile. "You'd think I would be," she replied. "But I've always had this weird relationship with storms. I find them exhilarating and terrifying at the same time."

And right now, she'd clearly let the terror take over. Her wide eyes and shaky voice tugged at his heart.

He held out his arms, wanting to give her the choice. "Come here."

The speed at which she crossed the space between them

had him chuckling. Once she'd settled in next to him, he wrapped his arms around her and held on tight.

She felt...good. Better than that. Right. As if she belonged there, close to his heart.

They sat like this for a few moments, until thunder crashed again and her phone siren went off for a second time.

"Ugh." Pulling out her phone, she looked at the screen. "Another tornado on the ground, but it's way north of here."

"Is this normal?" he asked, eyeing her in disbelief. "Even for Tornado Alley?"

Before she could answer, the power went off, plunging them into complete darkness.

"I forgot the candles." Voice shaky, she sounded like she might be about to cry. Pierce could deal with a lot of things, but a woman's tears weren't one of them.

"We don't need them," he told her, pulling her back close. "It's all going to be okay. Listen to Albert snoring. He's letting you know everything is fine."

Her hiccupping laugh made him kiss the top of her head.

"You're right, you know," she murmured. "Animals always seem to know when it's going to get bad. Thank you for reminding me of that." She snuggled into his side and put her head on his shoulder. He couldn't help but breathe in the clean, floral scent of her hair.

This should have felt...cozy. Except somehow, the lack of light made everything seem more intimate. Or maybe that was all in his head. Either way, he continued to hold her, telling himself he was offering only comfort while his arousal continued to grow. Talk about awful timing.

Another crash of thunder, another slash of lightning, briefly illuminating the bedroom outside the closet.

Cassie burrowed in deeper. She couldn't have gotten any closer unless she climbed on his lap.

That thought sent a bolt of heat straight to his groin. His breath caught, his heart thudded in his chest. When she went still, he felt certain that she knew.

Unable to speak, afraid to do anything that would scare her off, he kept himself as motionless as he could, even as his body throbbed.

One thing for certain—making love would definitely distract her from the storm. But would she even want to?

While he hesitated, trying to be a gentleman, she gave a little cry.

She moved first, twisting in his arms enough to face him. In the complete and utter darkness, the soft whisper of her breath on his face and the insistent press of her breasts against his chest set him on fire.

And then she found his mouth in the dark and kissed him. Not a gentle kiss, or a timid one, but the kind that could only lead to one thing.

Chapter 10

Cassie had never wanted a man more than she wanted Pierce Spade in that moment. Well, if she were being honest, she'd had a hankering for him from the moment they first met. But he'd made it clear that nothing could happen between them, and she'd intended to honor that. No matter how reluctantly.

But here in the darkness, wrapped tightly in his arms while the storm raged outside, she felt the shift in him. Desire simmered in the air between them and not all of it was one-sided.

She took a chance and a deep breath before making the first move.

The instant she settled her mouth over his, fire ignited. As always, the heat of the kiss had her craving more. She shifted again, settling herself over him, straddling him. The instant she felt the force of his arousal, her entire insides melted. Electricity shot through her veins.

"Your clothes," she managed to get out, in between kisses and caresses.

"In the way," he finished, his voice rough. "Yours too. Take them off. But wait. I want to see you."

He must have fumbled for his phone in the dark, because a moment later, his flashlight came on, illuminating the small space. And him. The shadows highlighted his muscular body, giving an otherworldly but sexy-as-hell vibe.

"Damn," he muttered, the shadows hiding his eyes. "You are so beautiful."

Lust emboldened her. "So are you," she said. Then, feeling as if her entire body was on fire, she moved back. Gaze locked with his, she slowly pulled her shirt over her head and yanked off her jeans. Glad of the partial darkness, she went back to him, leaving on her bra and panties, ready to help him shed his clothing.

But when she reached for the waist of his jeans, he grabbed her hand and kissed her again. "Not yet," he rasped against her mouth. "I need…"

Lust made her unstoppable. She grabbed his T-shirt and tried to lift it over his head, breaking the kiss.

He laughed. "Wait. I need protection." Removing his wallet, he procured a condom. Then, as she reached for his shirt again, he helped her. She took advantage of this by stroking his engorged body through his jeans and then releasing the top button. He groaned. "You can see what you're doing to me."

"I can," she agreed, reveling in a delicious sort of wickedness. "But I have no idea how I'm going to get that zipper open," she murmured. "Where there's a will, there's a way."

As she stroked him, she managed to ease the zipper down. Once she had him free, he arched into her hand with a groan.

"This," she hissed. "I need to feel you inside of me."

"Condom first," he managed, tearing open the wrapper.

"Let me." She took it from him. Relishing his tortured expression, she eased it over the swollen length of him, inch by inch.

His tortured groan only fed into her desire. When she

finished with the condom, she let her fingers linger on him for a moment. "I want you," she said again. "So badly."

Another groan and then he pushed against her hand. She flushed, heat spiraling through her.

Though she'd never considered herself a bold person, with him, in this moment, she became one. Sliding her panties to one side, she straddled him, guiding his arousal into her warm and ready body. Honey and heat, desire and other more elusive emotions swirled around them.

The instant he connected with her warmth, he muttered something unintelligible and went still. "I need a second," he rasped.

"One second," she said, holding herself motionless for exactly that. And then, she rose above him, only to come back down, sheathing him inside her. With a cry, he abandoned all attempt at maintaining self-control.

Arching himself up for her, she rode him like a cowgirl on a bucking bronco, giving in to the passion and the power of both of their arousals. Not fire and ice, they were flame and inferno, each of them nearly mindless with passion. He in her, she on him, lost in the motion and the moment.

When he rolled her over so he could be on top and plunged into her, she gladly relished the transfer of control. With each thrust, she arched her body, curving toward him, and welcomed him with every ounce of herself.

She'd heard other women say they saw the stars, but until this very moment, she'd never believed them. Not only stars but the galaxy, the universe.

The storm raged outside, mirroring their lovemaking. Thunder shook, or maybe it was their own movement. She didn't know and didn't care. In this moment in time, only Pierce and she existed.

As her climax began to build, she cried out. Shuddering, her entire body shattered as she found the peak. Over the edge, tremors rocked her body. She held on to him for dear life, riding the crest and going over the edge into free fall. She grabbed him and tried to hold him close. But like her, he appeared to be past the point of no return. When her body found release, clenching around him and raining honey, he went wild.

The shudders that took him mirrored her own. Fierce with emotions she refused to consider, she welcomed him. For the first time in her life, she wished she had more light, so she could see his face. Instead, she watched the shadows dance.

After, they simply held each other.

Lying with him, locked in his embrace while their skin cooled and their breathing slowed, Cassie realized she finally understood the difference between having sex and making love.

Never before had anyone made her feel this way. Complete. Cherished. Sensual.

"I'm—" he began.

"Shhh." Placing her finger against his mouth, she shook her head. "No apologies. No regrets. Understood?"

Gaze locked on hers, he slowly nodded.

"Good." She stretched and kissed him again, one quick press of her mouth on his. Then she moved away, pushing herself up off the floor.

Outside, the storm appeared to have moved on, but they still had no power. Using her phone's flashlight, she made her way into the bathroom. After cleaning herself up, she checked the weather app before going back to the closet.

"All clear," she said, keeping her flashlight on while grabbing her discarded clothing and trying to get dressed. "The danger has moved on, so we don't have to stay in here."

"Good," he muttered. He got up, retrieved his own clothing, and disappeared into the bathroom, using his own phone to guide him.

Meanwhile, Albert still slept. Cassie decided to leave him there until he woke.

Once she'd made her way into the kitchen, she lit a bunch of candles for light. They created a warm glow, making the small house look cozy.

Albert appeared, apparently waking up to realize she wasn't there.

"Do you want to go outside?" she asked. She'd house-trained her pet pig the same way people trained a dog, and Albert knew not to go potty inside the house.

With a grunt, he trotted to the back door. She opened it, peering outside. A light rain still fell, but the thunder and lightning had moved off to the east.

Since Cassie knew Albert would find the mud, she closed the door. It wasn't cold, just wet, and her pig loved his wet earth.

Pierce appeared, fully dressed. He went directly to the refrigerator and grabbed a bottle of beer. "Do you want one?" he asked.

"Sure."

After opening them, he put them down on the table and gestured at the chairs. "We need to talk," he said.

So much for keeping all of this lighthearted and simple.

"Do we?" she asked, dropping into a chair and grabbing her beer. "I mean, we're both single adults. What happened, happened. I enjoyed it and I think you did too. There's no need to make this a bigger deal than it is."

He stared at her for a moment before taking a long drink of his beer. She couldn't tell if he felt relieved or suspicious or what.

"Very cosmopolitan of you," he finally said, his tone bland.

"Is it? I can't tell if you mean that as an insult or a compliment." Taking a deep breath, she struggled to keep her voice even. "Either way, what is it you want from me?"

"Want from you? Shouldn't it be the other way around?"

She shouldn't have been disappointed, and she definitely shouldn't have been hurt. But all her life, Cassie had been fighting for herself, going on the defense against those who wanted to bully or ridicule her because she wasn't like them.

She'd thought Pierce would be different. Clearly, she'd been wrong. "Let me get this straight." Her tone dripped sarcasm. "Just because you're a famous author and I'm what, a nobody pig farmer's daughter from nowhere, Texas, you think I'm going to try and get something from you because we had sex?"

Taking a deep breath, she found herself blinking back tears. Which wasn't unusual, as she usually cried when she got angry and upset.

"Wait a minute." Pierce held up a hand. "I'm not sure how you inferred all that from an offhand comment I made. That wasn't what I meant at all."

She crossed her arms. "Then what exactly did you mean by saying I was being cosmopolitan?"

His sheepish expression mystified her. "To be honest, my ego might have taken a blow. That's all."

Unsure what he meant, she kept silent, waiting for an explanation. When he took another drink of his beer, she did the same.

"I'm sorry," he finally said. "I have mixed feelings about what happened."

"Me too," she admitted. "But I don't expect anything from you, just like I believe you don't expect anything of me."

Grimacing, he shook his head. "Definitely not. Look, can we start over?"

"Start over?" She decided to tease him. "Do you mean pretend all of this never happened?"

He looked mildly horrified. "Not that part. That was amazing. I wouldn't want to forget it. I meant from when I said we need to talk. For some reason, I thought I needed to establish boundaries. Clearly, I didn't."

Again, that unwelcome ache in her throat. She pushed to her feet. "No, you did not. If you'll excuse me, I have a few calls I need to make. Hopefully, the power will come on soon."

Grabbing her beer, she left the room, phone flashlight in hand to light her way.

Sitting alone in the dark, Pierce sighed and took another gulp of cold beer. As usual, he'd managed to make a total mess of things. He should have held back, waited to see how she acted, and let her take the lead.

Instead, he'd been worried about establishing boundaries—after the fact. She hadn't seemed concerned, or even affected.

Which meant he was the one in trouble. He couldn't stop thinking about how well they'd fit together.

His body stirred, which surprised him. Damned if he didn't want her again. Which wasn't good. He needed to try and focus on something else.

The house felt different in the darkness. Quiet, without the hum of the refrigerator and the other appliances. He could hear the wind occasionally gusting outside, but no sounds of rain.

Texas storms, and especially tornadoes, weren't something he ever thought he'd get used to. Even the air had felt charged, prickling the nerve endings under his skin. He truly believed that this had carried over to color the passion he and Cassie had shared.

Otherwise, what could explain the intensity when they'd come together? He'd never experienced anything on that level, and part of him doubted he ever would again.

His phone rang, startling him since he wasn't sure if they'd have cell service. Still sitting alone in the darkness, he answered.

"Are you sitting down?" Michael asked, his tone grim.

The bottom dropped out of his stomach. "Yes. What the hell has happened now?"

"The first post went live an hour ago," Michael said.

"You sound nervous," Pierce commented. "Why?"

"I don't know. Maybe because I don't like trying to anticipate what this guy will do. Since we're doing a media blast, the mainstream networks will be sure to pick up the story."

Pierce nodded. "So even if he's not on social media, he'll hear that we're calling him a liar."

"Yes. And while we're doing all this, you're also getting a lot of free publicity. We prepared a list of your books, in order, and provided bestselling stats. We've made a big deal out of your fictional serial killers and mentioned how there are no comparisons to be made to him."

"Good," Pierce said. "And I assume along with all this, you're insinuating he's incompetent."

Michael's short bark of laughter made Pierce grin. "Yep. We stop short of calling him the worst serial killer in history."

"And law enforcement is okay with all this?"

"Yes," Michael replied. "The FBI is geared up for any action on your stalker's part. They figure he'll do something big to distinguish himself in the eyes of the world."

The thought of this was sobering. "I don't want any more innocent people to die."

"No one does," Michael said. "But the FBI has also had us drop false clues as to your whereabouts. They're setting a trap just in case. The hope is this guy will go there looking for you and they'll be able to arrest him."

Though all of that seemed like a good plan, it also seemed too tidy to actually work. Pierce knew if he'd written something along those lines in one of his books, his editor would have claimed such a thing wasn't believable and made Pierce revise.

Of course, real life was often stranger than fiction, so who knew?

"I hope it works," Pierce said.

"Me too." Michael went quiet for a moment. "They've scheduled a date to demolish what's left of your old building. They plan to build more apartments in the same spot."

He felt a stab of homesickness, mingled with sorrow. When he thought of the people who'd been killed and the others who'd lost all their worldly possessions, the thought was so painful he had to change the subject.

"I've been corresponding with the insurance company," he said. "They're dragging their feet, but I imagine they'll settle eventually. Luckily, I'm all right without their money. I can't help but worry about the others who might not be."

"I agree," Michael replied. Someone said something to him in the background. "I've got something personal right now, so I need to go. I promise to keep you posted if I hear anything."

After ending the call, Pierce wished Cassie would come back, so he could fill her in. But then again, maybe her absence was all for the best. He might be getting a bit too close to her. Especially since they were essentially ships passing in the night.

Speaking of night… The darkness made it feel much later. Maybe he should go grab his Kindle and read, since it was backlit. He got up and, following Cassie's earlier example, used his phone flashlight to get to his room. Once there, he closed his door and got undressed. Then he grabbed his Kindle, and climbed up onto his bed with the intention of reading.

He started out strong, but must have fallen asleep. Because sometime in the night when the power came back on, it woke him. Since his nightstand clock merely kept blinking, he grabbed his phone to figure out the time—3:15 a.m.

Yawning, he quickly reset the nightstand clock, pulled on a pair of sweatpants, and went out to the main part of the house to turn off all the lights. Cassie's bedroom door remained closed, so he got everything shut down himself. Wondering about Albert, he opened the back door and peered outside, but saw no sign of the pig in the darkness. Maybe Cassie had taken him into her room for the night.

Part of him couldn't help but hope she'd wake and come out. He wondered what she wore to sleep in, pictured a worn, soft shirt slipping off one creamy shoulder. Instantly aroused, he forced himself to think of something else to calm his body down.

Once he'd gotten the house shut down, he returned to his room, crawled back into bed, and tried to go back to sleep. Though he tossed and turned, plagued with images of her silky skin and passionate kisses, eventually he must have succeeded. When he opened his eyes again, sunlight streamed through the window. Which meant he'd slept later than usual.

A quick glance at the nightstand clock confirmed that—

8:00 a.m. For someone who'd grown accustomed to rising at sunrise or shortly after, this was definitely a change. Stretching, he tried to decide if he liked or hated it.

After reveling in a leisurely hot shower, he got dressed and headed to the kitchen for some much needed coffee. Once he'd accomplished that, he carried his mug into the other room.

Cassie sat on the couch, watching one of the morning talk shows, Albert snoozing on the floor at her feet. Pierce found himself admiring the way her long, dark hair framed her delicate face.

Surprised, he stopped in his tracks. "What are you doing here? I thought you'd be busy with your baking and deliveries."

She laughed. "I've been up since three thirty. Everything has already been made and delivered. I plan on taking a nap sometime today."

Feeling sheepish, he nodded. "I guess I slept right through it."

"I guess you did. Pierce," she said, barely looking away from the TV. "You need to see this. It looks like they've already put your plan in motion. The hosts just teased a segment to come later about Pierce Spade and his serial killer stalker."

"Oh, wow." Pierce dropped down onto the couch next to her, careful not to spill his hot coffee. The movement made her pet pig raise his head, but once Albert saw it was Pierce, he grunted and went back to sleep.

"You slept in today," Cassie said, her voice casual.

"I did," he agreed, matching her tone.

"Guess you needed your rest." She flashed an impish grin.

A bolt of desire struck him hard. Swallowing, he struggled to find a response, settling on a nod instead.

The commercials ended and the two female hosts began chatting about Pierce and his books. From there they talked about his stalker, a confirmed serial killer with "a big ego," who'd been insistent Pierce had featured him in one of his novels.

"The author emphatically denies this," the blonde host said, a hint of mockery in her voice and smile. This led to several quips about people who believed they saw themselves in fictional characters.

Then the conversation turned serious. Images of the apartment fire—believed to be arson—played. And the murders and tortures of several women, all in an attempt to get Pierce Spade to reveal his location.

"Apparently, he had to go into hiding to avoid this guy," one host said, shaking her head.

More talk show repartee ensued, most of it faintly snarky until one of the hosts pointed out that this was an actual serial killer they were discussing.

A chart went up, briefly showing the stats. "So far he's killed at least twelve women."

"That we know of," one of the hosts chimed him. "I don't understand why law enforcement can't seem to catch him. Obviously, he can't be super intelligent since he continues to push his copycat narrative."

They all laughed.

Watching with a kind of horrified fascination, Pierce realized he hadn't thought anyone would go this far. But then again, what had he expected? They'd set in motion a plan, and now that it had been implemented, why was he so shocked?

When he glanced at Cassie, he saw a similar shocked expression on her face.

"Your stalker's not going to like this," she said, frowning as she met his gaze.

"No, he's not," Pierce responded. "But this is necessary. And, it's only the tip of the iceberg. There will be coordinated social media posts and eventually mainstream news should pick this up and run with it."

"I really hope this flushes him out," Cassie said.

"Me too." Unable to resist, he gave her shoulder a quick squeeze. "Thanks to you and your idea, I'm actually hopeful for the first time in a long time."

Her breath caught and she tensed under his hand. He moved away, as if the slight touch burned him. In a way, he supposed it did.

Damn. Just being in the same room as her aroused him. Sharing space and keeping his hands off her would be difficult. He'd better get busy doing other things to keep his mind off her and his desire at bay.

Mumbling something about needing to eat, he went back into the kitchen and fried a couple of eggs. He ate that with two pieces of toast, washing the entire thing down with a second cup of coffee. Then he went and grabbed his notebook, a pen, and a measuring tape and excused himself. He wanted to take measurements out at the barn and sketch out some possibilities. He still thought this place could be turned into a seasonal writer's retreat. The lack of distractions in the bleak landscape might even work in his favor.

He spent several hours measuring and making notes. The longer he worked, the more excited he became. The possibilities of just this one space. Never mind all the others.

Sometime in the early afternoon, his growling stomach reminded him that he hadn't had lunch. He trudged back to the house, more relieved than he should have been to see Cassie's vehicle was gone.

After eating a quick sandwich, he switched gears and got his writing notebook. More and more of his next story had begun to appear to him and he needed to get it all down before writing the synopsis.

By the time Cassie pulled back into the driveway, he felt a sense of accomplishment. In addition to starting on plans for turning the farm into a possible writing retreat, he'd not only gotten a good start on fleshing out a possible synopsis but had taken out two steaks and marinated them. He'd noticed the gas grill on the back patio and intended to try his hand at cooking the steaks on it. He'd had a smaller version on his apartment terrace, so he figured he could manage this one.

Cassie came inside and smiled when she saw him. She wore what looked like painter's coveralls and actually had a smear of paint on her cheek. "I've been working on the bakery," she said happily. "Trudi got them to move up closing and we're aiming for two days, since I'm paying cash. They said they didn't mind if I made some improvements beforehand."

Though he came way too close to asking if he could see it, he managed to swallow back the words. "That's great. I hope you like steak. I'm planning to grill a couple for dinner."

Surprise flashed across her face but she nodded. "I like anything I don't have to cook," she said, grinning. Then she frowned. "Do you have any work for me?"

Momentarily confused, he stared. "Work? What do you mean?"

"When we first met, you said you wanted to hire me as your proofreader. So far, you haven't given me anything to read."

He couldn't believe he'd managed to forget about that. But then again, he hadn't really been writing.

"I've been having a little trouble getting started," he admitted. "Sometimes writing is like that. I really thought moving out here to a place with no distractions would have me writing gangbusters, but instead it's been the opposite."

They shared an early meal, the quiet camaraderie soothing Pierce's restless soul. The steaks were delicious and the baked potato and side salad complemented them perfectly. Cassie seemed relaxed and her buoyant mood lifted his own spirits. It had been a good day, he thought. Even though simply sharing space with Cassie kept him in a constant state of arousal, he managed to hide it well.

She seemed unaware of her own beauty and the sensuality that radiated with every movement she made. Now that he'd known her body intimately, instead of slaking his hunger, he only craved more.

If she felt the same way, she didn't show it. He decided he'd be content to wait, to see if she initiated anything again with him. After all, though they were both adults, she was his guest here in the farmhouse he'd purchased. If things were complicated, neither of them seemed willing to allow that kind of tension to make their days uncomfortable or uneasy.

Instead, he thought this felt...*homey*. Something he'd never thought he'd wanted or even needed.

But now, he actually kind of *liked* this. Spending time with her on a remote farm in the middle of nowhere. Sure, he couldn't wait to have his old life back, to return to Manhattan and the places and people he knew. The motion, the excitement—all of that he truly believed helped inspire him. New York City, with all its quirks, fed his soul.

But he'd also managed to find inspiration here, in Getaway, Texas. The quiet, at first unsettling, no longer bothered him. And the bleakness of the rugged landscape took on its own kind of beauty. Especially with Cassie around to brighten his days with her smile.

Suddenly restless, for the first time in years he found himself doubting what he believed he needed. He'd always been rock steady, craving the sameness of his familiar routine. Boring, even. But comfortable in his own skin.

Having a serial killer stalking him had shaken everything up. He'd foundered, lost and unable to find his way. He'd impulsively purchased a farm in a part of the country he'd only driven through, hoping the utter differentness of the place might bring him peace.

And it had. In a way he'd never expected.

He gave himself permission to enjoy this. Because for now, this was...nice. Maybe even exactly what he needed, serial killer stalker be damned. He'd enjoy this while he could, for as long as it lasted. Hopefully no one would get hurt when it ended.

Because he knew it would. He believed Cassie did too. They were from separate worlds. If the idea of living anywhere without her seemed bleak, he told himself that was due to his overactive imagination.

Chapter 11

That night, the national news carried Pierce's story. Watching with him, Cassie caught herself almost reaching for his hand when the anchor started talking about what he called Pierce's "challenge."

> "Since this serial killer, who has managed to evade law enforcement, has claimed that bestselling thriller author Pierce Spade has used his methodology in one of his novels, the author himself has clapped back. Claiming the killer is delusional, Mr. Spade has issued a challenge."

A photo of Pierce's "official" statement appeared on the screen.

> "This author not only fully denies all claims made by this murderer but challenges him or her to either provide proof of their accusations or to stop spreading lies about Mr. Spade."

Next to her, Pierce sat motionless, staring at the TV. She nudged him. "That's sure to get a reaction," she said. "I have to admit, it makes me a little bit nervous."

Expression troubled, he turned to face her. "Me too. Because there's no way to know what this guy will do now. I'm hoping it sends him off the deep end, he messes up, and gets caught."

"We can only hope." She sighed. "At least he has no idea where to find you, so he can't enact his retribution on you." She shook her head. "I admit, the thought of a serial killer showing up here scares the bejeebers out of me."

"Bejeebers?" One corner of his mouth lifted as he eyed her. "That's a new one for me."

Sheepishly, she shrugged. "I might have made it up, though I swear I heard it somewhere. Either way, it suits the occasion."

"It does." His warm smile started a spark low in her belly.

"And you don't have to worry," he continued. "Because I'm confident he can't find me. I've done nothing that might enable him to locate me. I pay with cash, don't use credit cards or my debit card, and I don't post photos to social media."

The husky timbre to his voice made her ache with longing. Clearly, he had no idea of his effect on her.

Gathering herself together, she managed to reply. "I know. You're careful. I'd expect nothing less from a bestselling thriller author. I just want him caught."

"Me too." Again, that sexy flash of a smile. "I have to admit I'm also selfishly hoping when he is, he finally reveals which book and which antagonist he thinks is modeled after him." He shrugged. "Weird as it may be, I'd really like to know."

She smiled back. "I don't blame you. Hopefully, he will," she said, her smile fading. "The important thing is getting him locked up so he stops killing people."

"Agreed."

"I can't imagine how terrified his victims must have been." Shuddering, she wrapped her arms around herself.

"I can," he replied, his voice quiet. "One of the curses of being an author is we have an extremely vivid imagination. While I'm not comparing that with what the killer's victims had to endure, I have nightmares. Envisioning what they must have gone through keeps me up a lot at night."

Again, she had to keep herself from going to him. The bleakness in his expression, the pain she saw in his eyes. If anyone needed a hug at this moment, it was him. But despite the fact that they'd been physically intimate, they'd tacitly agreed to keep emotion out of the equation. Both of them were short-timers in this house.

Instead, she decided to change the subject. "What are your plans for tomorrow? I'm going to work on the interior of my bakery after I take care of my deliveries in the morning. You're welcome to meet me there if you don't mind physical labor."

His pretend horrified recoil made her laugh. "Physical labor?" He spoke the words with the kind of inflection one might use to decry being dropped into a pit of vipers.

She shrugged. "You're pretty muscular for someone who acts like wielding a paintbrush might strain your fingers."

Both brows rose. And then he laughed. A deep, masculine sound that made her toes curl.

"I have nothing against helping you paint," he finally said. "Though I have to admit, I'm not very good at it."

"That's okay. It's not anything complicated. Just putting a fresh coat of paint on the walls. But I'm really just teasing you. I've only just started painting. There's still lots to do. You can help me tomorrow afternoon if you want. I'm meeting Trudi in the morning for a final walk-through before closing."

"How long would that take?" he asked. "In case I did decide to show up and help paint a wall or two?"

"I'm not sure. I can text you if you want."

He nodded. "Sure." He gave her the number of his new burner phone.

Trying to concentrate on watching TV, all she could think of was how badly she wanted to kiss him. Every nerve ending felt as if it was on fire. Finally, she excused herself and went to bed.

The next morning, she got up before the crack of dawn and began baking. Once she'd completed all the day's orders, she got them loaded up. Pierce's bedroom door remained closed. Oh well. If he decided to help her paint later, he knew where to find her.

All she could think of was him as she walked out the door and got into her car. Damn if she wasn't in trouble.

Driving into town, she tried listing all the reasons why she couldn't allow herself to fall for Pierce Spade. First and most important, he wasn't from around here and had no plans to stay. All her life she'd figured if she ever settled down and raised a family, if not in Getaway, it would be in Texas.

Not someplace like New York, which seemed as foreign to her as another country.

Shocked at the direction of her thoughts, she shook her head and chastised herself for even thinking along these lines.

What on earth was wrong with her? She and Pierce had only known each other for a short time. Sure, she'd never felt anything like the intense attraction between them. And yes, the sex had been out of this world. Leagues better than anything she'd ever experienced before. And likely would ever again.

The maudlin thought made her sad. But then the foolish-ness of it all brought her out of her mood. She had her entire life ahead of her. She'd taken a chance and a leap of faith, sold everything in order to make a fresh start. With the pur-chase of the building, her dream of running her own bakery would be one step closer to reality. She needed to focus on this, not on what likely was only infatuation.

She dropped off her delivery at The Tumbleweed Café first. They weren't yet open, but they always had a crowd for breakfast. They were her largest order and had begun to hint they might be increasing it soon.

After that, she delivered to Ella at Serenity's. While her breakfast rush was on a significantly smaller scale, she al-ways sold out of Cassie's baked goods.

Ella greeted Cassie with a tired smile. "I'm going to have to hire some help soon," she said. "It's gotten too busy for me to be able to keep up with cooking and serving."

"That's a good problem to have," Cassie said. "I wish I could stay and help, but I've got work of my own to do."

"Oh, no," Ella teased. "I was so hoping for free labor. Good luck and I'll talk to you later."

The two women hugged before Cassie left.

Feeling better, she drove to the building. Trudi hadn't arrived yet, but since Cassie had her own key, she simply let herself in.

The main area already looked lighter and more welcoming since she'd painted most of it. She'd cleaned the display cases too and they now looked brand-new. She couldn't wait until she owned this place. And if she sometimes felt overwhelmed at the amount of work she still had to do—ordering signage, putting up a website, developing her menu and prices, and eventually hiring at least one person to help her—she also felt a vibrant sense of anticipation.

As promised, Trudi had started a buzz around town about the wonderful bakery soon to open. Most everyone had tried at least one of Cassie's creations, either at The Tumbleweed Café or Serenity's. People had told Trudi they were eager to order for their family celebrations and various holidays. And without exception, everyone loved the name.

"Yoo-hoo!" Trudi poked her head inside the front door. "Ready to do that final walk-through?"

"I am," Cassie answered, beaming. "Since I'm the only one who's made improvements, it's kind of a formality at this point."

"But a necessary one," Trudi replied. She then rushed over to envelop Cassie in a quick hug, before stepping back and looking around with a critical expression. "I suggest you film this," she said. "That way, you can look back after you close and make sure nothing has changed."

Cassie stared at her, half wondering if the other woman was serious. "Changed? Like if the previous owners came in here right before closing and removed stuff?"

"I've had it happen." Trudi shrugged. "And while I don't think it will in this instance, it's my job to protect you."

"And I appreciate that." Getting out her phone, Cassie went to the camera and pressed Video, then Record. Then she and Trudi walked around the interior of the building. Trudi pointed out each feature.

When they'd finished, Cassie dropped her phone back into her purse.

"Are you excited for closing tomorrow?" Trudi asked, smiling widely.

"I am. It's going to be a big day."

Cassie walked Trudi back out to her car and watched as the other woman drove away. When she turned back to go inside, she eyed the neat storefront, marveling that soon it would belong to her. She couldn't wait.

As she walked back inside, again she found herself thinking of Pierce. She'd told him she would text him, but now she thought it would be better if she did not. This would be her new life, her moment to shine. And Pierce, as handsome and sexy and interesting as he might be, had left her no doubt that he did not intend to be part of it.

Pierce woke up to an empty house. While Cassie was gone, making her deliveries and getting everything ready for her new bakery, he tried to write. Instead, he ending up doodling on the notebook paper. From past experience, he knew words weren't going to come easily right at this moment, so he gave up. Instead, he found himself roaming the deserted farm with Albert waddling along at his side.

After the series of storms that had rolled through, the dust had turned to mud. Like its predecessor, it seemed to be everywhere. There were even great globs of mud on the sides of the outdoor structures, including the fencing. The wind must have flung them.

Looking at the land he now owned, Pierce shook his head. Despite the unremarkable view, the lack of forest and color, oddly enough he found this place beautiful. Despite his skill with words, he couldn't quite articulate why.

The fact that he felt an affinity to his place was a good thing, considering that this was now, however temporarily, his home.

Even though he stayed on the gravel path, by the time he reached the main barn he had muddy feet. And somehow, he'd lost track of Albert. A quick scan of the area revealed the large pig had managed to find a particularly muddy patch and now wallowed in it. In his element and hog happy.

The description made Pierce smile. He actually found himself wondering if he could manage to include a pet pig in his next book. He might have to change the planned location, but he thought it might be doable.

Turning to retrace his steps back to the house, he left the pig doing his thing. Once Pierce got to the back patio, he located a stick, sat down on one of the chairs, and started scraping dirt off his boots.

Finally, he judged he'd removed all he could and took off the boots, hoping the sun might dry the rest and make it come off easier.

Now that the fresh air and solitude had refreshed his soul, maybe he could write.

Going inside, he grabbed his notebook. After tearing out and wadding up the page he'd ruined with the doodling, he sat down and wrote some notes. Inspired, he kept going. He'd gotten a lot closer to having enough material to write a fleshed out synopsis, though lately he'd found it difficult to be truly creative. Part of it was the change in his surroundings. The traffic noise and cacophony of the city had been like a symphony to him, putting him into the writing zone. Here, he struggled, mostly because of the overall silence.

Another reason he had to admit, since he tried to be honest with himself, was procrastination. He still had a few weeks until it was due. He tended to do his best work under pressure.

Acknowledging this, he grimaced and put the notebook away. The fact that he couldn't start working on the book until he'd nailed the synopsis wasn't lost on him.

After wandering the house, checking the internet and social media in case there were any updates about his stalker (there were not), he debated texting Cassie to see if she might be ready for his help, but changed his mind. Instead, he decided to go into town and explore. If she texted before he got there, he'd head to her location. If not, well he'd been wanting to check out the bookstore on Main. Being around books made him happy. And small town, independent bookstores were his favorite kind of bookseller.

Before leaving, he took extra precautions with his appearance. Among the general public, like when he'd gone to the pub with Cassie, he felt certain the probability of anyone recognizing him was slim to none. But in an actual bookstore, around people who might have actually read his books, he wasn't as confident in his ability to evade detection.

Though he wanted to blend in, he didn't own a single pair of Wrangler or Levi brand jeans. His motorcycle boots, still out on the porch, could easily pass for work boots.

Opening the closet, he surveyed the stack of men's clothing Cassie had gotten him to wear before. Another pair of Wrangler jeans, the same belt with the large buckle, and a different Western shirt would work. Idly, he wondered why the snaps instead of buttons and made a mental note to research this at some point.

After he'd gotten dressed in what still felt like a disguise, he grabbed the same cap he'd worn last time and crammed it onto his head.

A quick glance in the mirror told him he once again looked nothing like his author photo or the man who'd done interviews with a few of the more popular talk shows.

He almost looked like a rancher or a farmer.

Pleased, he went out to his Jeep and climbed inside.

Driving down Main Street, he was struck once again by how this little town seemed to be thriving. Vibrant, charming, and busy, it almost seemed like a relic from the not too distant past.

He'd driven through several other towns this size, in Texas,

New Mexico, and Arizona. Many of them had boarded-up storefronts, graffiti on brick walls, and a general air of defeat. Not Getaway. Despite the name, he got a very real sense the residents were proud of their town. It showed in the way they kept up not only their residences but the businesses they frequented. Shop local was more than just a logo for them.

He found street parking right in front of the bookstore, which meant either he'd gotten lucky or the place wasn't busy. Probably the latter. In a farming and ranching community like this one, folks didn't have a lot of time to read. He'd actually been surprised to see a bookstore still in business. Even in larger cities, he'd seen small, independent booksellers go under. It had become much too easy to get reading material from an online retailer or one of the big-box stores.

Jumping out, he took a moment to study the window display. The arrangement of the books, along with other props, had been very well done. Artistic, yet simple, enticing the passerby into stopping in to check out one of the numerous books they had for sale.

A familiar cover caught his eye. His last novel *Too Broke to Die* had made the display. A good thing, but also not.

Tugging his baseball cap down, he took a deep breath, opened the door, and stepped into the store.

Immediately, the scent of paper and ink, mixed with something that smelled like eucalyptus leaves, filled his senses.

A young man, whipcord thin with messy hair, came out from around the counter. Smiling, he approached Pierce. "Is there anything I can help you find?" he asked.

Pierce smiled back. "No thank you. I'm just browsing."

"Sounds good. Feel free to look around. I'm here if you have any questions."

Thanking him, Pierce turned left. He nearly ran into a

display of all of his novels, the most recent staged front and center. Equally thrilled and concerned, he avoided looking for the clerk and pretended to inspect his own books.

"Those are really popular," the kid offered, from his spot behind the counter. "If you want to try one, I suggest you start with the new one. That would be *Too Broke to Die*."

Pierce nodded and forced himself to move on. Interesting, the suggestion to start with the latest book and read backward. Though each was a stand-alone novel, if someone had asked him, he would have suggested starting with the first book.

But then again, what did he know? He was only the author.

Bypassing the entire fiction area, he went to nonfiction. He never knew what kind of book might spark his interest, for research purposes only.

"If you're looking for metaphysical books, there's a store called Serenity's that has an awesome selection too."

The kid again. Earnest in his effort to help.

"Thanks," Pierce told him. "But like I said, I'm just browsing. I don't have any particular type of book in mind."

"Oh, sorry." The clerk gestured toward the section where Pierce had stopped. "I saw you standing in front of those paranormal/metaphysical books and thought I could help you out."

"I appreciate that." Pierce nodded. Though he didn't want to be rude, he also didn't want to stand around talking to this stranger either. "I'm just eager to check out your stock, that's all. I'll know when something catches my interest."

The kid took the hint. "Oh. Okay. You're not from around here, are you?"

"No." Short and sweet, Pierce turned away. Hopefully,

they could leave it at that. Especially since he had no intention of getting into his life story.

Moving past the paranormal section, he also bypassed religion and spiritual studies. Since his next project was, at this point, only a bunch of ideas that he still hadn't strung together, he had no idea what kind of research would be needed.

Instead, he migrated over to fiction. Starting with the section marked Bestselling Books. They were shelved alphabetically. He made a point of looking through each shelf, starting with the *A*'s. John Grisham had a new one out, so he decided to purchase that.

When he got to the letter *S*, he spotted all of his own novels. Bypassing those, he grabbed a book with an intriguing premise by an author he'd never read and carried that and the Grisham back to the checkout counter.

"Good choices," the kid said, smiling. "Are you sure you don't want to try one of the Pierce Spade books? I've read every single one of them and can promise you that you won't be disappointed."

"High praise," Pierce replied, meaning it. "But I'm not in the mood for a thriller. These two will do it for now."

"Okay." Giving him his total, the clerk appeared startled when Pierce paid cash, but accepted it.

"How's business?" Pierce asked. "I admit to being really surprised that a town this small could support an independent bookseller."

"Yeah." With a tight smile, the clerk nodded. "We do all right. By the way, my name is Stoney," he said, handing over the bag with Pierce's purchases in it.

Since Pierce had no intention of giving his name, he simply nodded. "Nice to meet you, Stoney. Hopefully, I'll see you the next time I come in."

Then he turned and left, before Stoney asked any more questions. On the way out, he checked his phone just in case he'd missed a text from Cassie. He hadn't.

Michael called just as Pierce got into his Jeep.

"Have you seen the news? Your stalker slash serial killer is retaliating."

"I have not," Pierce replied. "What's going on?"

"The guy has made a video and sent it to all the major networks. But TMZ ran it first."

"A video?" Confounded, Pierce waited to hear more.

"He keeps his face blurry and uses a voice distortion machine. But in it, he not only refutes all your claims that he's lying but challenges you to a face-to-face meeting to settle things."

Incredulous, Pierce exhaled. "Why would he think I'd want to do that?" Then a thought occurred to him. "Does the FBI think I should do this? Maybe be bait to try and help catch him?"

Michael snorted. "Hell no. It's clear this guy is off his rocker. They're analyzing the video, looking for clues that might reveal his location."

"Seriously, I don't get any of this. What does he hope to gain?" Pierce asked.

"He claims he deserves credit and a cut of your royalties for the book that he thinks is all about him. And he'd kept some sort of detailed log of his most recent killings, so you and he can collaborate on another book."

"Collaborate?" Pierce dragged his hand through his hair. Every time he did this, the short length momentarily surprised him. He'd worn it longer for so long. "As if I'd write a book with a murderer."

"Exactly," Michael agreed. "And not just that, but you have more than enough of your own ideas."

"Everyone knows that coming up with ideas is the easy part. It's the actual writing of the book that's hard." Pierce thought for a moment. "It's been so hectic that I haven't been keeping count. How many murders has this guy committed?"

"That we know about? Twelve. The FBI is frothing at the mouth, they want to arrest him so badly."

"I want him caught too," Pierce said. "Probably as badly as they do. I wish I could do something to help." He thought for a moment. "Why don't you run my idea past whoever you deal with at the Bureau. I think it's a good one."

"What? You becoming bait? That's a terrible idea," Michael replied. "Just because this guy has fixated on you for whatever reason doesn't make it your responsibility to help capture him. That's what law enforcement is for. That's their job, for Chrissake."

While he loved how readily Michael defended him, Pierce knew his agent didn't understand. "I still feel a sense of responsibility for all of this."

"Look, Pierce. This guy has killed before you wrote whatever book he's claiming is about him. He's a serial killer who has been careful enough not to get caught."

Pierce had to acknowledge Michael's point. "True. I'm still struggling to understand what made him fixate on me."

"You write books about people like him. Sure, you and I both know they're fiction, but he doesn't seem to get that. He sees someone who has achieved bestselling author status with these stories. In his eyes, that likely means fame and fortune. I'm sure he craves notoriety for the murders he's committed, but he'd have to get caught for that to happen. Since he doesn't want to be captured, I'm sure he came up with this as another way to get the attention he clearly craves."

"Wow," Pierce said. "I'm impressed. I had no idea you were so good at analyzing people."

Michael laughed. "I represent a couple of psychologists who write popular self-help books. Since I try to read all of my clients' works, I may have picked up a thing or two."

He and Michael said their goodbyes and Pierce drove home. Once there, Albert greeted him with a friendly grunt, bumping against Pierce's leg for attention. Scratching behind the swine's ears, Piece shook his head. Damned if he wasn't getting to like the pet pig.

The sound of tires on gravel alerted him to Cassie's arrival.

Cassie breezed through the door, humming under her breath.

"Hey," she said, smiling when she saw him. "Did you have a good afternoon?"

"Sure." He eyed her paint-spattered coveralls. "You never texted me to come help paint."

Though her smile wavered, she kept eye contact. "I decided not to. I enjoy it, and I really don't need any assistance."

Stung, he kept that to himself and nodded. "It's all good. I went and visited the bookstore instead."

"Are you sure that was a good idea?" she asked. "Did Stoney act like he might have recognized you?"

"He didn't. I'm confident of that."

"Good." Cassie studied him for a moment. "I guess you got lucky. Stoney is pretty sharp. I shop there quite often. He always has a list of new books for me. Without exception, he's been right about each one."

"He's good at his job," he commented, hiding his surprise. "Maybe you and I can go together sometime. Bookstores are my favorite place."

Her brows rose. "Maybe." She moved past him. "I need to shower and change."

He watched her go, tasting regret, though he wasn't sure why. Instead of calling after her, as he almost impulsively did, he went to his own room and closed the door. Maybe now he could manage to get some writing done.

Sitting down with his notebook and his favorite pen, he looked back over all his notes. The characters, the story, the villain, and the various twists and turns he planned to put into the novel.

Keeping his focus on the page, he began writing the synopsis. Sometimes when he got in the middle of one, he learned he didn't have enough material. Not this time. He'd procrastinated for so long, he had way more than he really needed.

So it would be a very detailed synopsis, which usually meant a great book.

Once he had everything jotted down, he got out his laptop, typed the synopsis from his handwritten notes, and proofread it. A quick spell-check, and he emailed it off to Michael with an apology for sending it so late.

Done. Finally, freaking, done. Now he could actually get started on writing the book. He had bits and pieces of chapters written, scenes that he'd need to move into place later.

After heaving a satisfied sigh, he grabbed another, brand-new notebook. At the top of the page he wrote *Chapter 1*.

And then he began to write.

Lost in his newly created world, his fingers and the pen couldn't keep up with the story in his head.

"Pierce!" Cassie, calling his name. "Come here. Hurry!"

Setting down his work, he jumped up and yanked open his door. He sprinted into the living room, skidding to a halt when he saw Cassie sitting on the sofa, watching TV.

"You need to see this," she said, her eyes wide and voice excited as she pointed at the television. "They just teased that they have news about your stalker/serial killer."

He hurried over. *Breaking News* flashed across the screen, before a reporter came on. "New York City police have announced they apprehended a suspect in the serial killer case. As you may recall, this individual alleged that bestselling author Pierce Spade copied his methods and wrote them in one of his novels. The author recently issued a statement insisting this was false and challenging the killer to prove it. Police suspect that this may be why this murderer made his first mistake after numerous killings."

"They *caught* him?" Pierce asked, disbelief and hope warring inside him. "They actually caught the bastard."

"It seems like it." Cassie jumped up and wrapped her arms around him in what she no doubt meant to be a celebratory hug.

He stood still, processing, not sure if he could actually believe it. Meanwhile, the television cut to a press conference with the New York City police chief. With a grave look on his jowly face, he repeated what the reporter had just said.

"You're *free!*" Cassie said, pulling back to look up at him. With her sparkling eyes and joyful smile, her beauty lit up the room and took his breath away.

What could he do then but kiss her?

Chapter 12

Cassie thought she might melt into a puddle right then and there. But just as he bent his head to cover her mouth with his, his phone rang, startling them both.

She gave a little laugh and stepped away.

"Michael," he said, after checking his phone. "He must have seen the news too. I need to take this."

With a small nod, she started to turn away.

"Wait," Pierce said. "I'll put it on speaker. I want you to hear this."

Bemused, she turned around and dropped back onto the couch.

"Hey, Michael," Pierce said. "I've got you on speaker, just so you know."

"Fine, whatever. Are you watching the news?" Michael asked. The urgency in his voice combined with his New York accent made him sound intense. "Looks like they caught the guy."

"I saw," Pierce replied. "I also noticed they haven't identified him. That tells me they're not a hundred percent sure they have the right person."

"Talk about raining on my parade," Michael complained, his tone half joking. "Can't you just take the win and celebrate like the rest of us?"

"Not until I know they actually caught the right guy." Pierce glanced at Cassie, almost as if he was asking for her agreement. Slowly, she nodded yes.

"I'm sure they'll let us know," Michael said. "If I hear anything else, I'll be in touch immediately."

"I appreciate that. Did you get my email?"

"I did," Michael replied. "It's about time you sent me that thing. I've been fending off calls from Jamal on a weekly basis."

"Sorry," Pierce said. "I've had a lot going on. It's a good one, I think. I've already started writing it."

"Great. I'll send it to Jamal once I take a look at it." With that, he ended the call.

"You don't say goodbye?" Cassie asked, genuinely curious.

Brows raised, Pierce looked from her to his phone and shrugged. "Not if it's not necessary."

The news segment had ended. She used the remote to turn off the TV and tried to avoid staring at Pierce. Judging from his rigid posture, he hadn't liked the fact that he'd almost kissed her.

Or, she thought, trying to be more positive, he hadn't appreciated the way Michael's phone call had interrupted them. She hadn't liked it either. She'd wanted that kiss with every fiber of her being.

But the moment had definitely passed. At least while they were in the same room, she knew she had to pretend the almost-kiss had never happened. Especially now, when it appeared that Pierce's self-imposed exile might be over.

She mumbled some excuse and retreated to her bedroom. Only once she'd closed the door behind her did she release the breath she'd been holding.

He'd almost kissed her. Her dang traitorous heart had

leaped into her throat and her entire body had buzzed with anticipation. She'd wanted that kiss, craved it in fact. Still did. More than she knew she should.

And then Michael had called and ruined everything. But if she were honest with herself, his appalling timing had been for the best. If Pierce's stalker had truly been caught, he'd have no more reason to continue hiding out at the pig farm he'd purchased. She remembered spotting some notes he'd left on the kitchen table that seemed to indicate he might be considering turning it into a writer's retreat or something.

That idea might either be brilliant or deluded. On the plus side, the isolation and monotonous landscape would provide little to no distractions. And aspiring authors would definitely sign up for a retreat hosted by one of the world's most popular authors.

On the downside, the closest airport was several hours away and reaching Getaway by car would be a trek for even the most dedicated fan.

Three sharp knocks on her bedroom door startled her out of her thoughts. "Cassie? Are you okay?" Pierce asked.

"I'm fine," she lied, hoping he'd take the hint and leave her be.

"Do you have a minute?"

Briefly, she considered telling him no, she did not. But since she couldn't make herself stop thinking about the kiss that should have been, she got up and opened the door instead.

"What's up?" she asked, her voice as bright as her utterly fake smile.

His blue eyes met and held hers. "I'm sure you heard that I finally completed and turned in a synopsis."

"I did. Congratulations, I guess. You also said you've started writing the book."

He smiled. "Yes, I have. I tend to write each chapter by hand and then type it into my computer. Which means it will be a little while before I have anything for you to proofread."

"I see." Taking a deep breath, she nodded. "It's all for the best, really. I know when we first met, you'd said something about hiring me to assist you. I've honestly been too busy with the bakery to have been much use anyway." Even though she would definitely have made time to read his stuff. She loved the prospect of getting to read one of Pierce Spade's novels before it had been published. Plus she could have used the extra cash.

"I'm really sorry," he said. "I can still pay you, if you want."

"Not without me doing the work." Her swift response hopefully hid her anger. "Like I said, I've been busy too. Believe me, I get it."

"If you're sure…"

Crossing her arms, she nodded. "Is that all you needed?"

"No." The smile came back, just as bright. "I'm feeling like I need to celebrate the possibility of my stalker finally being caught. Even if the news turns out to be premature. Not to mention your big closing. Would you go with me to get something to eat and maybe have a couple of drinks?"

Oh, damn. Like a date. Except between friends. She needed to remember that.

Leaning on her doorframe, she considered his words. "Where to?" she asked.

"I don't know. I was hoping you could suggest a place." His slow smile ignited a spark. Which she promptly quashed by reminding herself that they were just friends.

"When?"

He shrugged. "Tomorrow night?"

"Sure," she heard herself reply. "Do you like Tex-Mex?"

"I do, though where I'm from it's not really authentic."

"It is here." And her absolute favorite cuisine. "The best place is called Tres Corazones. Three hearts. They have killer margaritas too. How about we go around seven?"

"Sounds good. Do we need reservations?"

She almost laughed. But then she realized he was serious. She suspected he'd forgotten just how small a town he now lived in.

"They don't take reservations," she answered. "Sometimes it can be a bit of a wait, but I promise you it's worth every minute. And it shouldn't be too busy on a Wednesday night."

"It's a date," he said. His husky voice once again seemed to reach deep inside her and summon desire. "I'll drive and it'll be my treat."

With that, he turned away before she could comment.

As she watched him walk down the hall, she knew she should be glad he didn't turn around. Because if he had, he'd have no doubt seen the desire simmering in her gaze, so strong it felt painful.

That's what all of this—whatever this might be—felt like. Nothing good could ever come of it, yet she couldn't seem to make herself turn off her aching craving for him. Day or night, Pierce stayed in her thoughts. She dreamed of him nightly, and when they were apart, she found herself counting the minutes until they could be together. She could no more control her need than she could make herself stop breathing.

At a time when her focus should be on making her life-long dream of opening a bakery a reality, mooning over an unattainable man was the absolute last thing she needed to do.

Since keeping busy had been the only distraction that worked, she went to the kitchen and began doing some prep work for her morning baking. Though she prided herself on making most of her baked goods fresh the day of the delivery, since tomorrow was her big closing, she needed to do all she could tonight.

Mixing and measuring, the familiar dance of baking soothed her. She'd double-checked her orders and, as was usual for early week, there weren't as many pies or cakes as there were leading up to a weekend.

Once she had the first batch in the oven, she took the time to wonder where Pierce might have gotten off to, but decided not to go looking for him.

Almost tempted to cancel their dinner plans tomorrow night, she finally decided she might as well go. He could celebrate the capture of his stalker, and as for her, buying her own bakery was definitely something worth celebrating.

By the time she had everything made, Pierce still hadn't put in an appearance. His bedroom door remained closed, which meant he was either deep in his writing or taking a nap. The latter thought made her smile.

Not in the mood to cook anything for dinner, she rummaged around and made herself a sandwich. She had a big day tomorrow and she wanted to be well rested.

In the morning, since she'd already baked everything, she slept in a little later. When she got up, she made coffee, snagged one of her spare muffins, and loaded up her truck. Then, she changed, wanting to spruce up a bit to meet Trudi at the bank for closing. She grabbed one of her favorite dresses and actually put on makeup and jewelry. She couldn't wait to sign the papers and take official possession of the keys. Trudi had promised to take a photo, which Cassie planned to frame and hang in her back office.

After making her deliveries, Cassie arrived at the bank forty-five minutes before it opened. She sat in her truck scrolling her phone until Trudi's Lexus pulled in.

Arm in arm, the two women walked into the bank. Since Cassie banked there, she went and got a cashier's check for the amount and carried it into the conference room.

The closing went by in a blur. As she had when she sold the farm, Cassie signed paper after paper, initialing here, putting her signature there. When it was all done, Trudi had her pose with the keys to her new property and snapped several photos.

"It's all yours now," Trudi said, grinning from ear to ear. "I can't wait to be one of the first to get in line at Cassie's Creations."

Tears filled Cassie's eyes, but she managed to smile and nod. Paperwork in hand, she hurried out to her truck and drove to her building.

Her building.

Now to get to work. In her hustle to get the place ready for her eventual grand opening, there always seemed to be a hundred or more little things she needed to do.

Hard work was good for the soul, she told herself. And, if she were completely honest, for her libido. Only with physical activity could she make herself stop thinking about Pierce and how badly she'd wanted that kiss. And more. Much, much, more.

Five o'clock came and went. The new refrigeration system had been delivered and installed, which meant the time had come for her to begin ordering supplies in earnest.

Since she'd created a detailed spreadsheet in order to keep up with inventory, she noted items there as she ordered. She felt a sense of pride when she completed her first bulk order, to be delivered in three days.

The website design had been placed in the hands of a capable company and was set to go live in one week. Though Cassie had agonized over her menu, she loved that she had the ability to make changes. Eventually, she planned to have weekly specials, flavors of the month, and things like that. Just thinking about all her plans had her vibrating with excitement.

This was happening. And she didn't need to be letting her infatuation with Pierce distract her from enjoying the moment her dream came to fruition.

She'd just finished inputting her notes into the spreadsheet and making a "To Do" list for tomorrow when her phone announced a text.

It was from Pierce. True to form, her foolish heart skipped a beat. Don't forget dinner tonight. See you soon.

Even that, a simple reminder about a friendly meal, had her feeling restless with anticipation. Taking a deep breath, and telling herself to calm down, she texted back a confirmation.

Then she locked up her bakery and headed back to the farm to clean up and get ready.

Walking into the house, she saw no sign of Pierce. Since his bedroom door was closed, she guessed he was either writing or taking a nap. The immediate image of him sprawled out in the bed, sheets twisted around his naked body, made her knees go weak.

Somehow, she managed to walk on past his room to her own.

Chiding herself, since he was most likely writing, she got cleaned up and went to get dressed for dinner. Though she'd changed, she managed to get paint on the dress she'd worn to closing, so she'd need to find something else.

Eyeing her meager supply of outfits, she tried to decide whether to dress up a little or wear her same old, everyday jeans and T-shirt. Tres Corazones wasn't a fancy type of eating establishment, so she'd be fine in jeans. But since she knew her time with Pierce was limited, she really wanted to make him see her in a different light.

She ended up choosing a black denim, casual dress. Since she wasn't the type of woman who enjoyed high heels, she stepped into a cute pair of sandals. Adding long, silver dangly earrings and her favorite grouping of bracelets, she did her makeup. Though she usually went with a natural, fresh-faced look, for tonight she decided to go all out.

When she'd finished, she eyed herself in the mirror. As the saying went, she cleaned up good.

Satisfied, she went to find Pierce.

When she strolled into the living room, he looked up from his phone and did a double take. "Damn," he commented, drawing the word out into two syllables. "You look amazing."

Pleased, she thanked him. Then, unable to stop smiling, she asked him if he was ready to go. "I know it's only six thirty, but there's usually a wait, even on a weeknight."

Still appearing bemused, he got up. "I'm ready."

When they reached his Jeep, he opened the passenger door for her. Climbing up in a dress meant she flashed a good bit of leg. It felt gratifying the way Pierce couldn't drag his gaze away.

Finally, he closed her door and went around to the driver's side. Once he got in, he started the engine but made no move to put the shifter in Reverse. "You look amazing, Cassie."

As usual, his husky voice made her toes curl. "Thanks again," she said, glancing at him with a smile. "You don't look so bad yourself."

He wore a pair of dark blue jeans, with cowboy boots that looked brand-new. Even his Western shirt appeared new. But somehow, all of this suited him. Though she'd grown up around ranchers and cowboys, Pierce was the sexiest one she'd ever seen.

The way his gaze lingered on her had her body tingling. Dangerous territory, for sure.

She cleared her throat and made a show of glancing at her fitness watch. "We'd better get going. The wait gets longer the later it is."

Finally, he shifted into Reverse. After backing up the Jeep, he got it turned around and they headed down the long driveway.

Once they reached downtown Getaway, she gave him directions to Tres Corazones. As she'd expected, the parking lot was packed. Several vehicles were already slowly cruising it, waiting for someone to leave.

"Now what?" Pierce asked. "Do they have overflow parking somewhere?"

She pointed to the grassy field on the other side of the lot. "A lot of people park there. As long as it's not muddy, it's an option."

"Since it recently stormed, what happens if it is muddy?"

"You can get really stuck," she responded. "I think that's why no one is parking there tonight. Even the guys with four-wheel drive are having second thoughts."

"Hmm. This Jeep has four-wheel drive. I think we'll risk it."

Before she could advise against that idea, he turned the wheel and hopped the curb. "I've got traction," he said, parking. "I think this will be just fine."

Another truck joined them. Then another.

"They all like your idea," she said. "Hopefully one of them could pull out all the others if they get stuck."

Pierce opened her door and helped her from the Jeep. This time, he kept his gaze on her face, which made her smile.

When her feet hit the ground, they didn't sink into mud. "That's a good sign," she commented, pointing. "Though I'm glad I didn't wear heels."

"It's not too muddy," he replied, grinning. "I think we'll be fine." He took her arm and they walked away, toward the restaurant. "I hope they have a bar where people can wait until their name is called."

About to answer that they did, the sound of tires spinning had them both turning around.

The truck that had pulled up next to them had gotten stuck. Tires spinning, it spewed clumps of mud and dirt all over Pierce's Jeep.

"Should we help them?" Pierce asked, glad he hadn't washed the Jeep earlier. He'd intended to, but time had gotten away from him.

"Help them how?" Cassie asked. "Look. One of the other trucks is setting up to try and pull him out."

Arms crossed, Pierce eyed the scene. "What if he gets stuck too?"

"Then they'll have to call Larry's Tow Service," she explained. "His brother Lou owns the used car lot in town. Larry lives for these kinds of calls."

"I see," Pierce said, even though he didn't. "Then let's go eat. I don't know about you, but I'm starving."

She linked her arm with his and smiled up at him. "Me too."

For a moment he couldn't speak. Hell, he could barely breathe.

They made it nearly to the door when Cassie made a

strangled sound that might have been laughter or something else.

"What?" he asked, stopping and looking at her. "Are you okay?"

"I am," she replied. "But I just realized we might not be able to get home after we have dinner. If that truck got stuck, we likely will too."

"Maybe, maybe not." He shrugged, not really concerned. "The truck is heavier than my Jeep. Also, he seems to have parked in a muddy spot. I don't think we did. At least the ground didn't feel like it when we got out."

"Good point, I guess. If you're not going to worry about it, then I won't either."

He almost kissed her cheek. Stopping himself just in time, he pretended to be glancing over his shoulder toward his Jeep. The second pickup truck appeared to be having some success pulling the first one from the mud.

Cassie looked back too. "Whew," she said. "I'm glad that worked out for them."

"Me too." He squeezed her arm.

She suddenly seemed to realize how close they were standing. With an apologetic look, she moved a few feet away.

By now, they'd reached the ornately carved, dark wood door. He grabbed the bronze handle and held it open for her. With a grateful smile, she moved past him.

As he stepped into the restaurant, immediately the sounds and scent of fajitas sizzling made his mouth water.

As they waited for the hostess to return to the host stand, he looked around. There were colorful decorations on the walls, tables with chairs painted red, green, yellow, and blue, and an area in the back where someone made homemade tortillas. Almost every table was occupied by laughing people.

Many were enjoying large margaritas or beer with a lime. The festive atmosphere immediately lightened his mood.

A smiling young woman came up and greeted them, before leading them to a booth near the tortilla area. She left them with menus, explaining that their server would be with them shortly.

After Cassie sat, she heaved a satisfied sigh. "It's been too long since I've eaten here. This is one of my absolute favorite restaurants."

Staring at her, he could have sworn she glowed. Maybe it was the lighting, but damn she was beautiful.

"What's good here?" he asked.

His question made her beam. "Everything. You really can't go wrong. Just get whatever sounds good to you. I promise you won't be disappointed."

The waitress came by to take their drink orders. Cassie ordered a margarita, Pierce went with a beer. Once the young woman left, Pierce leaned forward, pitching his voice so hopefully she was the only one who could hear. "I want to thank you, Cassie. You've been incredibly welcoming and I appreciate all you've done to keep my secret."

Her smile wavered. "You almost sound like you're telling me goodbye."

"That wasn't my intention," he replied.

"Which is understandable," she continued. "Especially since they might have actually caught your stalker."

"We don't know that yet," he heard himself say. Just then, the waitress returned with their drinks.

"Are you ready to order?" she asked.

Even though Pierce had barely glanced at the menu, he nodded. He'd already decided he'd simply get whatever Cassie chose.

"I'd like the Carne Asada taco platter," Cassie said. "With rice and refried beans."

He told the waitress he'd have the same. Once she'd gone to put their orders in, he took a deep breath and met Cassie's gaze. "I like you, Cassie. A lot. Probably more than I should have."

"Ouch." She winced. "Are you about to say *It's not you, it's me*? Because news flash. If you're trying to break up with me, we were never together. There's no need for you to put either of us through this."

Here, he had two choices. He could attempt to laugh off her statement and agree with it, or he could tell her the truth.

"Truth is, I think we have something special between us," he said, waiting for her to either confirm or deny it.

Her green eyes widened but she didn't speak.

"I'd like to give us a try." He swallowed. "What do you think?"

Instead of replying, she took a drink of her margarita. "You're going back to New York. Why are you bringing this up now?"

When she wiped at her eyes, he felt it like a punch to the gut. "I didn't mean to make you cry."

"Didn't you?" Bitterness colored her voice. "Your timing absolutely sucks."

The waitress arrived with the meals, which gave him some time to gather his thoughts. She set two platters of perfectly cooked tacos down in front of them. "Enjoy!" she said, smiling brightly, before dashing off to help another group of people.

Cassie eyed her food as if her appetite had completely abandoned her. At least she'd stopped crying, though that didn't make him feel any better.

"Cassie, I—"

"Don't." She picked up her fork and waved it at him. "Let's try to enjoy these tacos and save the serious talk for later, okay?"

Stung, he nodded, watching as she dug into her refried beans. She ate with gusto, as if nothing in their discussion bothered her.

Finally, he grabbed one of his tacos and took a bite. The perfectly seasoned steak along with the grilled peppers and onions made an out of this world combination.

Once he started eating, he didn't want to stop. The food was that delicious. Though he'd initially planned the meal as a celebration at the news of his stalker's arrest, he'd managed to ruin it by attempting to discuss a relationship she clearly didn't want.

Fine. He'd get the evening back on track.

"I'm glad you agreed to come out and celebrate with me," he said. "If what the news is reporting is true, I'll finally be free."

Her head snapped up at that. "Congratulations," she said, her voice dry. "I'm really happy for you."

"And you're now the proud owner of Cassie's Creations," he added. "How does that feel?"

Eyes wide, she stared. "You remember the name."

"Of course I did." Again the waitress stopped by, saving Pierce from saying something he might regret, like how could she think he'd forget anything that important to her.

"Would you folks like dessert?" the waitress asked.

Pierce looked at Cassie.

"No, thank you," Cassie said.

"We'll just have the check." Pierce almost got out his credit card without thinking. Luckily, he managed to rein himself in. Even though it seemed like his stalker might be in police custody, until he had absolute confirmation, he couldn't be too careful.

"I'll be paying cash," he said, when the waitress eyed him quizzically.

Cassie stood as soon as he'd settled the bill, clearly ready to go. He reached to take her arm and she sidestepped.

They walked outside and to his Jeep in silence.

He waited until she'd gotten buckled in before turning to face her. "Thanks for recommending this place. I really enjoyed the food."

Glancing at him, her frozen expression briefly thawed. "I'm glad," she said. "I wasn't sure you got to eat much Tex-Mex way up north."

Before he started the engine, he decided to try again. "I don't suppose you'd ever consider going to New York?"

"Are you inviting me to visit?" she asked, her tone bland.

Damn. He decided he might as well be honest. At this point, he had nothing left to lose and everything to gain. "Cassie, I have feelings for you."

She looked at him. "You do?"

"Yes." Though his heart pounded, he kept his voice firm. "And I hope that it's not all one-sided."

"Are your feelings for me strong enough to make you consider staying here in Texas?" she asked. "Since you're aware I've been working really hard to make my lifelong dream of owning a bakery become a reality."

When she put it like that…

"You could open a bakery in New York," he offered, trying not to sound desperate. "New Yorkers love quality baked goods as much as anyone else."

The sadness in her gaze made him catch his breath.

"Getaway is my home. These are my people. If—*when*—I have success, I want them to be a part of it."

Unsure of how to respond to that, he simply nodded.

"What about you?" she asked. "You have plans to turn the farm into some kind of writing retreat. Can you see yourself staying?"

"I don't know," he answered, even though he did. How could he trade the hustle and bustle, the bright lights and buzzing energy of his city for this? A patch of dusty land in the middle of nowhere.

Her gaze never left his face. "I think you do know. You love your home as much as I love mine."

Now he started the engine, hoping to distract himself from his slowly growing despair.

"What about the mud?" she asked. "Go slowly. There's less chance of getting stuck."

He nodded and shifted into Drive. They moved forward with no issues whatsoever, down off the curb and onto the pavement. Resisting the urge to peel off, he drove them back to the farm, wishing he'd never tried to open the topic.

Some things, it seemed, were better left unsaid.

As if on cue, his phone rang. Glad for the interruption, he answered. "Michael, what's up?"

"I just got off the phone with the Special Agent in Charge. He thinks local law enforcement picked up the wrong guy."

"What?" Stunned, Pierce glanced at Cassie. She sat up straight, her posture tense.

"Yeah. They're still interrogating him. But the FBI said his answers are not consistent with their investigation. But he's sure trying to get them to think he's their guy."

Pierce's heart sank. "A copycat."

"Yes. That means your stalker is still out there."

Now Pierce was really glad he hadn't used his credit card to pay for dinner. He swore under his breath.

"I'll keep you posted," Michael promised. "But for now,

don't make any plans to return home." With that, he ended the call.

"Looks like you're stuck here a little while longer," Cassie mused. Then, her voice gentled. "I'm sorry. I know how badly you were looking forward to going home."

Home. For the first time he realized the truth of that old saying. Home wasn't always a place. Sometimes home meant more than a location. Certain people could feel like home.

He felt that way about Cassie.

Shock and disbelief ran through him. Everything that had been happening with his stalker had put him through the emotional wringer. He wasn't even sure he was in the right emotional condition to feel this way about Cassie, never mind consider making a monumental decision such as staying here permanently.

So he said nothing, despite knowing that doing so might cost him.

Chapter 13

For the next three days, Cassie and Pierce acted like friendly strangers. Every time they were in the same room, they made pleasant small talk, the kind you'd make with a casual acquaintance. He smiled as he kept a careful distance from her while she ached with words she didn't dare say.

She absolutely *hated* this. Not only should they not have gone out for that celebratory dinner, but they never should have attempted to define their "relationship."

Luckily, getting ready to open Cassie's Creations kept her busy. She made sure she didn't spend a lot of time at the house, and she bugged Trudi every few days to let her know if any new houses came on the market. There were none. Cassie actually found herself considering one of the ones she'd rejected, just to get away from the uncomfortable atmosphere at the farm.

Pierce appeared spectacularly unbothered by the sexual tension that sizzled between them whenever they were in the same room. Which meant it all had to be one-sided, despite his brief attempt to discuss a potential relationship. Clearly, being with her hadn't meant that much to him. At least not enough to make an attempt to stay awhile in the place he'd just purchased.

Thinking back on that night, she thought she'd handled the

conversation well, letting him believe she had zero interest in moving beyond the casual-acquaintances-with-benefits stage. She'd be embarrassed if she thought he knew the truth, but these days he appeared to be existing in another reality. One that in no way, shape, or form, included her.

Which even she had to admit was probably for the best.

"Sorry," he said, when she'd had to repeat a question. "I'm thinking about my work in progress. That's how it is for me, once I've started writing. I have one foot in reality and the other in my new, fictional world."

She couldn't fault that. Except... They'd made love. Not just ordinary sex between two lonely, single people. It had been spectacular, knock-your-socks-right-off-your-feet, *love-making*. Not. Just. Sex. Not by a long shot.

Though judging by Pierce's behavior, her thoughts about that had apparently been one-sided too. The old insecurities that she'd thought she'd kicked long ago reared their ugly heads. Who was she to think a man like Pierce Spade would find her interesting? An intellectual, big-city author would naturally have no interest in the small-town, hick daughter of a pig farmer. In his mind, he likely considered their night of passion a one-off. Adults satisfying their needs and then moving on. Which was definitely one way of looking at it. She just wished she could get herself there.

All for the best, she continued to tell herself. Not only was she smack-dab in the middle of a fresh start and a new life, but Pierce Slade would hightail it back to New York City first chance he got.

From sunrise to sunset, Cassie worked hard to get one step closer to making her dream a reality. Once she had the interior of her new building ready, she had to order supplies, make inventory, and arrange to have the sign she'd had made installed.

By the time Saturday morning rolled around, she could barely get herself out of bed. Exhausted, once she finished baking and delivering her orders, she decided to take the day off from working on the interior of the bakery and do something for herself. Maybe get a pedicure or a massage and go out for brunch.

Thus energized, she tossed back the covers and went down the hall to the kitchen. First cup of coffee on board, she got busy. Two hours later, with the sky still dark outside, she had everything made. She took a quick shower. That done, she decided to let her hair air-dry and went back into the kitchen for her second cup of coffee.

Unfortunately, Pierce had gotten there ahead of her. The first sight of him, sitting at the table with his dark head bent over his phone, sent a jolt straight through her chest.

"Good morning," she managed, keeping her back to him as she made her cup of coffee. "I'm about to head out to make my deliveries."

"Morning," he replied. The husky timbre of his morning voice had her insides thrumming.

Telling herself to get that nonsense out of her head, she decided to ignore him. After she stirred her coffee, she summoned up a bright smile and headed outside to get into her truck.

Once she'd made her stops, she drove back to the farm. Today, she thought, would definitely be a three-or-more-cups-of-coffee day.

Glad to find the kitchen empty, she refilled her mug and walked outside to watch the sun rise.

Five minutes later, the slight squeak of the back door told her Pierce had decided to join her. She didn't look up from her phone as he dropped into the chair beside her.

"You seem kind of quiet today," he mused, in the fake,

friendly voice she was growing to despise. "Normally these days you're bustling around on your way to your bakery."

"I decided to take the day off," she told him, bracing herself as she met his eyes. It seemed like a sin for a man to be so handsome and sexy, plus have the ability to write amazing novels. Like the perfect package. Just out of her reach. Sad that she kept needing to remind herself of that.

"A day off?" This time, his smile seemed genuine. "Good for you. The pace you were going would burn anyone out."

Though tempted to bristle at that, since she knew he was right, she nodded. "I needed a break. I'm thinking I might get a pedicure or something. I don't get manicures, because long fingernails just get in my way."

Realizing she just might be babbling, she stopped talking and took a long drink of her coffee. Instead of looking at him, she pretended a keen interest in the familiar landscape where she'd grown up.

Yet she felt his gaze on her, as physical as an actual touch. "What?" she finally asked, hiding her complicated emotions with annoyance.

"Would you be interested in visiting the bookstore with me?" he asked, his tone as bland as his expression. "I was thinking of going today. Turns out I need some more reading material."

Tempted, she forced herself to consider before answering. On the one hand, she loved the bookstore and she hadn't been in a while. And she truly needed to see if Stoney, who she knew was sharp as a tack, had recognized Pierce. She wouldn't put it past the kid to have realized Pierce's true identity and kept it to himself.

But on the other…did she really need to be spending her free time with a man who didn't feel the same way about her as she did him? Someone with whom she'd been walking on eggshells for the past several days.

"Well?" he asked. "What do you think? Are you game?"

What the hell, why not? "Yes," she replied, as casual as him. Truthfully, she really wanted to go. "What time?"

"When do they open? Ten?"

She shrugged. "Probably. I like going right after they open. Especially if they got new stock in the night before."

His smile lit up his light blue eyes. "Then it's a date. I'll even drive."

A date. His choice of words made her swallow hard. Luckily, he had no idea how badly she really wanted to go on a date with him. Or once had wanted. No longer, or so she told herself.

"Sure," she managed, draining the last of her coffee in one gulp.

"How about I make us breakfast?" He got up without waiting for an answer. "Scrambled eggs and toast?"

For one brief moment, she allowed herself to indulge in a brief fantasy that this was her life. Breakfast together, then a shopping trip to one of her favorite stores.

Then, realizing he still waited for an answer, she nodded. "Sounds great."

When he turned away, she couldn't resist watching him as he walked inside the house. Just the way he moved, with his broad shoulders and lean hips, made her mouth go dry.

What the heck was wrong with her? Disgusted, she almost told him she was going to her room and never mind on the breakfast. But she needed to eat something, so she got up and followed him in.

A few minutes later, he carried over two plates of perfectly cooked scrambled eggs with two slices of toast.

"Here you go." Handing her a fork, he took his seat and proceeded to demolish his food.

She dug in too, finishing up shortly after him.

"I'll get the dishes," he told her, grabbing her plate and carrying it to the sink.

If she didn't know better, she'd think he was trying to make up for doing something wrong. Which definitely wasn't the case. They didn't have that kind of relationship. Or any relationship, for that matter. They were just two ships that passed in the night.

The sooner she got her head wrapped around that fact, the better. "Thanks," she said, keeping her tone casual. She made herself a fourth cup of coffee. "I'll meet you back here at nine thirty." Then she hustled away toward her room without waiting for an answer.

Closing her door, she sat down on the edge of her bed, coffee in hand. Since he'd no doubt be leaving soon, once they got definitive confirmation that his stalker had been taken into custody, she might as well enjoy their remaining time together. Even if her feelings were not shared, they could still be friends. As long as she could keep her emotions under wraps.

Eyeing herself in the mirror, she decided to change into her favorite pair of jeans, a fitted T-shirt, and boots. Then she sat down and applied a little bit of makeup. Just enough to enhance her natural look. Small gold earrings and a couple of bracelets completed her outfit.

Satisfied, she carried her empty coffee mug into the kitchen. Pierce still sat at the table, scrolling social media on his phone. But she noticed he'd grabbed an old baseball cap and put it on. Amazing how adding such a simple accessory made him look like any other farmer and rancher she'd seen around town.

"Any news?" she asked.

"Not yet." The frustration in his voice matched his expression. "First they announce they think they've caught him and they arrested the wrong guy. Then nothing. No follow-up or anything. I texted Michael to see if he's gotten any update. He hasn't either."

"I'm sure they're making sure to dot all their i's and cross their t's," she said. "They've got to do this just right so he doesn't get away on a technicality."

Eyeing her, he slowly shook his head. "Did you get that from watching a crime show?"

Sheepish, she nodded. "*NCIS*, I think. Though it might have been one of the others. I'm fans of them all. Either way, I hope you get some definitive news soon."

"Thanks." He stood and put away his phone. "You look nice. Are you ready to go?"

The way he tossed out the offhand compliment shouldn't have warmed her insides, but it did. She had it bad.

"I'm ready," she said, hoping he couldn't tell.

"Then let's go."

She followed him out the door. Once he'd unlocked his Jeep, she climbed up into the passenger side. Again, she silently admired the interior while he started the engine.

He waited until they'd turned off the gravel driveway onto the Farm-to-Market Road before glancing at her. "Are you okay? You seem a little…off."

While she knew she should have responded with some polite nicety, she didn't. Not this time. They were nearing the end of things and she might as well be as close to honest as she could. "I've got a lot going on," she pointed out gently. "So do you. But when it's all over and you're safely back in your big city, I'm going to actually miss you."

His silence filled her with an instant combination of regret and pain. More than she'd expected to feel, honestly.

"I'll miss you too," he finally replied, staring straight ahead. "But neither of us knows what the future will hold."

Too little, too late.

Not sure what to make of that cryptic statement, she simply nodded before turning her attention to the side window and the landscape they were passing by.

Pierce had never considered himself a particularly empathetic person. He figured he was too much of an introvert for that. Observant, yes. Sometimes he could be detached, and often felt like a spectator in life, sitting in the shadows watching the show.

But not lately. Something had changed in the short time since he'd met Cassie. If he were a writer of romance novels, he'd say colors appeared brighter, the world more vibrant. Since he wasn't, he likened his heightened awareness to some kind of almost spiritual awakening. Maybe the change in location had helped. He'd gotten away from the crowds and noise of the big city and found something unexpected and wonderful in the remote countryside.

Except he knew his new domicile wasn't the only reason he felt different. Truth be told, while living in West Texas might have been part of the changes inside him, getting to know Cassie had cracked what he now realized had been a shield of ice around his heart.

No other woman had ever made him feel the way he did when they were together. He sincerely doubted he'd ever find another woman who would. And he wasn't sure he even wanted to.

Then why hadn't he been able to tell her how he felt? He suspected all his recent trauma had made him wary.

The way she answered his simple question rocked him to his core. *I'm going to actually miss you.* And when she'd attempted to bare her own soul, he'd stalled and frozen.

For a few seconds, he couldn't find his voice. When he did, he simply repeated her words back to her, aware she wouldn't have any idea how deep they went. The thought of losing her, of never seeing her again or hearing her voice, suffocated him. He wasn't sure how he'd cope.

Since he couldn't tell her that, for the rest of the drive they talked about books. He asked her what books she'd grown up reading, and if there were any she'd read more than once.

A few of her choices surprised him. Ray Bradbury had been a secret favorite of his, along with several other, old-school SF writers. She too had delved into those books, as well as some fantasy. And of course the classics that everyone read as assigned reading in high school or in college.

But when pressed, she admitted without a trace of self-consciousness that romance would be her absolute favorite genre. Then she listed several authors as auto-buys who he'd heard of but had never read.

"I can loan them to you," she said, flushed with enthusiasm when he told her this. "I have what I call a Keeper shelf. All my favorites are there."

About to decline, he thought better of it. "I might just take you up on that. Maybe it's time to broaden my horizons."

Her delighted peal of laughter had him smiling all the way to the bookstore.

Just like last time, he found parking right in front. Gazing at the store, he felt the same sense of anticipation he always had at the prospect of browsing books.

"This is going to be fun," Cassie said, opening her door. "It's been a minute since I've gone book shopping."

"I hate when that happens," he said, joining her. "I felt

that way when I came here the last time. For as long as I'm here, I intend to rectify that."

For as long as I'm here. Cassie's smile faded away at the reminder, making him feel terrible. After all, it wasn't like he didn't have a choice. He could still write his books whether he lived here or in New York.

This realization, or maybe the fact that he now might even consider staying in Texas, made his step falter. Nonetheless, he reached the front door and held it open for Cassie.

Bright smile back in place, she moved on past him. "Stoney!" she exclaimed, greeting the clerk as if he was a long-lost friend. "How have you been? It's been way too long since I've seen you."

"Cassie!" Grinning from ear to ear, the kid came out from behind the counter and, to Pierce's utter surprise, he and Cassie hugged. "Great to see you!"

Once the two finished their quick embrace, Stoney's gaze drifted past to settle on Pierce. "Hey there," he said. "I remember you. But I don't think I ever got your name."

"Oh, let me introduce you," Cassie said. "Stoney, this is P—"

"Paul," Pierce interjected, before she could slip up and say his actual name. "I'm Paul. Sorry I didn't introduce myself the last time I was here."

Stoney eyed him and then slowly shook his head. "You're from up north, aren't you? I can tell by your accent."

Another reason why he should have kept his mouth closed. "Yep. Rhode Island," he replied, picking a state at random. "But I live here in Getaway now. I'm the one who bought Cassie's farm."

"Oh?" Stoney looked from one to the other. "Now the two of you together makes sense. Well, let me know if there's anything I can help you find."

After he wandered off to his spot behind the counter, Cassie and Pierce avoided making eye contact. For his part, Pierce was afraid he might break out laughing. He figured Cassie might feel the same.

She went directly to the romance books section. He decided to take a look at the new fantasy releases. His conversation with Cassie on the way there had made him realize he hadn't read anything in that genre for a long time.

He'd just picked up a book that sounded promising when Stoney appeared. "There's an entire series of those," he pointed out. "The book you're holding is book three. Would you like to see the others?"

Surprised, Pierce shook his head. "Thanks, but I see them right here on the shelf. I'm just browsing."

Stoney shrugged. "Suit yourself, man. I'm just doing my job." And he moved away, no doubt to talk to Cassie.

Unsure whether or not he should feel bad at the interaction, Pierce picked up the other two books in the series. As a devoted follower of the various bestseller lists, he'd seen this author dominate all of them with one or the other of these books. He might as well give them a try. After he finished, he could always share them with Cassie.

The thought of actually sharing a book with her made him feel warm inside.

In the past, when he finished reading a book, he'd made a practice of leaving it in the apartment lobby. His doorman, Frank, had set up a small table for the residents to take and leave books. The building library, he'd called it.

Lots of the residents had participated. Pierce felt a sting of sadness knowing that building, along with the neighbors he'd gotten to recognize, was all gone now. Thanks to his serial killer stalker, who still hadn't been identified or caught.

Since he ran the risk of becoming maudlin, he moved

on over to the thriller section. Might as well check out his competition.

Several of the new releases sounded interesting and he added them to his stack of purchases.

"Did you find anything?" Cassie asked, her arms full of books. Her eyes lit up when she spotted his haul. "Looks like you got as many as I did. Let me see."

She leaned over and inspected the top book in his stack. "Oh, I heard those are good." Her smile turned teasing. "Maybe not as good as a Pierce Spade, but close."

He shook his head. "You're funny."

"Would you mind letting me read them when you're done?"

"Not at all," he replied, smiling as he checked out her stack. She'd grabbed three romance novels, another book that he'd noticed shelved under Contemporary Fiction, and several hardback books with colorful photographs of food on their covers. "Looks like you got a few cookbooks there along with your fiction."

"I did." She blushed. "Actually, I collect cookbooks. Specifically, ones on baking. I've gotten some amazing recipes that way. Others, I've tweaked and made my own."

He loved how cute she looked when she blushed. Damn, he wanted to kiss her. Instead, he focused on trying to sound sensible.

"Remember, those cookbooks are a business expense now," he pointed out. "Make sure and keep your receipts."

Her smile faded. Slowly she nodded. "I will."

Together they carried their books to the counter. Pierce stepped aside so Cassie could go first.

"Are you ready?" Stoney asked, beaming at her. Once she'd nodded, he began to ring up her purchases. "I heard the best gossip this morning," he said just loud enough so

Pierce could hear. "I'm not sure if it's true or not, but I heard that famous thriller author Pierce Spade is in town."

Pierce froze. His heartbeat sounded loud in his own ears.

"What?" Cassie looked and sounded genuinely shocked. As she should be. "Where did you hear that?"

"I stopped for breakfast at The Tumbleweed Café." Stoney shrugged. "You know how it is in there. A couple women at the table next to me were all excited about it."

Pierce noticed how carefully Cassie avoided glancing back at him. For his part, all he could do was wonder what he'd done, where he'd failed. He'd been so careful.

"Did someone see him around town?" Cassie asked. "You know how big a fan I am of his. If he's here, I wonder if he'd sign some of my books."

Stoney paused in his ringing up of her purchases to laugh. "Me too, sis. Me too. I'd love for him to come in and sign my stock."

Pierce noticed he didn't answer Cassie's question.

"Where was he seen?" he asked, regretting it instantly since Stoney looked past Cassie to study him.

"I'm not sure," Stoney finally admitted. "You know how rumors are. Sometimes they're pretty far from reality. But in this case, since there's absolutely no reason someone like him would be in Getaway, I have to wonder if it's true."

"Good point," Cassie agreed. "I wish I knew who thinks they might have seen him. I'd sure love to talk to him or her." She paused for a moment. "Even better, I'd love to run into him myself."

The hint of mischief in her voice had Pierce hiding a smile despite his shock. "Me too," he said.

"Just go have lunch at the café," Stoney suggested. "You know as well as I do that everyone will still be talking about it. Maybe you can find out more." He finished ringing up Cassie's purchases. "That'll be $124.39."

"Maybe I will." Cassie didn't even wince at the total. Instead, she handed over her credit card.

Once Stoney finished, he handed it back to her along with the receipt and all her purchases, neatly bagged. "If you do, you'd better stop by here and fill me in."

"I'll do that." Cassie stepped aside so Pierce could place his books on the counter.

As Stoney began ringing them up, Pierce kept his expression impassive. Part of him wondered if the kid would suddenly eye him and ask him if he really was Pierce Spade in disguise. Since this bookstore was the only place Pierce had gone alone, being recognized by someone who worked around books made sense.

Otherwise, he had no idea who might have recognized him and when.

Stoney finished ringing up Pierce's purchases and gave him his total. Pierce got out his wallet and dug out cash. He paid, Stoney counted out his change, and then handed over his purchases, nicely bagged. Pierce thanked him, and he and Cassie walked outside, neither one talking.

They both got into the Jeep and locked the doors.

"What the—" Cassie began.

"Wait," he interrupted her. "Let's not talk about that until we've left town. I don't want to take a chance of being overheard."

Slowly, she nodded.

After pulling away from the curb, he drove slowly down Main Street. Once they'd left the commercial part of town behind, he turned to her. "What the hell? Do you have any idea who might be saying they saw me?"

"No. I don't. Maybe it'll be okay. Gossip has a way of fading, especially if it's unfounded."

He shook his head. "You're saying no reaction is the best reaction?"

"Maybe so." She touched his arm, no doubt intending to offer comfort. "What do you think?"

Think? Her soft fingers lingering on his skin drove all rational thought from his mind. Luckily, she moved her hand away.

"I think we need to figure out a way to discredit the rumors." He took a deep breath. "I don't want to take a chance on having my stalker show up here. That would be putting other people's lives at risk. Including yours."

She studied him for a moment, considering. "I think the main thing would be finding out who started the rumor. If I can do that, I have a much better chance at putting this thing to bed."

Her choice of wording caused his body to stir. Swallowing, he managed to find his voice. "Sounds good."

"I'll get to work on that right away," she said. "In the meantime, you'd better call Michael."

"Right? This time, I get to be the bearer of bad news."

He used the car to make the call.

Michael picked up on the first ring. "I was just about to phone you," Michael said. "What the hell have you been doing out there? Have you checked social media lately?"

"Social media?" Startled, Pierce glanced at Cassie. "No, why?"

"Because it's all over the place that the famous thriller author Pierce Spade has been spotted in a small West Texas town called Getaway. One of the posts has even gone viral. It looks like your cover has been completely blown."

Chapter 14

Completely blown. For the space of a heartbeat, Cassie couldn't breathe. Dimly, she registered that Pierce and Michael were still talking, their low conversation clipped and furious.

By the time she could find her voice, the call had ended. A quick glance at Pierce, his jaw tight with tension, told her the situation was every bit as awful as it seemed.

"Damn it." Pierce hit the steering wheel with the palm of his hand. "I just don't understand how this went from local gossip to a viral post on social media."

"I have a pretty good idea." Swallowing, she forced herself to continue. "We need to go back and talk to Stoney," she said. "He's very active on more than one platform. From what I understand, he has a large following."

Pierce whipped over to the side of the road and parked. "You think it was him?"

"Well, it's a distinct possibility." She struggled to keep her voice level. "Especially since the post went viral. Whoever posted it initially had to have a lot of followers. And honestly, I don't know of anyone else here in town who's that active on the socials."

"Then let's go back." Checking to make sure no other

cars were coming, Pierce made a U-turn, tires screeching on the pavement.

If he drove faster than Cassie considered safe, she didn't say a word. She couldn't blame him. The potential for disaster loomed over them, endangering everything Pierce had worked for.

With tension palpable between them, neither spoke. Cassie noticed Pierce jiggling his leg, his agitation obvious. For herself, she kept her hands clenched in her lap, her knuckles white from the tension.

When they arrived back at the bookstore, Pierce parked in the exact same spot as before. She jumped out as soon as he shifted into Park. Though she wanted to bolt inside, she forced herself to wait for him to join her.

Moving with purpose, he led the way. But once he opened the door, he stepped aside to allow her to precede him. Judging from his rigid posture, he had a very tight grip on his emotions.

If he could, so could she. She'd be diplomatic at first, until they could learn what Stoney might have done. If he'd been responsible for the post, he wouldn't have any idea how his actions might have endangered not only Pierce but all the people close to him. Herself included. Like so many influencers, she suspected that, for Stoney, it was all about likes and follows.

Seated at the back counter, Stoney looked up when they entered. "Back so soon?" he asked, smiling. "What'd you forget?"

Cassie glanced at Pierce, unsure if he'd want her to take the lead on the questions or if he'd prefer to handle it himself.

A quick dip of his chin let her know he wanted her to start.

"I wanted to ask you about what you said earlier," Cassie began, taking care to keep her voice neutral. "About the possibility that Pierce Spade might be here in town."

His face lit up. "Okay. I posted about that, and for the first time since I've been an influencer, the post went truly viral. It had over three million views last time I checked."

"Would you mind taking it down?" Cassie asked, clenching her teeth. "Immediately?"

"What?" Stoney eyed her, his incredulous expression letting her know he thought she might have lost her mind. "Why would I want to take it down?"

"Because you're putting a giant bull's-eye on an innocent man." Keeping her voice firm, Cassie relayed the bare bones of what Pierce had been going through.

When she'd finished, Stoney looked from her to Pierce. "How do you know all this?"

Then, before she could answer, he pointed at Pierce. "I knew you were him. You being with Cassie threw me for a minute, but you have a very unique facial structure. That's why I took a picture of you when you were here earlier. I used AI to change your hair and add a beard, like in all your author photos. It was a match. How was I supposed to know to keep it to myself? You being here in our small town is big news, like it or not."

"You could have asked me first." Pierce crossed his arms and glared. "That means we guessed right. It *was* you who started the rumor."

"I just report the news. I don't create it," Stoney replied, lifting one shoulder in a casual shrug. "And I've gained a ton of new followers for now. I'm internet famous."

When Pierce took a menacing step toward the kid, Cassie grabbed his arm. "Stoney, we really need you to take that post down. I told you a little bit about Pierce's stalker. This person is also a serial killer. With your post, you could be bringing a dangerous criminal to Getaway. You're risking other people's lives as well as mine and Pierce's."

Stoney's jubilant expression crumbled. He looked from one to the other. "I get it now, but taking it down won't change anything. Stuff lives forever on the internet. One screenshot and share, and it's still up there."

Cassie swallowed. He was right. And judging from Pierce's expression, he knew it too.

"Then make another post," Pierce demanded. "Explain you were mistaken. Or even better, say you've heard Pierce Spade has moved on, traveling to New Mexico or Arizona. I don't care where. Just make it sound like I'm no longer here."

The two men locked gazes. Cassie found herself holding her breath again.

Finally, Stoney slowly nodded. "I'll do it, but on one condition."

"Name it," Pierce said.

"I get an advance reading copy of your next book, signed by you."

Any other time, Cassie would have found this amusing. But now, with the stakes so high, she didn't dare even smile.

Slowly, Pierce held out his hand for Stoney to shake. "I have a book scheduled to come out in June," he said. "I'll make sure you get an ARC."

"Deal." Grabbing Pierce's outstretched hand, Stoney shook.

Once they'd sealed the agreement, Stoney grabbed his phone and began typing. "I'll make another Breaking News post," he said, animated. "And then later, I'll go live with updates on your—I mean, Pierce Spade's—whereabouts."

"Thank you." Pierce looked at Cassie. "Anything I'm forgetting?"

Pleased that he'd even asked her, she considered. "I can't think of anything right now. But we need to stay on top of this. For all we know, we might already be too late."

Though she could tell Pierce didn't want to believe that, she also knew if he really thought about it, he'd know the truth. There was someone out there, a serial killer, obsessed with Pierce. They were no doubt monitoring the internet, watching for anything pertaining to him. Heck, they likely had set up alerts.

That's why they needed to get the word out as quickly as possible that Pierce had left the area. Because if they waited too long, Cassie would bet every dollar she had that Pierce's stalker would be on the way to Getaway. Heck, he probably already was.

They got into the Jeep and Pierce started it up without a word. He pulled out onto Main Street and once again didn't speak until they'd left the downtown area behind.

"We're screwed, aren't we?" he asked, the defeat in his voice reflected in his expression.

"Probably, yes. I think so." She saw no reason to beat around the bush. "I actually expect your stalker to arrive in town sometime in the next twenty-four hours."

"Even if Stoney posts something about me leaving to head somewhere else?"

Noticing how tightly he gripped the steering wheel, she sighed. "Even so. Because he'll want to check things out himself. Then, if he doesn't find any sign of you, I'm sure he'll move on."

"I need to alert your sheriff," he said. "It's time to get local law enforcement involved."

"Rayna? Good idea. She definitely has her finger on the

pulse of things." She pulled out her phone. "I can call her if you want."

"Maybe we should stop by and talk to her in person. I have a lot of explaining to do." He sighed. "She doesn't even know who I am and why I'm in Getaway. I was hoping to keep it that way."

"Which isn't going to be possible any longer," Cassie said. "Unless you want to take your chances and try to wing this alone." Swallowing hard, she looked at him. "Which I think is a bad idea. It's time to bring in the sheriff. Rayna is good at her job. She can help."

Slowly, he nodded. "Do you mind if we stop by there now and see if she's available to talk?"

"Not at all."

"Can you point me in the right direction?" he asked.

"It's just off Main, a few more blocks. I'll tell you when to turn."

"Good. Once we talk to the sheriff, I think we'll be in a much better position. That way, if anyone new arrives and starts asking around town about me, she'll know."

Cassie couldn't help but grimace. "She will, but so will everyone else. I know you've heard this before, but I can't understate how fast gossip moves in this town."

They pulled up to the sheriff's department and parked.

"At least it doesn't seem too busy," Pierce commented.

"Small-town life," Cassie replied. "Not too much crime, aside from the occasional serial killer."

He glanced at her, his expression making it plain he wasn't sure if she was joking or not.

"Past serial killers," she elaborated.

Once inside, they asked Debbie Smythe, a woman with whom Cassie had gone to school with, if the sheriff was in.

"Hey, Cassie. Good to see you. Let me check." Instead of picking up the phone and calling, Debbie got up from the front desk and, after motioning them to sit, went through the doorway leading to the back room.

A moment later, she returned. "Follow me," she said. "Rayna has a few minutes and can see you now."

The back room had several desks, all close together and only separated by half partitions. Two of those were occupied by uniformed deputies, one of whom waved as Cassie and Pierce passed.

"Do you know everyone around here?" Pierce muttered.

"Small town," Cassie reiterated.

They reached Rayna's small office. Inside, the sheriff sat behind a cluttered desk, her luxurious red hair in a messy bun. She stood as Cassie and Pierce entered.

"Cassie Denton!" Rayna came around the desk and enveloped Cassie in a hug. "What brings you here? And who's your friend?"

Taking a deep breath, Cassie performed the introductions.

Shaking Pierce's hand, Rayna frowned. "Why does your name sound familiar?"

"That's what we came here to talk to you about," Pierce replied.

"Sit." Rayna gestured toward the two chairs she had in front of her desk. "I'm all ears."

Cassie let Pierce explain. She watched Rayna's expression. Either the sheriff had completely mastered maintaining a poker face or she'd heard much stranger stories in her career.

When Pierce finally finished, Rayna leaned forward. "Honestly, I knew about your stalker—it's been all over the news. I wasn't aware you'd moved here to my town. I wish you had filled me in sooner. I totally understand you wanted to remain anonymous, but I have contacts at the FBI. I could have worked with them to ensure you remained safe."

"Understood," Pierce responded. "But the FBI doesn't even know where I am. I disappeared on my own. My agent is acting as the intermediary between me and law enforcement. We are only alerting you now out of necessity, as it would appear my stalker might be showing up here in Getaway."

"I see." Rayna briefly looked at Cassie before returning her attention to Pierce. "And you say Stoney, the kid who works at The Bookstore, is the one who outed you?"

"He is," Cassie replied. "He said he used AI to alter a photo he took of Pierce when he visited the store. He was able to make it match up with his author photo."

"Brilliant. I need to hire that kid. He'd make an excellent law enforcement officer." Rayna stood. "If I hear of anything, I'll let you know immediately. Unfortunately, if some strange guy shows up and starts asking around about a famous author, that's not against the law and I can't arrest him."

"Could you detain and question him?" Cassie asked. "Maybe check to see if he has any outstanding warrants?"

"Now that I can do." Smiling, Rayna checked her watch. "Unfortunately, that's all the time I have today." Getting out her phone, she asked Pierce for his number. After she'd entered that, she got Cassie's. "I'll be in touch."

Her quiet confidence made Cassie feel slightly better. As she and Pierce got up to go, she murmured a quiet thank-you. Pierce did the same.

Once they'd walked outside, Pierce unlocked his Jeep and they got in. "I like your sheriff," he said.

"She's your sheriff too," Cassie pointed out. "But yes, Rayna is awesome. And I think she's right. We should have enlisted her help sooner."

Driving home, Pierce's thoughts warred between an urge to pack up and put as many miles as possible between him and this town and the desire to dig in his heels and fight.

He'd honestly believed this entire situation would have been resolved much quicker than this. The purchase of the farm had initially been made on a whim, but the more he'd thought about it, the happier he'd been about his decision.

Especially since he'd met Cassie Denton. Now the thought of leaving her tore him apart.

But the knowledge that by staying he could be putting her life in danger, hurt even worse.

"Penny for your thoughts," Cassie said, startling him into remembering she was beside him in the passenger seat.

"My mom used to say that," Pierce replied, still distracted.

"Where is she now?" Cassie asked. "You've never mentioned anything about your parents before now."

"Parent, singular. My mother raised me on her own. She passed away when I'd just finished writing my first book. She always supported me, but she never got to see me published."

Slowly, Cassie nodded. "I'm sorry. That's rough."

"Thanks. It's been several years, but that's my biggest regret." His mother had loved to read and she'd passed that love along to him. She would have been thrilled when Pierce's first novel had been published and even more ecstatic to learn he'd made numerous bestseller lists.

He'd always had the fanciful hope that she'd been able to

see all this from the afterlife. He could picture her cheering him on.

"Is that what you were thinking about?" Cassie asked.

Circling right back to her original question. He had to admire her tenacity. "No," he admitted. "I'm actually wondering again if it's time to finally confront this person who's been stalking me relentlessly. This self-proclaimed serial killer who'd even begun murdering women in my name." He didn't even try to keep the bitterness from his voice.

"Are you really considering trying to arrange some kind of meeting?" she asked.

"That's just it. I don't know." Teeth clenched, Pierce kept his attention focused on the road. "With every single book I wrote, I did a ton of research on serial killers. I read books by FBI profilers, watched hours of documentaries, and knew many of the more infamous killers' methods by heart. But this person, who insists I stole his life for a book without giving him proper credit, hadn't managed to garner too much attention from law enforcement. In fact, until this guy started harassing me, the FBI didn't even have him on their list."

"Seriously?" she replied. "What about now?"

"Now the Bureau's profiler has done a complete work-up on him. They'd profiled him as a young male, constantly striving for attention and furious at women for what he likely believed as their unfair rejection of him. This is what had likely driven him to kill for the first time. Just like with all other serial killers, the rush of power has kept him killing again and again."

"Just like in one of your books," she said.

"Yes. Just like in one of my books." Sometimes reality was far worse, but he kept that factoid to himself.

They'd reached the turn that would take them down the

gravel road leading to the farm. Once they'd left the pavement, he slowed since there were a lot of ruts and potholes. While he knew his Jeep could handle them, he didn't like bouncing Cassie around.

When they finally pulled up to the house and parked, he felt mentally exhausted. "I just don't know what to do," he told her, shutting off the ignition. "I constantly battle this in circles. I hate the idea of fleeing and hiding and don't want to spend the rest of my life looking over my shoulder. But there's all those other innocent victims to consider."

"Hey," she said, touching his arm. "First off, you don't know that this guy would stop killing even if he succeeded in capturing you. A serial killer doesn't simply stop."

Since she had a point, he nodded.

"Don't make any rash decisions," Cassie continued. "Rayna's involved now. Plus, we've got Stoney putting out some false information to hopefully stir this killer in another direction. Maybe we'll get lucky and nothing will happen."

He didn't want to tell her he no longer believed in luck, so he nodded again.

Once inside the house, she went directly to the kitchen, grabbed a couple of cans of Diet Dr Pepper, and plunked them down on the table. "Want one?" she asked, opening hers and taking a long drink from it. "Sometimes these just hit the spot."

"Sure, why not?" Dropping down into one of the chairs, he did the same. "I'm starting to really like these," he said, holding up the can.

"You're welcome," she said, smiling. "Now let's talk about something more positive. How's the writing coming?"

"It's going," he said cautiously. Despite everything, now that he'd gotten started, Pierce wrote. Often, Cassie would find him, pen in hand, hunched over his notebook at the kitchen table first thing in the morning. He'd grown to love that first sight of her, her hair all tousled and sleep still in her eyes. He looked forward to that moment every single day.

"I suppose it must be going well, especially since it takes you so long to register my presence in the morning. It's kind of endearing when you finally look up, with that dazed and almost lost expression on your face."

"Endearing?" he asked, incredulous. And touched, though he'd never admit that out loud. Maybe those early morning moments meant as much to her as they did to him. The thought made his heart race.

"Yes." Her smile seemed genuine. "You probably don't remember, but the first few times that I interrupted you, you blinked, clearly surprised to see me. Oh, you apologized, but the second I turned away to do something else, like get a cup of coffee, you'd go right back to it. Absorbed in a world of your own making, you didn't even notice when I left the room."

"I'm sorry." The automatic apology was genuine. He'd long ago realized most people didn't understand how an author's mind worked or how lost they could get while writing out a scene.

"Don't be." Her smiled widened. "I actually find it darn cute. You're creating something millions of people will someday read. This inside glimpse into the lifestyle of a bestselling author fascinates me."

Which meant it wasn't personal. Just like that, his brief flash of happiness deflated.

"I love watching you work," she continued, clearly oblivious. Which in retrospect, he felt was a good thing.

"I'm usually a lot more prolific," he told her, slightly uncomfortable with all this talking about himself.

"At least you're working again, right?"

Slowly, he nodded. "There's that."

"Don't let all this mess with your writing," she said, her earnest expression matching her voice. "You've been really into it lately. I'd hate to see you lose that spark."

"Thanks." Touched again, he exhaled. "I'm surprised that you understand, though I guess I shouldn't be."

This made her laugh. He felt he could drown in the warmth of that sound of pure feminine mirth. "When we first met, I asked you be my proofreader," he continued. "Not a lot of writing went on for a good while, but now I've got a few chapters done on my next book. If you're still up for taking a look at them, I can email them to you. I just finished typing them into the computer."

He found himself waiting with bated breath for her response. "If you're too busy with the bakery, no worries. I completely understand."

"What? Too busy. Never." Expression thrilled, she nodded. "I'd love to take a look at your first draft. I'm no editor, but I am an avid reader. I've read everything you've ever written."

"Great. I'll send them over in a few. But I should let you know, I expect you to be honest. If you don't think something is working, tell me. I promise, I can take it."

"I can do that," she replied. "But you're such a good author, I doubt I'll find any mistakes."

Now he laughed. "You'd be surprised. That's what a good assistant and then later, a great editor, is for. To keep me from making a complete and utter fool of myself."

Her skeptical expression told him she didn't believe a word of what he'd just said.

"Let me send them over." Getting up, he went and retrieved his laptop, opened it, and powered it on. "What's your email address?"

She told him. A few keystrokes and then he looked over at her. "I've sent it. It should be in your inbox."

Eyes wide, she stared at him. "Excuse me, but I've got reading to do," she said, grabbing her drink and heading off to her bedroom. "I need privacy to do that. Thank you for trusting me to look at your work."

And then she left the room. A moment later, he heard the sound of her closing her door.

The kitchen felt oddly empty without her. Resisting the urge to reread what he'd just sent Cassie, Pierce closed his laptop and grabbed his notebook and favorite pen.

For years he had written the same kind of books. Fast-paced thrillers, heavy on the action, with strictly nuanced character development and emotion. Zero to no romance.

But this book felt...different. Still written in his trademark style, but the female protagonist Mallory Drake seemed softer somehow. And a definite spark existed between her and the male FBI agent helping her work the case.

Romance? Where he once would have scoffed, this time he decided to continue writing and see where it went. As long as he didn't let the sexual tension overcome the suspense, he actually thought the book would be better for it.

He'd gotten well through the fifth chapter when he realized he'd written a lot of Cassie's characteristics into Mallory Drake. He'd even given her the same hair and eye color. Now that he'd asked Cassie to take a look at the first three chapters of the work in progress, he couldn't help but wonder if she'd notice. Part of him hoped she would.

The relationship he'd had with his previous editorial service, which he'd liked to use before ever sending the book to Jamal at his publisher's office, had been strictly business. They'd only actually met face-to-face a few times. She'd been an English major and worked for a small publishing house as an editorial assistant. Her meager salary had led her to start a side hustle, and with him as her most recognizable client, her editorial service had taken off. She'd become so popular and had so much work that she'd been able to quit her main job and devote all her time to her own business.

As she added more and more bestselling authors to her client roster, Pierce's work no longer seemed to be her priority. She hired several freelance editors and the first time she assigned one of them to his work, he'd decided the time had come for him to move on. He just hadn't hired anyone yet.

And since, at that time, he'd just turned in one book and hadn't started working on the synopsis for the next, he hadn't needed to.

Though he wasn't sure what Cassie might bring to the table, who better to take a quick look at his first draft than an avid fan. She claimed to have read everything he'd ever written, which meant she'd be super familiar with his style.

Which also meant she might notice the subtle changes he'd unconsciously made.

What if Cassie hated the changes? Would she feel comfortable enough to tell him the truth?

When Pierce had first started writing, he'd had moments of near-crippling doubt. He'd worried about whether he was a good storyteller, if his character development and descriptions were enough to elevate the prose above ordinary. He'd always believed if he reached success with his books, those doubts would go away. And for the most part, they had.

Except in this book, he'd bared more of his soul. He loved Cassie and had allowed that love, that trust in another human, to shine through in her fictional doppelgänger. He had no idea how she'd react to that or if she'd even notice.

Hell, he wasn't sure how *he* was reacting to that revelation. He. Loved. Cassie.

Finally admitting this, even to himself, felt as if a huge weight had been lifted off his shoulders.

In his heart of hearts, he couldn't help but hope she'd see his emotions laid raw on the page.

Chapter 15

The instant she opened her email and downloaded the attachment from Pierce, Cassie caught her breath. Heart pounding, she clicked the icon to open the file.

When the document filled her screen, she eyed the words *Chapter One* at the top of the page. She would be reading this work, not as a fan, but in order to proofread.

The word made her smile. Proofread. Looking for problems, typos, or other mistakes. She'd have to point out to Pierce any errors she found. Somehow, she doubted a writer as prolific as Pierce would make any mistakes.

Excited, she immediately started reading.

When she finished—three chapters was definitely not enough—she got up from her bed and stretched. She'd have to read it again. The first read-through, she'd been so enthralled with the story, she hadn't really been looking for anything. A few typos had jumped out at her, but she'd kept going since she needed to see where the story went.

Something about this one seemed different from all the other Pierce Spade thrillers she'd read. Deeper, as if his writing had matured and moved to another level. While she didn't know how the rest of the story would go, she suspected that this one would be one of her all-time favorites.

She especially liked the main character, Mallory Drake.

She shared many of the same character traits and values and this made her feel a deeper connection to the fictional woman.

But Pierce hadn't hired her to gush over his work. He'd been clear with what he wanted. A critique and a proof-reading.

Notes. She realized she'd need to make notes. In fact, a notebook similar to the kind Pierce used would be helpful. She wondered if he had extras.

Energized and eager, she hurried back into the kitchen. But Pierce had gathered up his things and retreated to his room.

Though she briefly debated knocking, she didn't want to disturb him. Surely she could find a pad of paper some-where.

After rummaging in the kitchen for a few minutes, check-ing both junk drawers, she finally located one wedged in between several of the old cookbooks that had belonged to her father's eldest sister.

Then she went back to her own room to begin reading it all over again, this time making notes.

By the time she'd finished, it was long past her bedtime. Peeking out into the living room, the quiet, dark house told her Pierce had retired. As for Cassie, she'd even forgotten to eat. When she opened the refrigerator, she saw that Pierce had made a salad for her, with a note taped to it.

Enjoy! See you in the morning.

Touched, she sat down at the table and scarfed down her meal.

After rinsing out her bowl, she did some prep work, tak-ing dough out of the fridge to rise and mixing up a couple of quick breads to bake in the morning. Then she hurried to wash up and brush her teeth, before going back to her room and crawling beneath the sheets.

The next morning, she woke in a great mood. She'd dreamed of Pierce's story, finding herself existing in that world. This made her smile.

She hurried through her morning preparations, humming to herself. She checked her order list again and got busy baking. Three pies, two quick breads, and a couple of dozen muffins later, she drank her coffee and waited for Pierce. Every morning, she looked forward to seeing him first thing before she left to make her deliveries and then head to her bakery and before he'd started his writing.

This morning was no exception. After loading up her car, she found him already seated at the table with a large mug of coffee when she wandered in.

When he looked up from his phone, his haggard face and exhausted eyes stopped her in her tracks. "Are you all right?" she asked.

Before answering, he dragged his hand through already tousled hair. "I guess so. I just didn't sleep well last night." He shrugged and took a deep drink of his coffee. "There's a whole lot of nothing going on with regards to catching my stalker. Unfortunately, I have a really vivid imagination."

She could imagine. "They'll catch him eventually," she said. "You have to believe that."

"Do I? I mean, I hope so. But the lack of any results thus far doesn't exactly inspire confidence."

Since he had a valid point, she went and made her own cup of coffee to give herself time to figure out what she wanted to say. Generic platitudes would only insult Pierce's intelligence. Since he appeared to value her input, she could only speak what she perceived to be the truth.

"I agree, unfortunately. All we can do is hope that sooner or later, your stalker will make a mistake."

Instead of replying, he snorted.

Once she'd added the right amount of creamer and sweetener to her coffee, she turned to face him. "I've done a couple of read-throughs on the work you sent me. I've made some notes, but I want to go over it one more time to make sure I didn't miss anything."

"That bad?" he asked, grimacing. Then, before he could answer, he held up his hand. "Don't tell me. I'll just wait until I see your notes."

"It's really good," she said softly. "I know you've had a lot going on, but honestly, you've elevated your writing. This book has all of your usual style, but *enhanced*. I don't really know how to explain it, but what I've read so far is good."

His skeptical expression suggested he wasn't buying it. "Cassie, I'm used to criticism. You can't be a published author without developing a thick skin. You don't have to sugarcoat anything. That's why I wanted you to read it. For your unbiased opinion."

Realizing he wasn't going to listen to anything good she had to say, she took a drink of her coffee and nodded. "I'll get my detailed notes over to you before the end of the week. I've got a lot going on with the bakery, but I'd prefer to do one final read-through before I consider myself done."

Narrowing his eyes, he nodded. "By then, I should have a couple more chapters done. I'll be sending them to you as soon as I feel they're ready."

Again she fought the urge to tell him how much she enjoyed his writing. Instead, she decided to ask him about something that had been puzzling her.

"How do you do it? With everything going on, how are you able to focus enough to create a whole other world?"

He tilted his head, considering. "Honestly, writing is my escape. It always has been. Creating a new book allows me to retreat from whatever is going on in this world, into one of my own making."

A ghost of a smile flitted across his handsome face, bringing an ache to her chest. "I know you don't think you know what it's like, but I bet there's times when you're baking that you get lost in what you're doing."

"True," she replied, weighing the validity of the comparison. "I always say I get in the zone."

"Exactly. And that's what writing is like. I'm putting words on paper, you're mixing ingredients to bake the best cake or whatever. Creating. Just different kinds."

Slowly, she nodded. "I think I get it. I never thought of it that way."

Their gazes locked. For a moment, time seemed to stand still. For a moment, she could envision them coming together in a fierce embrace, chest to chest, mouth to mouth.

Then Pierce looked away, breaking the spell.

"Speaking of your work," he said, his voice a bit huskier than normal. "How's the bakery coming?"

Relieved to be back on safer ground, she swallowed before answering. "It's getting closer and closer to becoming a reality. All of my supplies have come in. Even though I've still been baking for The Tumbleweed Café and Serenity's here, I hope to transition to that location soon."

She checked her watch. "Speaking of that, I need to get going if I intend to make my deliveries on time."

"That's amazing." He gestured around the kitchen. "I'm guessing you'll be taking all these mixers and things over there when you do?"

This made her laugh. "Yes. And no more sample taste tests for you."

He made a face. "I guess I can always stop by the bakery when I get a craving."

"Now that you definitely can do." She smiled. "It'll be open soon. I've even gone so far as to pick a date for the grand opening. I've had flyers printed up and my friend Ellie has agreed to leave some on the counter at Serenity's as well as her café."

"What about the Tumbleweed? Have you talked to them about putting out flyers?" he asked.

"Not yet. But since I'm delivering pies there again tomorrow, I'll bring it up then. I'm sure they won't mind helping me out, especially since I'm one of their most reliable suppliers. On a small scale. Hopefully, I can change that and they'll increase their orders."

"If they sell out of your stuff daily, I'd think they would," he said. "And honestly, Cassie, your baking is out of this world."

Now she blushed, uncomfortable with the praise. "Thanks. I'd better get going," she told him. "It's going to be another busy day."

Glad she'd already loaded up her truck, she practically fled. As she drove to town, she reflected on how much her life had changed in such a short time. While some of the changes had been planned and eagerly anticipated, others had not.

Never in a million years would she have guessed she'd meet and fall in love with her favorite author.

Wait. She barely kept herself from swerving on the road. Fall in love? What the…?

But then as she straightened out her tires, she realized she'd simply admitted the truth. She loved Pierce Spade. And the thought of anything happening to him, including him packing up and going back to New York, made her heart feel like it had been ripped out of her chest.

As usual, she dropped off The Tumbleweed Café's order first. They were super busy getting ready to open and barely acknowledged her as she entered the back door. After leaving their goods on the counter, she hurried over to Serenity's, where she knew Ella would be equally busy but much more welcoming.

This morning, Ella seemed a bit distracted. She motioned to Cassie to leave the baked goods on the back counter.

"Are you okay?" Cassie asked, slightly concerned.

Ella raised her face. "I am. But I've got to hire someone else soon. This pace is killing me. I've got a million things to do before I open and not nearly enough time."

"I won't keep you then." Cassie hurried out to her truck.

Someday, she thought she could see herself in a similar position. Once her bakery took off, she too would need to hire help. Quite frankly, she couldn't wait.

Pulling up to her building, she sat for a moment in her truck, talking several deep breaths to calm herself. Then she turned off the engine, hopped out, and got ready to go to work. Time to lose herself in her work. Because Pierce had been exactly right. Though their creative endeavors were completely different, in that one way they were the same.

The crew arrived with her new sign and she showed them where to install it. Stepping back, she got out her phone and took pictures, needing to document the moment. She planned to share it to her newly created Cassie's Creations social media page.

Once the sign was up, the installers left. She took one final photo, then did a quick post, along with the caption *Coming soon!*

She spent the next couple of hours puttering around, making a few test batches of quick breads since those were the easiest to do. She planned to stop by the Tumbleweed for lunch and see if they'd put out her flyers, so she might as well bring along some fresh baked goods to sweeten the deal.

And while she was there, she'd keep her ears and eyes open for talk about any strangers asking around town for Pierce Spade. She might even stop by The Bookstore on the way back, just to check in on Stoney and see how things were coming along.

The quick breads turned out perfect. After loading them up in her large, insulated carrier, she put them in her truck. Then she drove over to the Tumbleweed. Though at eleven thirty, the lunch rush had just started. The parking lot already appeared crowded.

Pulling out her insulated carrier, she carried it around to the back door, which led directly to the supply room and an area where the manager kept a small desk near the time card machine. They never kept that door locked, so she walked right inside.

Harriet, the manager currently on duty, looked up from her work and beamed. "What are you bringing us now?" she asked.

Setting her carrier down, Cassie unloaded the quick breads. "There's strawberry, lemon, and a pumpkin spice," she said.

"Let me get these to one of the line chefs, so they can get them into the display case."

"Sounds good." Cassie pulled out one of her flyers. "Oh, and here. I wanted to show you this. I'm hoping they'll let me leave a few near the front counter. I'm hoping to have a grand opening soon."

"'Cassie's Creations,'" Harriet read out loud. "I like it."

She held out her hand. "Give me all the flyers you brought and I'll make sure they're set out."

Cassie grinned and handed them over. "I appreciate you."

"Right back at you." Harriet blew her a kiss. "Everything you make is downright delicious. Your bakery is bound to be a big success."

"Thank you. I sure hope so."

"Now go and grab you some lunch," Harriet ordered.

Happily, Cassie made her way to the counter and grabbed a barstool.

After indulging in a tuna melt with creamy tomato soup, Cassie paid her check and headed home.

The empty and quiet house had her looking out the back window for Pierce. As she'd suspected, she spotted him sitting on the back porch in one of her father's old rocking chairs. He had his head down, busy writing in his notebook.

She stood for a moment, simply watching, her heart full. Sometimes, she allowed herself to pretend that all of this was permanent. She and Pierce living together on the farm, him writing and setting up his writer's retreat while she got her bakery up and running. A perfect life.

Except none of it was real. And once Pierce left and went back to New York, she'd not only need to find a new place to live but figure out a way to deal with her own heartbreak.

Writing some books felt like pulling teeth. Others, Pierce could scarcely write fast enough to keep up with the scenes playing out in his head. This book, as of yet still untitled, was the latter.

He loved everything about it. The story, the characters, even the villain.

Sitting outside under the porch cover, he wrote and breathed in the fresh spring air. The lack of humidity felt refreshing and the wind had died down, so dust wasn't blowing around for once. All in all, a great day.

He registered Cassie's truck barreling down the gravel road, but the writing was going so well he didn't want to stop. Even though his heart skipped a beat at the prospect of seeing her, he had to get this scene on paper before it vanished from his head.

As usual, he must have lost track of time. When he looked up again from his notebook, he had no idea how much time had passed. Checking his watch, he realized it had been several hours. Cassie had arrived back home shortly after one and it was now three thirty.

His stomach growled, reminding him he hadn't eaten since breakfast.

Closing the notebook, he got up and stretched. He'd go rummage around the kitchen and find something to snack on.

When he walked into the house, the smell of bread baking and something else simmering on the stove made his mouth water.

Cassie looked up from the stove and smiled. "Your writing must be going well. You've been at it for a good while."

Smiling back, he put his notebook down on the table and approached her. "It is. I have a couple more chapters to send you."

"Awesome." She turned her attention back to whatever she was stirring. "I'll get those notes over to you soon. I hope you don't mind that they're handwritten."

"Not at all." Moving closer, he sniffed appreciatively. "What are you making?"

"Beef stew for dinner. Plus some simple French bread to go with it. I had a craving for stew, and since we had all the ingredients…"

"I love beef stew, especially with fresh bread." Unable

to contain his enthusiasm, he pulled her into a quick hug and kissed her neck. "Thank you, thank you, thank you."

Though at first, she immediately stiffened, his effusive gratitude finally made her relax and giggle. "You're welcome," she said, returning her attention back to the Dutch oven full of food. "It still needs to simmer a few more hours, but should be done by dinnertime."

"Sounds great." He moved away, grabbing his notebook on his way. "I need to go get cleaned up, then I want to check in with Michael and see if there's been any news."

"Keep me posted."

"I will." He glanced at her once more before heading to the pantry and grabbing a protein bar. Unwrapping it and taking a bite, he waved at her and left the room. The straight line of her back, her long hair swinging as she moved from the stovetop to the counter, beguiled him. He ached to return and pull her close again, this time for a real embrace and kiss.

Since he didn't have the right to do that, he forced himself to continue on to his room.

Closing the door, he sat down on the edge of the bed and put his head in his hands. What the hell was he doing? An impossible situation had become dangerous, and all he could think about was how badly he wanted Cassie.

After a quick shower, he returned to his room and scrolled social media. When he saw his name trending on one of the platforms, he frowned. Was it because of the so-called sighting in Getaway?

But when he clicked on the first video, his heart stopped. There, in a clearly manipulated video, he saw himself admitting to someone off-screen that he plagiarized his own books.

Immediately, he called Michael.

"Have you seen what's floating around on social media?" Then, before Michael could answer, he continued. "That's not me!" He heard anguish, fury, and sorrow all tangled up in his voice. "I swear to you, I never said those things. Or did them. Every single book I write comes straight from my imagination."

"I know." Michael sounded equally angry. "I've seen your synopses. Hell, I've seen your notes. You don't plagiarize anything. Not one word, sentence, or description. Give me a second. I haven't seen what you're talking about."

"It's trending." Pierce waited while his agent checked social media.

A moment later, Michael swore. "They're using AI. They've manipulated your image and your voice to make it appear you've said things you haven't."

"But why?" Pacing now, Pierce yanked open his bedroom door and stalked into the living room. There, Cassie looked up from her phone, a horrified look on her pretty face. Which meant she too had seen the video.

"It has to be your stalker." Michael cursed again. "I'll ask my contact at the FBI to look into that video. It has to have been made using AI."

Pierce cursed. "That makes sense. I remember seeing a news segment on how they could use AI to make a person look like someone else."

"It's another attempt by your stalker to try and flush you out into the open. No doubt he figures you'll need to make some personal appearances, whether on TV or a podcast, to explain your side of this."

"That would make sense," Pierce said. "How else am I going to correct this awful misinformation?"

"Not by getting yourself killed," Michael countered. "You can film a statement or something. But first, let's see what the FBI comes up with. If they say that video was created with AI, which they will, we'll release a statement."

Swallowing back a curse word of his own, Pierce agreed.

"I'll keep you posted," Michael once again promised. He took a deep breath. "Stay focused. They are going to catch this guy. He's ramping up his attacks on you."

"I'm trying," Pierce said. "But BS like this can ruin an author's career, as you well know."

"You've got me in your corner, you know that. And Jamal. As your agent and editor, our statements will carry a lot of weight."

"I'm going to make my own statement," Pierce promised. "The sooner I get out ahead of this, the better."

"True. Just be careful and don't give away anything about your location." Michael paused. "By the way, how's the writing going?"

"Great," Pierce answered. "Or it was." They both knew controversies like this could wreak havoc on a writer's creativity, not to mention their sales.

"Well, keep after it." Michael ended the call.

Cassie made a sound, reminding him that she'd heard the last part of the conversation.

"You saw the video." It was more of a statement than a question.

"I did," she replied. "And I know that wasn't you. I'm not sure how they did that, but you'd never say those things."

"Thanks." For a moment he couldn't force words past the lump in his throat. "I appreciate that."

"I have faith in you," she said, her soft voice matching her gentle gaze.

Humbled, he could only nod. "Thank you," he finally managed. "I just don't know how I'm going to clear my name.

If people actually believe this, my writer's retreat will be dead in the water before I even start it."

"You're still thinking about turning the farm into a retreat?"

Slowly, he nodded. "I've been sketching out ideas for the place, though I haven't even talked to any contractors yet to get estimates."

She didn't press. And he didn't mention that if he did go through with those plans, he'd be spending a fair amount of his time here in Texas. But until he got that manufactured scandal with all the lies cleared up, those plans would be eternally on hold.

"Let's get to filming that statement," Cassie said, holding up her phone. "Have you given any thought as to what you want to say?"

"I want to categorically deny every word. Explain that wasn't me, touch base on what's been happening, and why I think whoever made that false video did it."

"Good." She nodded. "Since this is so important, why don't you make at least a list of what you want to say. I mean, yes, we can always redo the video, but the crisper it sounds, the better."

Slowly, he nodded. "That absolutely makes sense," he agreed. Grabbing the notebook that was never far from his side, he jotted a quick list of everything he wanted to say.

When he'd finished, he read it out loud to Cassie. "Do you see anything I might have missed?"

"No." She lifted her phone. "Do you want to do it live or film it and post it later?"

"Which is more effective?" he asked.

"Live, I think."

"Then that's what we'll do." Glancing again at his notes, he swallowed. "I'm ready when you are."

"Okay. One, two, three, and go."

Looking directly at her phone, Pierce drew himself up. "Today I learned that a video had been posted with—"

Three staccato knocks on the front door interrupted him.

"Are you expecting anyone?" Pierce asked Cassie, motioning at her to turn off the live feed.

Slowly, she shook her head. "No. And I didn't hear any vehicles come up the driveway."

Just to be sure, he went to the front window and looked out. "You're right," he said. "No other cars."

"I don't think we should answer," she whispered. "What if your stalker managed to find out where you live?"

She had a point.

Pointing to her phone, she sighed. "Should we reschedule this?"

"What do you think?" he asked.

"I think we should go ahead and finish. We'd already gotten up to over a hundred thousand viewers before I shut it down."

Impressed and gratified, he listened for a moment. "Maybe whoever it was went away. Let's continue." He waited until she signaled that she was recording again before speaking. "A video is circulating purporting to be me saying some pretty awful things. First, that is not me. I've asked the FBI to look into it, but I feel pretty confident that both the image and the words were created using artificial intelligence technology."

He took a deep breath, looking directly at her camera. "I did not say those things. I do not plagiarize my books. I work very hard to come up with the stories and the people. All of it. I have my notes and my synopsis for each book to prove it. There has never been a case—ever—of me using someone else's writing and claiming it as my own."

Again, three sharp raps hit the door, more forceful this time.

"Excuse me a moment," Pierce said, aware they were still streaming live. "Once again, we're going to have to pause this. I apologize. If necessary, we'll reschedule for another day and time."

That said, he went over and looked out the peephole. "It's the kid from The Bookstore. Stoney." He looked again. "And he's got a woman with him."

Before Cassie could respond, he went ahead and opened the door. "Stoney? What brings you out here? And where's your vehicle?"

He hadn't even finished speaking when he realized Stoney's eyes were wide and frightened, his skin blanched with terror.

"Move," the woman ordered, prodding Stoney. As she did, Pierce realized she had a gun pointed directly at Stoney's head.

Chapter 16

Cassie made a quick decision and resumed the livestream. So far, she didn't think she'd shown anything that would give anyone watching the slightest clue as to Pierce's whereabouts.

And since Pierce had said Stoney was at the door, this could make the livestream more interesting. Stoney claimed to be an influencer and his videos had been what had started this situation.

But when Pierce's posture changed, Cassie realized something had gone terribly wrong. As Stoney and an unfamiliar woman moved into the room, she saw the black pistol pressed against Stoney's temple.

The woman's short brown hair framed a long face. Her tall, athletic body looked fit. But her expression, a mixture of bitterness and anger, revealed how dangerous she might be.

Cassie's heart stopped. "What's going on?" she asked, setting her phone down, propped up on a picture frame and still streaming. At least now, someone could call law enforcement if necessary.

An extremely pale Stoney looked from her to Pierce and back again. The stark terror in his gaze told her he realized the depths of the danger he was in. "I'm not sure," he croaked. "I don't know who this is. She showed up at the store, pulled a gun on me, and demanded I take her to you."

"Why?" Pierce stepped forward, his hard voice matching his glare. "Who are you and what do you want?"

The woman narrowed her gaze. "Don't pretend like you don't recognize me. We dated back in Manhattan and you damn well know it."

Pierce continued to stare at her, clearly not remembering.

"How long ago?" he asked. And then before she could respond, he shook his head. "Never mind. It's not relevant. What do you want?"

She laughed, a sound that chilled Cassie to the bone. "You still don't understand, do you? I've been looking for you a long time. Now that I've found you, I've come to make you pay."

When she glanced at Cassie, the absolute lack of emotion in her dark eyes sent a shiver of terror up Cassie's spine. "I think I'll start with your little friend here. Since all of my victims so far have been women, she'll be a perfect starting point."

"Victims?" Cassie gasped. "I just now realized who you must be. You're Pierce's stalker. The serial killer."

"Do you think?" The woman smirked. "It's about time someone figured that out. Considering how many people I've killed, you'd think law enforcement would somehow have come up with a guess. But no. Even when I ramped everything up, they simply bumbled around, looking for all the wrong people. I bet my FBI profile is way off base."

"Just a second," Pierce said, stepping in front of Cassie. "Serial killers are usually male. Less than 9 percent are women."

"Bravo. You've done your research. I'd expect nothing

less from an author. Even if you don't give credit where credit is due."

Now Cassie knew without a doubt she'd done the right thing to keep the livestream open. She didn't even dare to glance at her phone, but she knew a whole lot of people were no doubt still watching. Hopefully someone local who knew either her or Stoney would call Rayna for help. Right now, that was their only chance.

Dragging his hand across his face, Pierce grimaced. "I think it's finally time we got all this out in the open. You've been stalking and harassing me, committing murder and blaming me, and now you're here threatening people I love."

He cocked his head. "I bet you're the one behind that AI video of me supposedly saying I plagiarized all my books."

"I am." Her smirk widened. "Making that video was surprisingly easy to do. The thing is, a lot of people will believe it. Has your life been ruined yet? I bet it will be soon."

Instead of answering the question, Pierce shook his head. "The entire time you've been doing this, setting fire to apartment buildings, torturing and killing innocent people, and now trying to ruin my career, I still don't know why. All along, I haven't had any idea why someone I barely know— you—would feel compelled to do any of this. I need you to explain it to me like I'm five."

The woman recoiled as if he'd slapped her. "You're lying."

Was that hurt, mingled with the fury that Cassie heard in her voice?

"We dated! I helped you research serial killers. All those evenings we spent in the public library on Fifth Ave. How can you possibly forget all that?"

A glimmer of recognition crossed his face. "You worked there. At the library. Your name is… Ruth. I remember you now. Yes, you helped me with my research, but we never dated."

Ruth hissed and bared her teeth. "Another lie." She waved the gun toward Pierce and Cassie before bringing it back to Stoney. "You just can't help yourself. All of you, go sit on the couch. Now."

Silently, the three of them went and took seats. Pierce took one end, Cassie the other. Stoney sat in between them. It took a lot of effort, but Cassie managed to avoid glancing at her phone.

Muttering under her breath, Ruth paced in front of them, her shaky grip on the pistol making everyone nervous.

Along with nerves, Cassie also struggled to contain her own anger. For much of her childhood and adolescence, she'd dealt with bullies. They'd hounded her relentlessly, making fun of the fact that she lived on a pig farm. She'd learned to stay in the background and watch for weaknesses. Even the slightest crack in their armor could be their undoing.

This Ruth, while clearly mentally unstable, had already shown the crack in her psyche. She'd been obsessed with Pierce for years and had managed to build up a complete fantasy backstory with him in it.

Normally, a situation like this would generate sympathy. But this woman was a serial killer, someone who murdered and tortured other women for fun.

And judging by her past acts, neither Cassie nor Stoney had much longer to live. Pierce, who knew? Ruth might have different intentions toward him.

"What do you want, Ruth?" Pierce asked, making Cassie think he'd come to the exact same conclusion. "Obviously, you feel there is something I owe you. Please, tell me what that is."

For a second, Ruth's stone face crumbled. But she quickly regained her composure. "You," she answered. "I've always wanted you. With all I've done for you, you could have made me as famous as Jeffrey Dahmer, if you'd wanted. You used bits and pieces of my methods in your books, but you never even considered to make any of your fictional serial killers female. Not once."

Pierce winced. "Because of statistics," he said quietly. "Obviously, you're one of a kind. You just proved me wrong."

"You've always been wrong." Ruth's impassioned statement seemed at odds with her furious expression. "We were meant for each other. I've read your books. The way you describe the murders tells me that you and I are the same."

"We are *not* the same," Pierce insisted. "What I do is write fiction. You're a cold-blooded killer."

"That's not so different," Ruth insisted. "Surely you can see that."

While Ruth appeared occupied pleading her case with Pierce, Cassie kept avoiding glancing at her phone. Though until now, they'd wanted to avoid letting anyone know Pierce's location, the reason for that had already found him.

Time to do more to help anyone watching the livestream who might want to call the sheriff's office to help them.

"I suppose you saw Stoney's posts about Pierce being here in Getaway, Texas," Cassie commented, her tone conversational. "Is that why you sought him out once you arrived here in town?"

Visibly upset, Stoney swallowed hard when Cassie used his name. Belatedly, she realized she'd managed to direct Ruth's attention back to the terrified bookstore clerk.

"What do you think?" Ruth asked, clearly enjoying Stoney's fear. "I bet you're wishing you never decided to try and be a social media influencer."

Then, when Pierce shifted in his seat, half rising, Ruth swung her weapon around to point it at him.

"Don't even think about getting up!" Ruth barked. "Sit down and shut up. Now."

Pierce froze. Cassie could tell by the rigid set of his jaw that he didn't like it. But he still complied, dropping himself back onto the couch cushion and glaring at the woman holding the pistol.

"I've only killed women," Ruth said, her tone conversational. "Quite a few of them, in fact. You'll be number thirteen, once I kill you today." She gestured at Cassie.

"And you," Ruth continued, nodding at Stoney. "Will be my very first male kill. That will be weird, but I'm thinking killing you will be just as satisfying as any of my others."

"Do you remember any of their names?" Cassie asked, hoping she succeeded in hiding her revulsion and terror. "The ones you murdered. They deserve to be remembered."

"Of course." Ruth lifted her chin, her dark eyes gleaming. "I have every name written down, stored along with the trophies I took when they died. I haven't forgotten a single one of them."

Though her heart pounded so hard it felt like it might come out of her chest, Cassie forced herself to continue. "Give me a name," she challenged. "Prove to me that you haven't forgotten."

Ruth locked eyes with her, the iciness of her stare sending a chill down Cassie's spine. "Patricia Atwood. Candace Blevins. Sophia Mascaron. Those were my first three kills. There have been many more since. But those women were special to me. There was a special kind of beauty in the way they died. So much blood." She smiled, her gaze still cold and flat. "They initiated me into my power. Just as your death will help sustain it."

"I don't want to die," Stoney burst out, his voice shaking. "Please, could you let me go? I'm not involved in any of this and I've only met Pierce twice."

"No." Ruth barely looked at him. "And if you don't shut up, I'll kill you first."

Stoney swallowed and closed his mouth. His entire body shook so hard, Cassie could feel him trembling.

"None of us want to die," Pierce said. "Why don't you let them go and take me? I'm what you wanted anyway."

"Initially, yes." Ruth flashed him a sweet smile edged with steel. "But now I want them all."

Then, before he could respond to that, she used her gun to gesture at Cassie and Stoney. "All of you, get out your phones. I want you to drop them onto the floor," she ordered. "Now. While I can see you."

Damn. Hopefully someone watching the livestream had called Rayna. If not, they were all in really bad trouble.

Stoney pulled his phone from his pocket and gently tossed it onto the carpet. A moment later, Pierce did the same.

Cassie cleared her throat. "Umm, my phone is over there on the end table," she said, pointing. "Do you want me to go get it?"

"No." Ruth eyed the phone. Luckily, the screen had gone dark, but Cassie knew it was still recording. "As long as you're not able to touch it."

Not trusting herself to speak, Cassie settled for a nod. She wasn't sure how much longer she had before Ruth started her torturing and killing. She knew she'd volunteer to go first, because watching Stoney or Pierce suffer would be worse than anything else. Or so she thought.

Remembering all of the stories Pierce had written and the various creative and evil ways his villains had tormented their victims, her blood ran cold. Surely by now, someone who'd been watching the livestream of what had started out as Pierce's attempt to clear his name, would have called for help.

But even if they had, if Rayna and her deputies pulled up to the house in their clearly marked cars, Ruth would know. She'd have enough time to shoot two of them and take the other one hostage. Unless… Cassie shot a sideways glance to Pierce. Unless they all rushed her the moment the sheriff arrived.

Ruth would likely still be able to squeeze off a shot or two, but with any luck no one would die.

The only fallacy with this plan was the complete lack of sheriff's department vehicles.

Maybe help wasn't on the way. Or if it was, would it arrive too late to save them?

Pierce eyed the madwoman holding them hostage and considered the possible scenarios if he were to launch himself at her. She'd be able to squeeze off a shot, but the odds of her getting a fatal hit when startled seemed about fifty-fifty.

Better him than Cassie. Judging by the way she kept shifting in her seat, she'd come up with her own risky plan. Damned if he'd sit there like a lump on the couch and watch Ruth kill her. Or young Stoney, who was so terrified he appeared about to break down.

When Cassie had pointed to her phone on the table, Pierce remembered she'd been livestreaming his statement. He had no idea if she'd ended it or left it going. He suspected she might have let it continue, which meant anyone watching for his statement had witnessed Ruth's confessions.

That would be a damned good thing, but only if one of those viewers had thought to put in a call to the sheriff.

Which might explain why Cassie had made a point of stating the town's name earlier.

A movement at the side window caught his eye. Had someone gone past or had he just seen some sort of shadow? Ruth didn't appear to have noticed anything. Stoney had his head down, too involved in his own fear to have seen anything. And if Cassie had seen it, she gave no sign.

Damn, he hoped this meant help was on the way.

From what he'd heard, Getaway's sheriff Rayna Coombs was sharp. If she'd seen any of the livestream, or someone had described the situation to her, she'd know better than to drive up to the house with multiple sheriff's vehicles. No, she'd likely park someone on the other side of the pasture and walk herself and her officers up to the back of the house.

Hope, actual hope, lifted his spirits. He'd hold off for now on doing anything dramatic, like trying to jump Ruth so Cassie and Stoney could escape. Maybe, just maybe, Rayna and the cavalry would arrive in time to save the day.

Next to him, Cassie's sudden tension told him she must have seen what he had. Slowly, he reached for her hand.

But the instant he curled his fingers around hers, Ruth took a step toward them. "Enough of that," she ordered, her weapon pointed at Cassie. "You. Get up. Now. I've decided to kill you first."

Slowly, Cassie got to her feet. As she did, Pierce squeezed her hand once before releasing it.

Pierce knew if the sheriff didn't make a move, he'd have to. No way did he intend to stand by and let this woman hurt Cassie.

As if she'd heard his thoughts, Cassie glanced back at him and gave the tiniest shake of her head. "I want you to know I love you, Pierce. In case I never get another chance to tell you."

Stunned, Pierce opened his mouth to say it back to her. But before he could get out a word, Ruth grabbed Cassie and shoved her into the wall. Cassie stumbled, but managed to stay on her feet.

"Love?" Ruth sneered. "You really are beyond help. Do you honestly think a man like him knows how to love anyone beside himself?"

Then, as Cassie straightened, Ruth brought the pistol up to aim at her. "I hope you like pain," she commented. "I plan to shoot you in several places. Each will hurt and bleed. Maybe you'll bleed to death, maybe not. Eventually, I'll put you out of your misery. But first, I plan to enjoy watching you suffer."

Pierce knew he had to act now, or Ruth would follow up her words with action.

"Don't," he said, pushing himself up and off the couch. "You'll have to go through me first."

He threw himself at Ruth, between her and Cassie, trying to knock the pistol away before she could squeeze the trigger.

As the gun went off, the side window shattered. Cassie screamed. Stoney dived to the floor. And Rayna and two of her deputies kicked in the door and came through with their guns drawn.

As Pierce slammed into Ruth, grabbing for the pistol, she twisted around, attempting to bring her pistol up to get off another shot.

"Drop your weapon!" Rayna ordered, just as Pierce's momentum knocked Ruth to the floor. The pistol went flying.

From that instant, everything seemed to happen at once.

Rayna and one of deputies grabbed Ruth and cuffed her. The other deputy half helped, half lifted Pierce to his feet.

"You've been shot," the deputy said. He radioed for medical assistance, helping Pierce over to the couch.

Cassie's concerned face was the last thing Pierce saw before he lost consciousness. "I love you too," he tried to say, but wasn't sure if the words made it past his throat.

The next time Pierce opened his eyes, he lay flat on his back in what had to be a hospital bed. Machines beeped all around him. He turned his head and realized Cassie slept in a chair at his side.

Something, maybe his movement or a change in his breathing, woke her. "You're awake," she said, her sleepy voice joyful. "How do you feel?"

The question made him frown. "I'm not sure." He moved a little, experimenting. Stretching, a sharp stab of pain in his side made him wince. "What happened to me? Was I shot?"

Cassie took his hand and kissed the back of it. "Yes. Luckily, the bullet missed your vital organs. But the doctors were able to get it out. They have you here under observation for now."

Feeling groggy, he nodded. "As long as they haven't admitted me, they'll let me go home."

"You sound as if you speak from experience," she teased, still gripping his hand. "I wanted to ride with you in the ambulance, but Rayna insisted I take my own truck so I'd have a way to get us home. I'm glad she did."

"Me too."

"What about Stoney? Is the kid okay?" he asked.

"He's fine. He dived for the floor and crawled into the kitchen. A little shaken up, but unhurt."

Just then a doctor came into the room. "You're awake," he said, smiling at Pierce. "Fantastic news. We got the bullet out and you didn't have any major damage. You've had some IV antibiotics and painkillers. We'll send you home with a prescription for more."

He then glanced at Cassie. "He'll need his bandage changed and the wound kept clean. I assume you'll be able to help him with that?"

"Of course." Cassie squeezed Pierce's hand. "I'll do whatever needs to be done."

"Good, good." The doctor glanced down at his notes. "Let me sign off on his release. A nurse will be in shortly to help you with your discharge."

As soon as the doctor left the room, Pierce sighed. "Thank you for being here for me. I need to let Michael know what's happened."

"Oh, I'm pretty sure he knows." Cassie held up her phone. "The livestream caught everything. Last time I checked, we had over two million views. I've had news stations from every major network contacting me for the story. I had to turn off your phone too."

Not sure whether to be alarmed or relieved, he sat up a bit straighter. "What did you tell them?"

"I didn't. That's your story to tell. The good thing is, everyone knows you didn't really plagiarize your novels."

He nodded. "And my stalker, a dangerous serial killer, is finally in police custody."

"Yes." She met his gaze. "In the end, it turns out Ruth was infatuated with you. She thought you were a couple just because she gave you a lot of help with your books when you went to the library. So weird."

"But when I never gave her credit or liked her the same way she liked me, her delusions turned into murder. So it wasn't that she was a serial killer who thought I was writing about her as a killer and copying her. It was that she only started killing to get revenge."

"An awful situation." A shadow crossed her face. "But now you're free to return to New York and live your life in a way that makes you happy."

Before he could respond, a nurse came in, smiling. "Lucky you. Dr. Pederson has signed your discharge papers. I'll just need your signature on a few of them, and we can get you out of here."

He signed, the nurse smiled. "Go ahead and get dressed."

Cassie grabbed his clothes from a wall locker and handed them to him. "I had to have Rayna bring a man's T-shirt and pair of sweats, because your clothes were ruined." She grimaced. "There was a lot of blood, so I had to toss them."

"You thought of everything," he said, grateful. "Thank you."

"No problem. Do you need help getting dressed?" she asked, drawing the curtain around the bed closed with her still inside.

Grateful, he shook his head. "I think I can do this. I'm not in a lot of pain yet." He paused, considering. "Though it's good to know you can help if I need you to."

"I'll be right out here," she said, stepping outside of the curtain. "Holler if you need me."

Her word choice made him smile. Right then and there, he resolved to use the word *holler* in one of his books.

Somehow, he managed to get his clothes on. Standing on shaky legs, he separated a part of the curtain and stepped through. "I'm ready to go," he said.

Like magic, an orderly appeared with a wheelchair. "Have a seat," the burly guy said cheerfully. "Ma'am, if you want to go get your car, I'll have him down at the side entrance."

"That's not necessary," Pierce protested, gesturing at the wheelchair. "I think I can walk."

"Hospital policy." The guy patted the chair. "Are you ready?"

"Sure." Pierce sat.

While the orderly wheeled Pierce to the elevator, Cassie stayed with them. When they reached the lobby, she hurried off to get her truck.

Once she'd pulled up to the entrance, and the wheelchair had been pushed near the curb, Pierce struggled to his feet. His legs still felt surprisingly weak, but he made it the few steps to her truck. Opening the door, he climbed inside unassisted. The orderly smiled and waved goodbye as Cassie pulled away.

Before exiting the parking lot, Cassie handed him his phone. "It's still off," she said. "But you're going to see a bunch of missed calls and I don't know how many texts."

Cradling the phone in his hands, he debated. Instead of immediately turning it on, he shoved it into his back pocket. "I'll look at it later," he said. "Right now, we have more important things to discuss."

"We do?" Hands on the steering wheel, she kept her gaze straight ahead. They pulled out onto the parking lot and began the long drive back to Getaway from Midland. There'd be miles and miles of mostly deserted two-lane roads. Plenty of time and space to say what needed to be said.

"Did you mean what you said back at the house?" he asked, making his tone deliberately gentle.

"You mean when I honestly believed I was about to die?" Still keeping her full attention on the road, her quiet voice gave no hint of her inner thoughts or emotions.

"Yes, then."

Instead of answering, she accelerated. "You said something too," she pointed out. "Right before you passed out. Do you remember?"

"Remember?" He took a deep breath. "I meant every word. I love you, Cassie Denton. I know we haven't been together very long, but I honestly believe we can have a future together."

"I do too," she admitted, pulling over onto the shoulder and stopping. Once she'd shifted into Park, she put the truck's flashers on and turned to face him. "But not if you're going back to New York. I'm staying here, in the town where I grew up, and opening my bakery."

He nodded. "I know."

"And as much as I wish I could, I'm not cut out for long-distance," she continued, a hint of anguish now in her voice. "I only told you I loved you because I really wanted you to know before I died. That's all."

"Same," he said, hiding a smile as his heart felt about to burst with tenderness. "But I've come to realize a few things. Life without you would be merely existing. No matter if I went back to New York City or moved to anywhere else. I've come to love it here, but only if you're with me."

She clenched her hands together tightly in her lap. "Does this mean you're staying?"

"Only if you want me to." He thought for a moment. "I'll have to go back to settle the insurance claim on my apartment. And eventually, testify in Ruth's trial. I'd love for you to come visit New York with me. But that's what it would be, a visit. Getaway will be my home. If that's all right with you."

"I think you know the answer to that," she said. "But only if you truly believe you can make a life here. Because I'm also not good at short-term flings."

"I do," he said, feeling as if the words might be prescient

of another vow he'd make somewhere down the line. "But only if you'd be willing to provide your baked goods to my writing retreat once I have it up and running."

This finally coaxed a laugh from her. But still, she hung back, almost as if afraid to truly believe.

"I love you," he repeated. "And more than anything, I'd like to make a life here in Getaway with you by my side. What do you say? Want to give us a shot?"

She covered her face with her hands, her shoulders shaking.

"Are you crying?" he asked, bewildered. "Cassie, don't cry."

Reaching for her, he embraced her as best as he could with the console between them. "Say something, please."

"I'm not crying." Voice muffled behind her hands, when she lifted them away from her face, her eyes were shiny but without tears. Her quick smile flashed and then vanished as she locked her gaze on his.

Outside on the highway, a large tractor trailer passed them by, the wind created by its passing rocking her truck.

"What is it?" he asked, pushing away a stab of desperation. "What's wrong?"

"I need you to be sure. I want you to know that I'd never ask you to give up everything you love."

He didn't even have to consider how he'd respond. "You are everything I love," he said.

With that, she gave a happy cry and wrapped her arms around his neck. "Yes," she breathed, tears finally spilling from her eyes. "I want you to stay."

Joy flooded him. He kissed her then, the press of her lips against his setting him on fire.

When he broke away, they were both breathing heavily.

"Let's go home," he told her. "We need to be somewhere else so we can celebrate this properly."

Wiping her eyes, she nodded. "Then I'll get us home as quickly as I can."

Home. No longer an abstract, but a genuine place. The place his heart resided. In a small farm at the end of a dirt road. With her, his Texas love.

* * * * *

Get up to 4 Free Books!

We'll send you 2 free books from each series you try
PLUS a free Mystery Gift.

FREE
Value Over
$25

Both the **Harlequin Intrigue®** and **Harlequin® Romantic Suspense** series
feature compelling novels filled with heart-racing action-packed romance
that will keep you on the edge of your seat.

YES! Please send me 2 FREE novels from the Harlequin Intrigue or Harlequin Romantic Suspense series and my FREE gift (gift is worth about $10 retail). I may cancel anytime by emailing ReaderServiceInfo@Harlequin.com or by calling 1-800-873-8635. If I don't cancel, I will receive 6 brand-new Harlequin Intrigue Larger-Print books every month and be billed just $7.19 each in the U.S. or $7.99 each in Canada, or 4 brand-new Harlequin Romantic Suspense books every month and be billed just $6.39 each in the U.S. or $7.19 each in Canada, a savings of 20% off the cover price. It's quite a bargain! Shipping and handling is just 75¢ per book in the U.S. and $1.75 per book in Canada.* I understand that accepting the free books and gift places me under no obligation to buy anything—they are mine to keep for free no matter what I decide.

Choose one: ☐ **Harlequin Intrigue Larger-Print**
(199/399 BPA G3CD)

☐ **Harlequin Romantic Suspense**
(240/340 BPA G3CD)

☐ **Or Try Both!**
(199/399 & 240/340 BPA G3CE)

Name (please print)

Address   Apt. #

City   State/Province   Zip/Postal Code

Email: Please check this box ☐ if you would like to receive newsletters and promotional emails from Harlequin Enterprises ULC and its affiliates. You can unsubscribe anytime.

Mail to the **Harlequin Reader Service:**
IN U.S.A.: P.O. Box 1341, Buffalo, NY 14240-8531
IN CANADA: P.O. Box 603, Fort Erie, Ontario L2A 5X3

Want to explore our other series or interested in ebooks? **Visit www.ReaderService.com or call 1-800-873-8635.**

*Terms and prices subject to change without notice. Prices do not include sales taxes, which will be charged (if applicable) based on your state or country of residence. Canadian residents will be charged applicable taxes. Offer not valid in Quebec. This offer is limited to one order per household. Books received may not be as shown. Not valid for current subscribers to the Harlequin Intrigue or Harlequin Romantic Suspense series. All orders subject to approval. Credit or debit balances in a customer's account(s) may be offset by any other outstanding balance owed by or to the customer. Please allow 4 to 6 weeks for delivery. Offer available while quantities last.

Your Privacy — Your information is being collected by Harlequin Enterprises ULC, operating as Harlequin Reader Service. For a complete summary of the information we collect, how we use this information and to whom it is disclosed, please visit our privacy notice located at https://corporate.harlequin.com/privacy-notice. Notice to California Residents—Under California law, you have specific rights to control and access your data. For more information on these rights and how to exercise them, visit https://corporate.harlequin.com/california-privacy. For additional information for residents of other U.S. states that provide their residents with certain rights with respect to personal data, visit https://corporate.harlequin.com/other-state-residents-privacy-rights.

HIHRS2603